A SHORT HISTORY OF
MODERN KOREA

A SHORT HISTORY OF MODERN KOREA

David Rees

HIPPOCRENE BOOKS
New York

ACKNOWLEDGEMENTS

Grateful acknowledgements are made to Unwin Hyman Ltd., for permission to reproduce two short passages by John K. Fairbank from *East Asia: The Modern Transformation* by Edwin O. Reischauer, John K. Fairbank & Albert Craig (Allen & Unwin, London, 1965).

Copyright © 1988 by David Rees

All rights reserved. No part of this publication
may be reproduced, stored in a retrieval system,
or transmitted in any form or by any means, electronic, mechanical
photocopying, recording, or otherwise, without prior
permission in writing of the publisher.

For information, address: Hippocrene Books, Inc.
171 Madison Avenue, New York, NY 10016

ISBN 0-87052-575-1

Printed in the United States of America.

For Rosemary Bromley

KOREAN PROPER NAMES

In accordance with general Korean usage, Korean surnames are given first. Thus, in the name Park Chung Hee, Park is the family name. Exception has been made in the case of personalities already better known by their name in a westernised form, such as Syngman Rhee or John Chang.

Contents

Introduction 1
Chapter 1 The Three Kingdoms 5
Chapter 2 Silla and Koryo 10
Chapter 3 Korea Under the Yi 17
Chapter 4 The Time of Isolation 29
Chapter 5 The Opening of Korea 41
Chapter 6 Japan and Russia in Korea 1895–1910 51
Chapter 7 Japanese Rule 1910–1945 63
Chapter 8 Korea Divided 73
Chapter 9 The Two Koreas 83
Chapter 10 Korea at War 96
Chapter 11 Trial of Strength 114
Chapter 12 Post-War Korea 1953–65 134
Chapter 13 South Korea's Economic Revolution 147
Chapter 14 The Beloved and Respected Leader 160
Chapter 15 The Problem of Security 171
Epilogue Seoul Past and Present 183
Select Bibliography 189

List of Maps

The Three Kingdoms AD 600 7
United Silla and Koryo 8th–14th centuries. 11
The eight provinces of the Yi Dynasty 14th–19th century . 19
Sino-Japanese Russo-Japanese conflicts 47
Korean War 1950–1953 97

Introduction

Koreans call their country Choson, literally 'morning freshness' or more familiarly, 'The Land of the Morning Calm'. The climate of Korea, as we might expect from this indigenous name is thus a favourable one, but it should be remembered that the weather from season to season depends on two significant factors.

These two factors are the cold Siberian air which flows south during the winter and the warm monsoon air from the Pacific which affects the shores of East Asia during the summer. Korean winters are therefore cold and dry, but there is much sunshine and little of the damp that so characterises the winters of northern Europe.

Conversely the summers are hot, with a rainy season in July and August. But although there are sometimes high winds during late August and September, Korea lies just outside the track of the typhoons that regularly affect Japan during this season. Both the spring and the autumn, or fall, in Korea are tranquil temperate periods when the full beauty of the country may be seen to its best effect.

The Koreans are an ancient and homogenous people, whose ancestors migrated originally from Central Asia and Manchuria. The Korean language is quite distinct from either Chinese or Japanese, and belongs to the Ural–Altaic language group which includes Turkish and Mongolian. For many centuries, however, the country's serious literature was written in classical Chinese, and Chinese loan words form about half of the vocabulary. The modern trend is for the substitution of Korean words and phrases for Chinese forms, and, in any case, modern Koreans write in their own phonetic script.

In keeping with the country's separate nationality, Korean history goes back over two thousand years, and from the unified Silla kingdom of the seventh century to 1945, Korea was one country. Thus neither the long centuries of domination by Imperial China, when Korea was an independent but tributary state within the Chinese Confucian system, or the modern annexation by Japan from 1910 to 1945 has affected the feeling that Koreans belong to a distinct people. Nor has the artificial division of Korea between North and South since 1945 removed the fundamental feeling that Korea is still one country.

Despite the country's indigenous name, the history of Korea has been anything but calm with successive invasions by the Chinese, the Mongols, and the Japanese. Today's division of Korea has added a new dimension to this turbulent past. Consideration of Korea's history is inseparable from consideration of Korean geography and the country's central location in North East Asia. The Korean peninsula extends southwards from the Yalu river, the boundary with China and Manchuria, for some 600 miles; the average width of the country is about 150 miles, although at its narrowest point this width narrows to about 100 miles. The total area of Korea is about 85,000 square miles, including some 3,000 islands and islets, mostly in the south and west, and thus the country is about equal in size to Great Britain or the State of New York.

Of this total area, the Republic of Korea (South Korea) comprises about 38,000 square miles, or rather less than half. But of Korea's total population of about 62 million people in 1985, some 42 million live in South Korea, and about 20 million in the Democratic People's Republic of Korea (North Korea). We should also note that several million Koreans live in Manchuria, and another 600,000 in Japan, a legacy of Japanese rule in Korea. A recent phenomenon is the emigration of nearly one million Koreans to the United States, most of them from South Korea.

As both warriors and visitors have often discovered in Korea, the land is mountainous, especially in the north. While these mountains are not very high, rising to over 9,000 feet in the Mount Paektu area on the Chinese border, the central Taebaek mountain range is often composed of the characteristically steep hills that dominated much of the fighting in the Korean War of 1950-53.

From the Taebaek range, hilly spurs and valleys extend westwards, and the South Korean capital Seoul lies in one of these valleys, that of the River Han. To the south of Korea, the hills tend to become more gentle, and here are found the river valleys of the Kum and the Naktong, which are old, historic centres of Korean life and civilization. In northern Korea, the Taedong river basin was another centre of Korean antiquity.

Historians have often commented that it is Korea's strategic position, rather than its size or wealth, which have aroused its neighbour's interest. A glance at the map will show that Korea lies at the crossroads of North East Asia. To the north, the country has a common frontier along the Yalu River for 500 miles with Manchuria, the north-eastern region of China. To the south of the Korean peninsula, the Japanese home islands of Kyushu and Honshu are about 120 miles away; the smaller Japanese islands of Tsushima in the Korea Strait between the two countries are visible from south-east Korea. To the west of Korea, the tip of China's Shantung province is about 130 miles from Korean Territory. In the far north-east of Korea, along the Tumen River, there is an 11 mile border with the Soviet Union.

Korea has thus long been a focus of international contention, as the country is a natural bridge between the continental states of Asia and the maritime powers of the Pacific. Traditionally in these matters, the Japanese have described Korea as 'a dagger pointed at the heart of Japan', while the Chinese have seen Korea as 'a hammer ready to strike at the head of China'. Over the centuries, Koreans have thus seen their fate decided by decisions made outside, rather than inside, their country.

In recent times, since 1945, all these age-old factors have been complicated by new global alignments in an age of advanced weapons and instant communications. Korea in an area where the vital security interests of America, Russia, China and Japan all converge and intersect. It is a commonplace observation in strategic discussion that Tokyo, Peking and Vladivostok all lie within 1,000 miles of Seoul. The continuing tension along the Demilitarized Zone (DMZ) which divides Korea, and which lies within 30 miles of Seoul, underlines these historic and strategic rivalries.

In recent years, while North Korea remains a closed society, South Korea has sometimes attracted world attention through increasingly vocal demands for internal reform. It should be remembered, however, that South Korea has faced very great adversities in the past generation. Following the destruction of the Korean War the economy remained very weak for a decade, unable to sustain an attempt at parliamentary government during 1960–61 (Chapter 12 below).

Following a military *coup* in 1961 South Korea enjoyed both political stability and economic growth which within twenty years turned the ROK into an advanced industrial country (Chapter 13 below). But as the ROK's prosperity grew, so expectations of a more democratic form of government naturally increased. These expectations culminated in the student riots and other disturbances in the summer of 1987 (Chapter 15 below).

South Korea's leaders then wisely bowed to the inevitable. On 29 June 1987 Mr. Roh Tae Woo, the Presidential candidate of the ruling Democratic Justice Party (DJP), announced his support for wide-ranging reforms including direct presidential elections. A few days later President Chun Doo Hwan endorsed these proposed reforms and stated that South Korea would now achieve 'an advanced form of democracy that we can proudly show the world'.

Since then solid progress has been made in drafting a new constitution. In August 1987 it was reported that agreement between the ruling and opposition parties had been reached on direct presidential elections. A national referendum then decisively approved these constitutional provisions in October 1987. In the elections on 16 December 1987 Roh Tae Woo was elected President of the ROK. There is every hope for a new democratic structure in South Korea.

In a wider context it should be stressed that despite all the vicissitudes in their history the Korean people, according to one well-known American scholar and writer, the late George McCune, 'have developed a national character with all the accomplishments of a common cultural heritage, language and way of life'. Another American scholar, Gregory Henderson, writing in 1968, has noted that Korean history is marked by 'exceptional historical continuity'.

It is this continuity that underlies our story of Korea.

Chapter One:
The Three Kingdoms

According to tradition, the mythical founder of the Korean people was Tun'gunwanggom, who was born of a father of heavenly descent and a woman from a bear-totem clan. The legend asserts that he lived in the third millenium B.C., and that he and his family ruled the Land of the Morning Calm for a thousand years.

Probably most of these tribes from which the Korean people descend lived originally in an area between the Taedong River, in what is now North Korea, and the Liao River in southern Manchuria. It was only much later that the Yalu and the Tumen Rivers became the accepted northern boundaries of Korea.

By about the fourth century B.C. the Korean tribal kingdom of Ancient Choson had emerged in this area between the Taedong and the Liao. The kingdom is so called to distinguish it from Choson, the name later given to the whole of Korea. The society of Ancient Choson was based on a relatively advanced iron technology for its tools and weapons, and a warrior ruling class had already emerged.

Chinese influence in the region was ever-present, and eventually in about 108 B.C. the Chinese Han dynasty conquered Ancient Choson and established four commanderies or counties. These units were essentially districts ruled by an administrator appointed by, and responsible to, the Chinese Emperor. The Han conquest was significant in that Chinese influence was to remain the predominant one in Korea. Moreover, from Han times to the modern period China has remained the foreign country with which Korea has had the closest relations.

This attempt to incorporate what is now north-western Korea into China was not successful. One by one the four Chinese commanderies were abandoned in the face of Korean pressure and by about 300 A.D. three distinct Korean kingdoms had emerged.

These kingdoms were Koguryo, which comprised most of today's North Korea and southern Manchuria; Paekche, based in south-west Korea, encompassing the Kum River basin; and Silla, which included most of south-east Korea and in particular the Naktong valley. (Silla was to incorporate the Kaya tribes to the west of the Naktong.) These three kingdoms, Koguryo, Paekche and Silla, then fought amongst themselves with the objective of establishing a single hegemony over the Korean peninsula.

This was a complex political and military process which took over three centuries. However, the three kingdoms soon achieved a high level of social and cultural development, stimulated by the example of China, where a sophisticated civilisation had already evolved. The three kingdoms sent tribute to the Chinese Emperor, and gradually a complicated, feudal society emerged in the Korean kingdoms. Each king was surrounded by a warrior aristocracy and a skilled bureaucracy which ruled over a peasantry providing the manpower for incessant military campaigning. There was a serf and slave class at the bottom of this society. The new aristocracy which served the Korean kingdoms was more powerful than its Chinese counterpart, where a meritocracy on the pure Confucian model was more in evidence.

Chinese Influence

In particular, Chinese influence on the Korean kingdoms manifested itself through three developments which have left a permanent mark on Korean society. Most important, perhaps, was the adoption of the Chinese language, with its ideograph or sign system, for all serious Korean written works. From the time of the early kingdoms to the fifteenth century, therefore, the literary language of Korea was Chinese while spoken language continued to be Korean.

A second Chinese importation was the Buddhist religion which with its emphasis on enlightenment and loyalty to the state soon became immensely popular. As Buddhism was an undogmatic religion, it soon quickly absorbed local beliefs and superstitions, and became quickly acceptable to all classes. Many Buddhist temples and shrines were now constructed throughout the Korean kingdoms; perhaps it should be remembered that the word Buddha is not a personal name, but a description meaning 'the enlightened one'.

THE THREE KINGDOMS 7

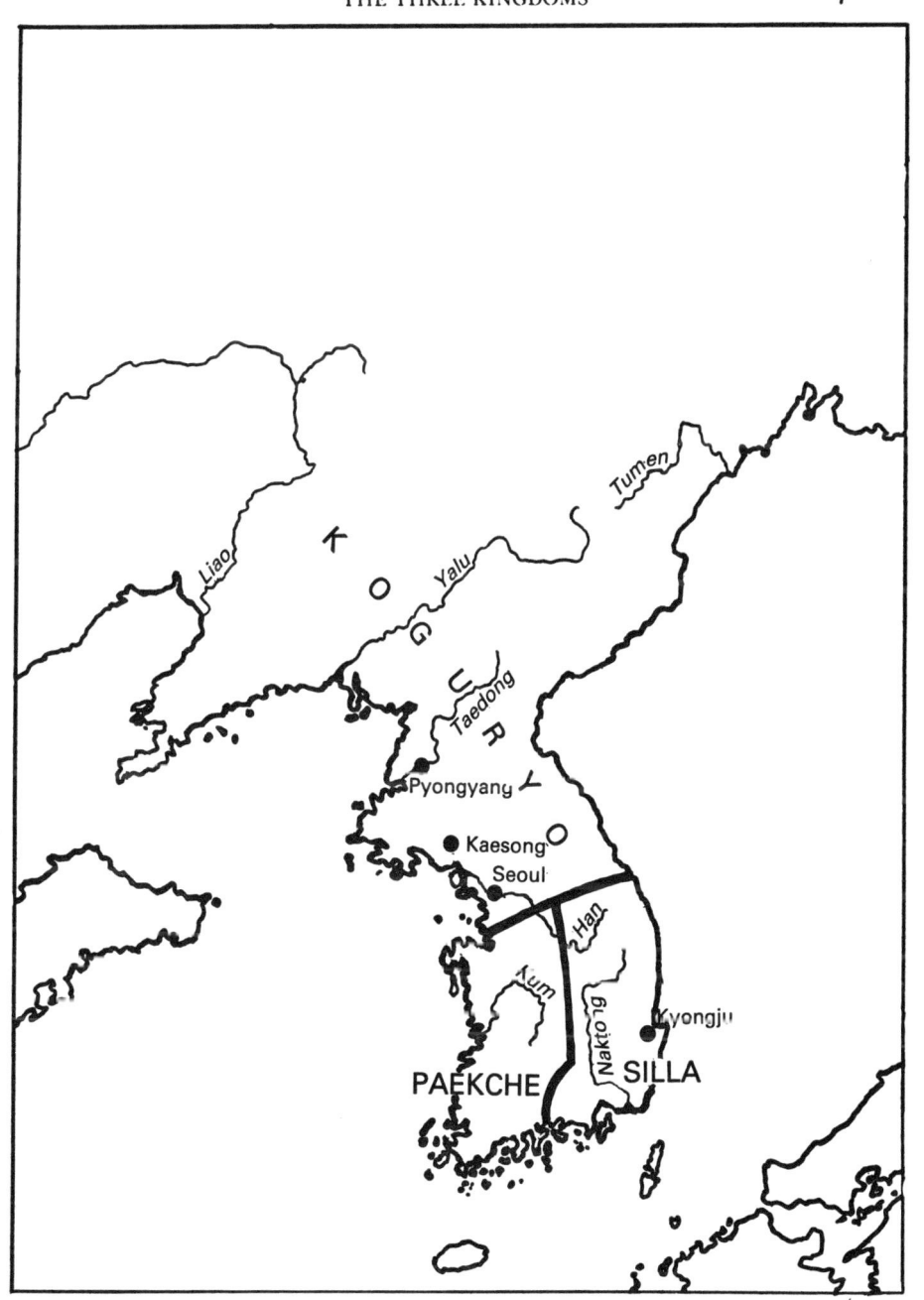

The Three Kingdoms AD 600.

A third cultural infusion from China into Korea lay in the learning and social philosophy of Confucius. With its stress on filial piety, on loyalty to the ruler, and to the established order, Confucianism had a major influence on social life generally and reinforced Korean forms of feudalism. Confucianism in particular emphasised the five relationships between king and minister, father and son, older and younger brother, husband and wife, friend and friend. The classic works of Chinese Confucian literature, and an examination system for the recruitment of civil servants, based on Confucian precepts, buttressed the system. Thus by about 600, the three Korean kingdoms were already run on Confucian lines.

For geographical reasons, the kingdom of Koguryo had the closest links with China originally. But Paekche also played a very important role in the wider dissemination of Chinese culture for this kingdom had close trading links with China. It was from Paekche that Chinese learning reached Japan.

In view of the fact that China was a more highly developed society than Korea, the influence of Chinese writing and thought is hardly surprising.

But in his authoritative *History of Korea*, Woo-keun Han has written of this period that 'the most significant fact is not that Korea adopted Chinese culture in such massive doses but that she managed to retain her own distinctive individuality and to adopt Chinese culture to her own purposes while many other people who came under Chinese influence were completely absorbed into the body of Chinese culture and their own culture ceased to exist'.

Silla Victorious

While Chinese cultural influence seeped into Korean life during the fifth and sixth centuries, it seemed as if the political rivalry between the three kingdoms would be won by the northern state of Koguryo. This kingdom not only threatened Paekche and Silla, but was also able in the early seventh century to repell an attack by the Chinese Sui dynasty. When the Sui, exhausted by its effects to dominate Korea, was succeeded by the Tang dynasty, Koguryo was still able to repell the Chinese between 644 and 659.

But the inter-Korean rivalry was won by Silla. This kingdom had been gradually increasing its political, military and economic potential. The south-eastern Korean kingdom had as its capital the legendary city of Kyongju, where relics of the Silla kings are an outstanding attraction for today's visitors. Kyongju was already a major centre of Korean arts and sciences by the seventh century, as it successfully adopted Chinese models of government and social organization to its own purposes. Now Silla displayed a high degree of statecraft as well.

In the late seventh century, Silla came to an alliance with the Chinese Tang rulers with the objective of eliminating its rivals. A Chinese army was sent to Korea, and a combined Tang-Silla force overthrew Paekche (660) and then Koguryo (668). Silla was now supreme in central and southern Korea, and the rule of the unified Silla dynasty is dated from 668.

Chinese ambitions to rule the whole of Korea were thwarted by Silla in 676. A Chinese army was expelled from Pyongyang on the Taedong River in northern Korea and the invaders sent packing to the Liao River far to the north. Korea south of the Taedong was now ruled as a politically unified country by a confident, powerful Silla. Further north, large parts of the former Koguryo kingdom had passed to the Parhae people during the eighth century. Parhae, which included large areas of what is now known as Manchuria, was reckoned a kingdom of Korean people. At first it posed no threat to the unified Silla kingdom which now concentrated on rebuilding the country after the wars of the seventh century.

Several generations later, in 735, the Chinese formally recognised the kingdom of Silla. The history of Korea had taken an important step forward, for Imperial China had come to terms with a single Korean kingdom.

Chapter Two:
Silla and Koryo

From its capital at Kyongju in south-east Korea, the Unified Silla Kingdom extended northwards to the Taedong River and the 'waist' of the Korean peninsula. Under King Kyongdok, who reigned from 742 to 764, Silla reached the peak of its power and prosperity.

Buddhism had been the official religion of Silla for some time, and now, with increased wealth generally, Buddhist monks began to enjoy a position of great power and privilege. It was a period of close Korean contacts with China, and some Buddhist monks went as far as India to obtain Buddhist scriptures. Other Korean traders and artists went to Japan, bringing with them further infusions of Chinese thought and learning. This was the great age of the Tang dynasty in China, but it is recorded that the temples of the Silla capital at Kyongju were as richly appointed as any in China. Royal patronage was an important factor in this outpouring of Buddhist art and architecture.

Near Kyongju, during the eighth century, there were four built on the To-ham mountain, which formed a natural barrier protecting the Silla capital from the east, two great Buddhist temples, the Pulguk-sa state temple and the Sokkuram granite cave temple. These temples remain two of the most perfect and celebrated Buddhist monuments in East Asia. The Pulguk-sa temple was partly destroyed in the Japanese invasions of the sixteenth century, but the stone parts of the temple, as originally built, remain. In particular, the Sokkuram shrine, with its figure of Buddha almost eleven feet high, its domed hall, and its delicate stonework, is a masterpiece of Buddhist art.

These two temples were built at the zenith of Silla's power and prosperity. The Silla royal family sponsored their construction,

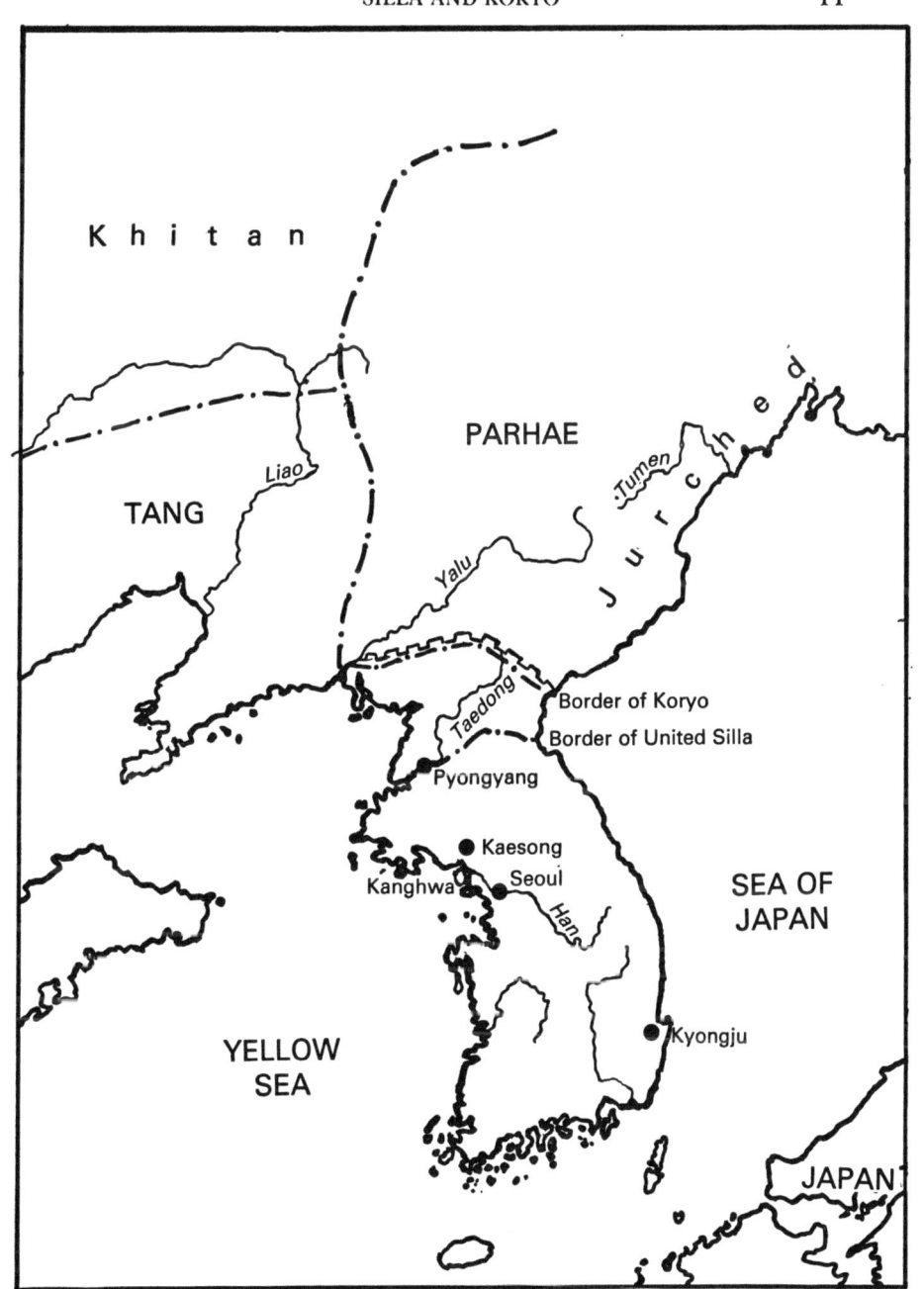

United Silla and Koryo 8th–14th centuries.

and execution of the project was the responsibility of Kim Tae-song, who had served King Kyongdok as chief minister. When he died in 774, the Silla kingdom completed the two temples. Other Buddhist memorials from this Silla period include large rock reliefs, which are relatively numerous, and which still attract worshippers. The Buddhist temple bells which were made in the Silla era include some of the biggest and finest ever made, some over ten feet high.

The Confucian Order

During the Silla period, Korea achieved full tributary status within the Confucian international order headed by Imperial China. We have already noted that the Confucian domestic order was dominated by the five personal and family relationships.

In the wider international context, according to M. Frederick Nelson's classic study, *Korea and the Old Orders in Eastern Asia*, 'to those accepting Confucian ideology, the world stood as a single unit. Under the aegis of heaven, according to this belief, there existed a pre-established world pattern wherein all things had a definite and proper relationship . . .' In this system, China was the Middle Kingdom, to whose ruler Heaven had given its mandate, to whom Heaven looked for the proper ordering of things. Under Silla, Korea was now to find its own distinctive place in this system.

This family of nations was governed by the same rules as the natural family, and hence under the Confucian familistic system, 'a nation's duties and privileges were governed by the same rules that preserved harmony in the family and in society'. China's relationship to Korea now became that of parent to son, although after the seventeenth century, this was usually termed that of elder to younger brother. The relationship was 'familistic and natural', and not legal in the Western sense, as there were no such concepts as the state and legal sovereignty in the Confucian order.

Korea did not achieve a place within this system until about the seventh century. Previously, the Middle Kingdom had regarded the Korean kings as barbarians to be conquered or manipulated as events dictated. But as Confucian culture came to dominate Korea, its kings came to consider investiture by the Chinese emperor as necessary to their right to rule. Nelson also writes that 'Korean rulers showed their respect by sending tribute to the Son of Heaven and accepting from him their investiture, along with gifts and admonitions concerning the preservation of the natural order'. Here was a pattern that was to govern Korean relationships with China until the late nineteenth century; it was only in 1895 that Korea became an independent state in the Western sense.

If reigning Chinese dynasties were overthrown by barbarians or usurpers, Korea gave up its allegiance to the Son of Heaven until the traditional relationship was re-established. When, for example, the Mongols conquered China in the thirteenth century they found it difficult to control Korea without the Confucian family relationship, and force and direct rule had to used. Japan, the third country of the Confucian system in East Asia, on the other hand, sometimes acknowledged and then renounced a tributary status in the Chinese Confucian system.

However, despite all its power, its artistic achievement, and its growing status within the Confucian family, the Silla dynasty went into a long, irreversible decline following the golden age of the eighth century.

For this fatal decline, three factors seem to have been responsible. Firstly, the Silla reigning family was plagued by family feuds and quarrels which completely dissipated its energy. Secondly, Silla was gradually threatened by the growing power of the Parhae kingdom to the north. This development helped to erode Silla's military power, so hastening the dynasty's decline. A third and very important reason for Silla's eventual fall was a series of peasant revolts, the inevitable result of misgovernment.

Early in the tenth century, a great rebel leader, General Wang Kon, became powerful in the Kaesong region to the north of the Han River estuary in central Korea. In 918 Wang Kon proclaimed the dynasty of Koryo at Kaesong, his native town. From this nodal point, the new regime could control a number of important strategic routes that linked the south and north of Korea.

After a prolonged political and military crisis, the last Silla king, Kyongsun, decided to abdicate and in 935 Wang Kon received the formal surrender of this monarch and his government. The local magnates were left undisturbed for the time being, the Silla aristocracy were accommodated, and the new dynasty was further legitimized when Wang Kon married a woman from the Silla royal family.

In this way, Silla was succeeded by Koryo; the second great dynasty in Korean history was now at hand.

The Koryo Dynasty

In line with Chinese custom, the Koreans gave their kings regnal or descriptive titles after their death, and it is by these names that the Korean kings are known to posterity. General Wang Kon, the founder of Koryo, thus became known to history as King Taejo, and this was also the posthumous title of the founder of the next Korean dynasty, the Yi. This was because the word Taejo was the Korean form of the Chinese expression for 'grand progenitor', or founder.

The age of the Koryo dynasty, from whose name derives the Western term 'Korea', was an eventful and significant age in Korean history. Following the establishment of regime, and the reorganisation of the bureaucracy on more centralist lines, Koryo embarked on a consistent policy of absorbing northern Korean lands which had been in the possession of the Parhae kingdom.

Parhae had been conquered in about 926 by the nomadic Khitan people, who then began raiding Koryo territory south of the Taedong River. But in a series of planned offensives later in the tenth century Koryo drove back the Khitan to the line of the lower Yalu River, thus largely establishing the northern borders of Korea in this region as they have remained to this day. Former Korean lands to the north of the Yalu were now considered lost. In the far north-east, Koryo claimed the Tumen River as the Korean border, but the rise of the Mongol Jurched people in this area precluded effective Koryo control.

Eventually, in about 1044, Koryo built a stone defensive wall across Korea from the lower Yalu to the Eastern Sea (or the Sea of Japan). There was continuing instability on the northern borders of Korea, and in 1136 Koryo recognised the suzerainty of the Jurched Chin dynasty which had conquered North China and Manchuria. For the next few decades there was comparative calm on Korea's northern borders.

The early Koryo period was characterised by the rise of an aristocratic landed class, the yangban, who were to contest the emergence of a strong monarchy. Another source of latent instability was the conflict between the warrior class and the powerful literary caste which provided the bureaucracy. But nevertheless, there were impressive cultural developments during the age of Koryo.

Buddhism was reconfirmed as the state religion and thus received protection and valued privileges from the Court. Many Korean historical works were written but some of the most valuable of these books did not survive the subsequent Mongol invasions of Korea. However, of great importance in the cultural history of Korea was the first printing of the Buddhist devotional work, the *Tripitaka*. This production in 6,000 volumes was made possible by the carving of 80,000 wooden blocks. Later destroyed by fire, the *Tripitaka* was re-printed, and survives to the present day. Moreover, during the late Koryo period, movable metal type was evolved in Korea, several centuries before this technique was discovered in Europe.

An important intellectual development during this period was the evolution of a sophisticated (and revitalising) interpretation of Confucianism which stemmed from the thought of the Chinese sage, Chu Hsi. This neo-Confucianism now emerged as the intellectual basis of an opposition movement to Buddhism, for the privileges enjoyed by Buddhist monks were generating resentment throughout Korean society.

But perhaps the most important cultural legacy of the Koryo period lay in the flowering of Korean ceramic art. Under the Silla dynasty, Korean ceramics had already developed from earthenware and ash-glazed pottery to early examples of the distinctive pale-green porcelain known as celadon. Chinese potters, of course, manufactured a wide range of ceramics, but now under Koryo, their Korean counterparts concentrated on producing uniquely refined celadons. With their inlaid, incised designs, even the Chinese regarded Koryo celadons as the finest made; the art reached its perfection under the rule of King Injong (1122–46).Many of these treasures have survived and may be seen in the Korean National Museum in Seoul.

The Mongol Invasions

The high civilisation of Koryo was ended by one of the great catastrophes in Korean history, the Mongol invasions. Korean life was affected for over a century, and the aftermath of this alien incursion led to the fall of the Koryo dynasty.

In 1202 Temujin, or Ghengis Khan, was elected leader of the Mongol horde. By 1215, eastern Europe had been ravaged, and the Mongols had even conquered China, where they became known officially as the Yuan dynasty. Korea was now affected by Mongol pressure, and at first the Mongols were bought off by tribute.

But in 1231 the Mongols launched a full-scale invasion of Korea, driving down the central mountains to the Han River. The Koryo capital at Kaesong was taken, and heavy tribute exacted. The Korean kings retreated to Kanghwa Island, in the Han estuary, but on the mainland resistance continued for decades during which most of the the major cities of Korea were sacked. Eventually, the country was pacified, and Koreans were even impressed to assist the abortive Mongol invasions of Japan in 1274 and 1281. The failed invasion of Japan, however, marked the Mongol high tide in East Asia.

The Mongols continued to bear down on Korea until the mid-fourteenth century, when the Chinese reasserted themselves under the Ming dynasty. By 1382, the Ming were in control of Peking, the Koryo kings had removed Mongol officials, and the Mongol era had thus come to an end.

But by now the Koryo dynasty was in a prolonged, insoluble crisis. Removed pro-Mongol officials plotted against the court. There was conflict between Buddhist monks and Confucian intellectuals. The Buddhist monasteries were in any case envied for their wealth.

Eventually the fall of Koryo was brought about indirectly by the ravages of Japanese pirates on the southern Korean coast. General Yi Song-gye gained much esteem by countering these pirates, and in 1388 General Yi seized local power in Kaesong. He then began to implement reforms with the backing of the Confucian elite.

In due course, General Yi was proclaimed King in July 1392, so ending the Koryo dynasty. The Yi dynasty was to last for over 500 years into the twentieth century, linking medieval with modern Korea, so that there are Koreans still living who were born under the Yi.

Chapter Three:
Korea Under The Yi

Following his assumption of power in 1392, General Yi Song-gye, the new ruler of the Korean kingdom, was recognised by the Supreme Council, the most important body in the Koryo administration. The Council stated that the Koryo dynasty was ended, and that General Yi was the legitimate ruler of Korea. The new king was later given the same posthumous title as the founder of the Koryo dynasty, Taejo, and it is by this name that posterity knows the first Yi king.

As part of his general policy of reform, King Taejo replaced Buddhism as the state religion by Confucianism. Confucian learning was given priority, and neo-Confucian scholars, well versed in Chu Hsi's doctrines, achieved great influence. These scholar-officials who were recruited by the new king in effect acted as senior royal advisers. The King had an interest in benevolent rule, for he was regarded as possessing the Mandate of Heaven. Many Confucian teaching institutions were set up as part of this policy of establishing a Confucian state.

Most of these Confucian scholar-officials came from the *yangban* or landed aristocratic class. The term may be used generally to describe this official-landed class or to refer to individuals. The yangban had begun to emerge as a class in late Silla times, and had contested the development of a strong Koryo monarchy in Korea as we have already noted. There were thus good reasons of state why King Taejo now made a determined attempt at land reform. This reform aimed at establishing the royal authority and at the same time bettering the living conditions of the ordinary peasant and small tenant farmer.

With the support of many of his Confucian officials, Taejo decreed that all land was to be held by the state and reapportioned. Royal officials could only hold land when they were actually in office. The general thrust of King Taejo's policy was thus aimed at creating a reformed, centralized monarchy based on the ascendancy of the King over the yangban landed magnates.

Founding the Dynasty

King Taejo moved to establish his authority in a number of other ways. Early in his reign he reaffirmed his country's traditional tributary relationship with the Ming rulers of China. The Chinese Emperor approved a new name for Korea, Choson, which was the title, as we have seen, of the earliest Korean state. It was in this way that Korea acquired its modern name of the Land of the Morning Calm. The dynasty founded by King Taejo is thus often called Choson by Korean historians, although in the West it is generally known as the Yi after the name of its founder.

Of great importance was King Taejo's decision to transfer the Korean capital from Kaesong, with its Koryo associations, to Hanyang (later Seoul), a hilltop fortress site in the lower valley of the Han River and near the Yellow Sea. Taejo had very early decided to move from Kaesong, but it was not apparent at first that Seoul would be the choice. One of the critical elements in the final decision over the new Yi capital was the ancient Oriental science of Geomancy.

This pseudo-science, which had great influence in China and Japan as well as Korea, stemmed not from Confucianism but rather from the Chinese religion of Taoism. Essentially, Geomancy taught that the physical outlines of a landscape had great influence on the people living there. But these 'marks of a propitious character' had to be interpreted by learned intermediaries, especially as 'wind' and 'water' elements had to be carefully assessed, as well as those of male and female.

Although King Taejo was disposed to establish his new capital in southern Korea, a Buddhist monk, Mu-Hak, who was associated with the King believed that the vital signs indicated Hanyang. Here was an attractive site guarded by a northern mountain (Pugak-san) and a southern mountain (Nam-san). After some deliberation, the preference of Mu-Hak, the Buddhist geomancer, proved decisive and the King adopted Seoul as his capital in about 1395. The site was in any case in the

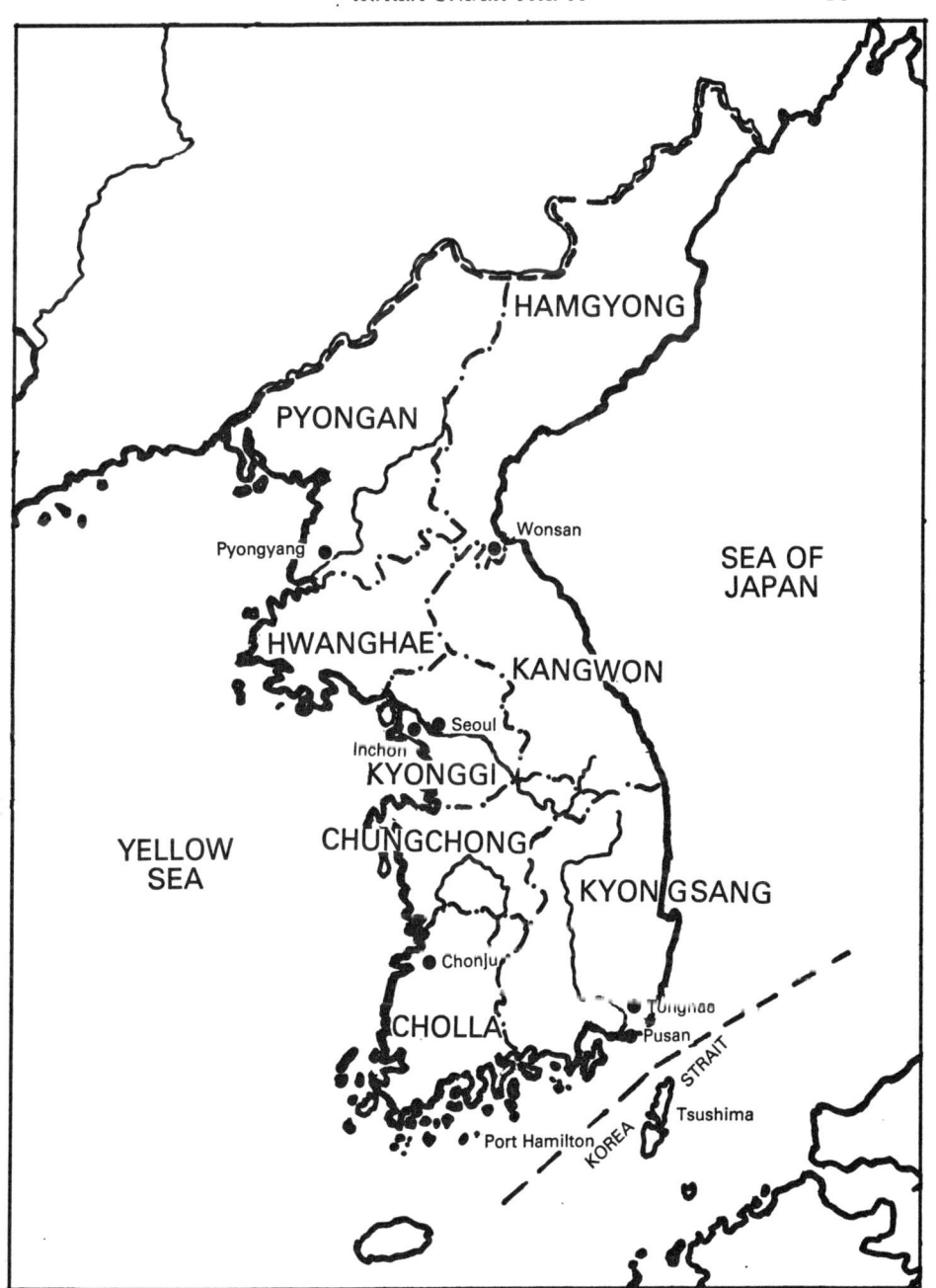

The eight provinces of the Yi Dynasty 14th–19th century.

strategic centre of Korea, with good access to both north and south of the country.

The government thus moved to Seoul, as it became known, and new palaces were built, including the Kyongbok Palace in the centre of the site. This palace became the main seat of royal administration. Apart from a few short periods, Seoul was now to remain the capital of the Yi kings through all their vicissitudes during the next five centuries.

Yet another historic administrative development initiated under King Taejo and his immediate successors was the permanent consolidation of north-east Korea as an integral part of the country. To be sure, the Koryo dynasty had claimed the northern border of the upper Yalu and Tumen Rivers in this region, but the Koryo kings had been unable to conquer the nomadic tribes of the area and bring the region into the Korean administrative structure.

With King Taejo, a determined effort was begun to solve this problem, and under Taejo's grandson, King Sejong (*reg.* 1418–50), the Korean north-east up to the line of the Tumen River was brought under royal control. Garrison towns were set up, civil officials moved in, and immigration from southern Korea was encouraged. And so to this day, the Tumen River remains the north-eastern border of Korea.

Another lasting administrative measure of the early Yi kings was the division of Korea into eight major provinces. In later years, these provinces were further divided into northern and southern parts. But the main provincial boundaries have survived into the present.

In each of these new provinces the Yi kings appointed an administrator, and beneath him were created magistrates with wide executive powers. A military headquarters was set up in each province staffed with army and sometimes naval officers. In the northern provinces of Pyongan and Hamgyong, for example, army officers were in control. But in the southern maritime provinces of Kyongsang and Cholla, whose coasts were affected by Japanese piracy, there were sometimes two naval commanders in the provincial military command.

Confucian Government

The centralized Confucian system of government which was

created by the early Yi kings in the first century of their rule was to survive, surprisingly unchanged, into the nineteenth century. Essentially this structure was based on classical Chinese Confucian lines adapted to Korean conditions and thus a strict hierarchy was an integral part of the system. It must be remembered that the Confucian cultural legacy remains strong, even in today's Korea.

At the pinnacle of government was the King who, like the Chinese Emperor, claimed the divine Mandate of Heaven. The King's authority was absolute and hereditary, for in the Confucian view his government brought about harmony between divine and human activities. Chinese Confucianism held that a ruler could be overthrown if the Mandate was violated by an unjust Emperor. In Korea, this teaching was modified to assert that even a tyrannical ruler could not be overthrown, although in practice Korean kings were deposed or murdered.

The King was surrounded by a mystique and protocol that proclaimed his divine origins. Immediately below the King was the Royal Secretariat and the State Council which supervised six ministries. These six ministries were concerned with Justice, Personnel, Public Works, Revenue, Rites and War. Under the Yi, the State Council was soon to lose its supervisory functions, and the Ministries were put under the King's direct control. The Council then became advisory only.

An important supervisory part of this government lay in the three Censorate offices. One was known as the Office of the Inspector-General and another as the Office of the Censor-General. The third was the Office of Special Counsellors which advised the King on matters connected with the Confucian classics and their relevance to government.

Serious criminal offences were dealt with by Royal Guards, who also functioned in cases of threats to the King and to national security generally.

According to the Korean historian, Woo-keun Han, who has described the system in detail, this basic administrative structure was set up during the reign of King Taejong (1400–18), who was King Taejo's son. The laws which governed the system were then duly codified and completed by about 1470.

The essence of the system lay in the stratified bureaucracy with its exclusive relationship between officialdom and the literate yangban, aristocratic caste. The bureaucracy encompassed nine grades, each grade sub divided into four, so making a class with thirty six ascending divisions. As promotion into the upper levels was extremely difficult, the Korean government was a relatively tiny elite which in practise perpetuated itself from generation to generation.

The power of this elite was further concentrated by the practice of senior officials holding several posts at the same time. This pluralism further increased the centralization of the system.

In line with Confucius's teachings, which exalted learning and especially literary scholarship, civil servants were held in greater regard than the military. But this demarcation was not always observed, as civil officials sometimes held military or naval rank. However, in general under the Yi kings it was the civil officials of the administration which held the senior policy-making positions.

Inherent in the Yi government was the device which allowed relatively junior officials to present petitions to the King, a method also used by some Confucian intellectuals in attempting to see that national policy followed the precepts of the Sage. Commoners could also appeal to the King, but in general these methods did not influence policy. The Yi administration thus remained both autocratic and the preserve of the yangban class.

Underwriting the system was the Confucian examination system which was apparently applied with greater strictness under the Yi than under earlier Korean dynasties. But the very complexity of the system turned it into an elaborate screening process which continued to emphasise yangban ascendancy. Although there were three examinations, civil, military and technical, the civil division was of course the most important.

In this category, there were two subdivisions, higher and lower, and the emphasis in both divisions was on the Confucian classics and literature. In the final, higher examination there were three stages held in the provinces, in Seoul, and before the King. Successful candidates were able to serve in all senior administrative posts, a great honour.

The emphasis on hierarchy and status in the Korean government was but a reflection of the firm divisions in society under the Yi dynasty. At the pinnacle lay of course the *yangban*, who inherited both power and wealth. Then came the *chungin*, a small middle class of minor officials. Below them were the *sangmin* (common people) who were largely farmers and thus formed the majority of Koreans. Lastly we find the *chonmin*, a menial class of slaves and generally underprivileged persons.

The Confucian system meant that there was an intense emphasis in the upper reaches of society on learning, which meant in practice the study of the Chinese Confucian classics. Familiarity with these classics was the avenue to power and prestige. Social distinctions were strict, and inter-marriage between classes virtually prohibited. There was an inherent Confucian prejudice against commerce and business which affected both Korean domestic and international trade. This bias against commerce reflected the Confucian precept that for an individual to change his status, for example by the accumulation of wealth, was abhorrent to society and even to heaven itself.

Thus although the Confucian legacy in Korean life and government emphasised national continuity and stability, it also gave to society a rigidity which even the reforming ambitions of the early Yi kings were unable eventually to overcome.

Cultural Achievements

A high level of cultural achievement was promoted by the early Yi kings, and in particular by King Sejong. The king was a strong believer in the Confucian precept that the study of literature and history was the path to the achievement of individual and collective virtue. This notable reign in the first half of the fifteenth century was also characterised by the development of new ideas in music, medicine, astronomy and other sciences.

Sejong gave practical effect to his innovative ideas by creating a royal research institute, the 'Hall of Talented Scholars' *(Chiphyonjon)*. The institute was modelled on Chinese examples, and compiled textbooks and instructional manuals on the Korean arts and sciences, besides providing tutors for the Korean royal family.

The historic cultural achievement of King Sejong's reign, which seems to have been the personal inspiration of the king, was the promulgation in 1446 of a Korean phonetic alphabet with 28 letters. This was officially called *Hunmin chongum*, 'Correct sounds for the people', and became generally known as *Hangul*. Prior to the development of *Hangul*, the only effective written language in Korea was classical Chinese, which was known as *Hanmun*.

Before the promulgation of *Hangul* in 1446, attempts had been made, as in the *Idu* system, to adapt spoken Korean speech into Chinese characters. But because the Chinese and Korean languages were structurally unrelated, and in particular because

Chinese was an ideographic or sign language, while Korean was phonetic, it was enormously difficult for Chinese characters to represent Korean speech. Hangul transformed the prospects of the Korean language for its 28-letter phonetic alphabet could be learnt in a few hours. A premium was thus placed on literacy, as Hangul was much easier to learn than Chinese with its thousands of sign-letters.

However, many Confucian scholars objected to *Hangul*, and Chinese remained the language of serious literature, of offical administration, and of polite yangban society. The Chinese cultural heritage thus remained predominant in Korea, in much the same way as Latin remained the official language in Western Europe at the close of the middle ages while individual European countries were developing their vernacular languages. Moreover, although the Yi court continued to promote Hangul, the forces of tradition were on the side of Chinese as a literary language. The phonetic alphabet thus came to be regarded as an inferior usage, and in effect was reserved for popular prose romances and other such works until the increasing modernization of Korea at the end of the nineteenth century.

With the development of general literacy in Korea in the present century, Hangul has now come into universal use. Many of the Chinese loan words in Korean have been turned into Hangul, and Chinese ideographs or signs are increasingly retained only for technical terms or proper names.

The visual arts as well flourished under the early Yi kings. There was a revival of Korean painting, which now advanced from its Buddhist or religious preoccupations and concentrated on secular, non-religious themes.

As part of this development, professional artists turned to portraits and landscapes, and their work became recognisably Korean in terms of content and technique. These professional painters often worked for the Yi Court and the royal family. Less professional artists, who were often literary men and poets, turned to scroll painting and calligraphy, a form that remained popular with Koreans down the centuries.

Thus in calligraphy, as in the wider artistic field, Korean artists under the early Yi dynasty outgrew their original Chinese models and began to develop their own naturalistic modes of expression. During the early Yi period, therefore, a Korean tradition began evolving in the arts which went on developing for the remainder of the dynasty's long life.

Korean ceramics under the Yi, while not so accomplished as those of the Koryo period, were still prized. The earlier demand for the distinctive green Koryo celadons seems to have declined in favour of a highly perfected white porcelain characteristic of the early Yi period.

Yangban Rivalry and Reassertion

The paternalistic administration of King Sejong, the inventor of Hangul, was probably a golden age. Although the cultural achievement remained, Sejong's reign was followed by a prolonged period of feud and rivalry within the Court and the yangban class.

This period of instability was characterised by a reassertion of the power of the traditional aristocracy, the yangban. The early Yi kings had embarked on a policy of land reform and had attempted to curtail the privileges of the yangban. An attempt was made to restrict the holding of estates by these nobles only when they held office. Both King Sejo (1455–68) and King Songjong (1469–94) attempted to continue this policy.

However, as the yangban class continued to hold very real power through their monopoly of office, they were in effect able to resist the royal policy and to continue to expand their estates, known as *nongjang*. The yangban put pressure on a series of kings to accept their privileges and at the same time by a series of extralegal devices continued to improve their position. One such device was the removal by the landlords of tenants from the official tax lists, so weakening the royal treasury. Another was the exclusion of yangban tenants from the draft or conscription rolls, so weakening royal military power. Thus the internal balance of power moved away from the King to the yangban class.

As the yangban increased in number through each generation, so the competition for official posts increased. Rivalry and ambition led to a number of feuds and purges within the official class, as powerful yangban sought to exclude their rivals from office. The yangban class was in any case divided between its loyalty to the Crown and to its respective clans. It was also difficult to institutionalize opposition under the Confucian ethic which emphasised authority. The net result of this yangban factionalism was that the monarchy was further weakened and that the creative energy of the early Yi kings ebbed away.

Historical analogies are not always apt. But in this particular respect, the Korean Kings of this period were not as fortunate as the Tudor monarchs of England who reigned at approximately the same time. These monarchs were able to establish their authority and also a centralized monarchy at the expense of the traditional landed aristocracy.

Eventually, however, a semblance of stability was restored during the early sixteenth century in Korea under the reign of King Chungjong (1506–44). But for the remainder of the Yi dynasty, the Crown was on the whole at a disadvantage in relation to the yangban who had reasserted their power.

Following Chungjong's reign, there was a revival of yangban factionalism. But within a generation, the internal problems of the Korean kings were relegated to a secondary place as relations with Japan came to the fore. Events within that neighbouring island empire at the end of the sixteenth century were now to have profound results for Korea.

Hideyoshi's Invasion

During the fourteenth and fifteenth centuries, south and west Korea were plagued by Japanese pirates on Kyushu and the Tsushima islands in the Korea Strait. The founder of the Yi dynasty, King Taejo, had distinguished himself as a young man in operations against these pirates. Successive Korean kings had thus sent envoys to the Shogun's court at Kyoto in Japan with the objective of controlling these marauders. It was the Shogunate, controlled at this time by the Ashikaga family, which ruled Japan as the emperor was but a cipher.

Progress was made in controlling the piracy, and during the early fifteenth century there was a regular exchange of missions between Korea and the Shogunate. Some trade developed between the two countries which was largely controlled by the *Daimyo* (lord) of Tsushima. A commercial treaty between Korea and the Daimyo in 1439 regularised this trade, and three southeastern Korean ports, later reduced to one at Pusan, were opened to commerce.

Despite these trading activities, the political arena in Japan during the fifteenth and sixteenth centuries was characterised by almost perpetual civil war in which rival Daimyo increasingly wrested authority from the Shogunate. But in 1573 there was a change in this pattern which soon affected Korea. A great Japanese warrior, Oda Nobunaga, overthrew the Ashikaga

Shogunate and began to impose his rule on the country. Although Nobunaga was assassinated in 1582, one of his followers, Toyotomi Hideyoshi, now succeeded in unifying Japan and was given the title of dictator.

Hideyoshi, although physically a near-dwarf, was a great military leader and he now decided on the conquest of China. When the Koreans rejected Hideyoshi's demand for transit rights in this ambitious plan, a Japanese army of 150,000 men invaded Korea in the spring of 1592. Within three weeks of landing at Pusan, the Japanese had taken Seoul. By July, Pyongyang had fallen. A significant factor in these successes was the use of muskets by the Japanese. These they had copied from the Portuguese who had landed in Japan in 1542.

In response to a Korean request, large Ming Chinese forces now entered Korea across the Yalu, and forced the Japanese back to the vicinity of Seoul. Korean guerrillas harried the Japanese, and under Admiral Yi Sun-sin Korean iron-clad warships, named 'turtle-ships' after their armoured decks, intercepted Japanese supply vessels in the Korea Strait. But the Chinese, too, suffered heavy losses and many thousands of Koreans died in the chaos of war. Japanese losses from disease were considerable.

During 1593, an armistice was agreed, but the Japanese, following further reverses, now only continued to occupy a toehold of Korean territory in the , south. The peace negotiations dragged on, and in 1597 Hideyoshi launched another full-scale invasion of Korea. But this time the invaders only succeeded in occupying the southern Korean province of Kyongsang and part of Cholla. Admiral Yi won a decisive action over the Japanese fleet, but was killed in action. Only after Hideyoshi's death in 1598 did the Japanese withdraw from Korea.

Hideyoshi's invasion had profound consequences for the three countries involved. Tokugawa Ieyasu, Hideyoshi's successor, was able to become the recognised dictator of Japan, and later Shogun. He was the founder of the Tokugawa Shogunate which ruled until 1868. For Ming China, the years of fighting in Korea with its unprecedented cost were soon to lead to the collapse of the dynasty when faced with the militant challenge of the Manchus.

Korea was the most affected. The physical devastation was immense, and it is believed that land under cultivation fell by two thirds. The southern Korean provinces were especially affected.

Temples, towns, and cultural treasures were all destroyed, while Korean potters, together with metal printing type and other artefacts were taken back to Japan. Resentment over the invasion naturally remained. But a treaty was signed with the Shogunate in 1609 which permitted limited trade between the two countries through Tsushima and Pusan.

The catastrophe of Hideyoshi's campaigns in Korea was compounded by the successive Manchu invasions of the country forty years later. Korea then withdrew from virtually all foreign contacts for over two hundred years, so acquiring the name of the 'Hermit Kingdom'. It is to this prolonged episode in Korean history that we must now turn.

Chapter Four:
The Time of Isolation

Within barely a generation of Hideyoshi's invasion, Korea was to suffer further foreign incursion, but this time from north of the Yalu. The Ming dynasty in China had been critically weakened by its efforts in repelling the Japanese from Korea; the Chinese rulers now faced the threat of the revived Jurched tribes of Manchuria, a people from now on known to history as the Manchus.

The Manchus hoped to conquer China and to set up their own dynasty in much the same way as the Mongols had done. Moreover, like the Mongols, the Manchus were clearly aware of the potential flanking threat to their ambitions from a Korea loyal to the old Chinese dynasty.

The Manchu Invasions of Korea

It soon became apparent that the decline of the Ming was terminal. Taking advantage of their early military successes against the Ming and also of dissension within the Korean royal family, a Manchu army crossed the Yalu in 1627 and seized Pyongyang. The invaders then moved south to Seoul. King Injo (1623–49) and his family fled to the traditional royal retreat of Kanghwa Island in the Han estuary. But prolonged struggle was not possible and peace negotiations were soon begun. The Koreans agreed to pay tribute to the Manchus, and also, in rather vague terms, to give homage.

The issue was finally decided during 1636–37 after the Manchus had won further victories over the Ming. By now the Manchus had proclaimed themselves the Ching dynasty of China and their envoys demanded that Korea should formally become their vassal. King Injo refused and consequently another Manchu host invaded Korea. Like the Mongols four centuries previously the invaders advanced through the central Korean mountains and southwards along the Uijongbu corridor which lies immediately north of Seoul.

This time King Injo and his family were unable to escape their fate. Although the King initially took up residence on Kanghwa Island, this royal sanctuary soon fell to the invaders. The King was then forced to renounce all allegiance to the Ming, and to make homage to the Manchu Ching dynasty. The Crown Prince of Korea, Prince Sohyon, was held by the Manchus as a hostage. Korea was also forced to assist the Manchus in their final military campaigns against the Ming regime, which was at last toppled in 1644. From Peking, the Manchus now ruled China as the Ching, a dynasty which was to survive until 1911.

These events, following the earlier Japanese invasions, were traumatic for Korea. The country was now to enjoy over two centuries of peace, but the fear of foreign countries was so great that foreign travel and foreign visitors were banned. It was these developments that gave Korea its name of the 'Hermit Kingdom'.

Foreign trade was also restricted and officially confined to China and Japan. Envoys and annual tribute were sent to the Imperial Court at Peking through the Korean town of Uiju on the Yalu, and then through Mukden in southern Manchuria to Shanhaikuan, where the Great Wall of China meets the sea. The demands of the Ching were not heavy, and the tribute ritual continued well into the nineteenth century.

Trade with Japan was allowed on a restricted basis through Tsushima Island and Pusan. Occasionally, Korean envoys were sent to the court of the Shogun at Edo (later Tokyo). Following the virtual elimination of Christianity in early seventeenth century Japan, that country was closed to foreigners on pain of death in 1638. Apart from the limited trade with Korea, the only external contact allowed by the Tokugawa Shogunate was a small Dutch trading post on the island of Deshima in Nagasaki harbour.

But Korea was even more effectively isolated than Japan. Korea relied on Peking for its foreign relations, and as an independent country within the Confucian system insisted that even the Sino-Korean border along the Yalu was kept tightly closed.

The result of this effective, self-imposed seclusion, underlined by geographical isolation, was that Korea was the last of the Con-

THE TIME OF ISOLATION 31

fucian states of East Asia to be opened to Western contact. The full implications of this policy of national isolation only became apparent in the later nineteenth century. By then it was no longer possible to insulate even the Hermit Kingdom from the outside world.

The Hermit Kingdom

Korea's time of isolation from the seventeenth to the later nineteenth centuries was characterised on the whole by political and social stagnation; but paradoxically the tradition of artistic vitality dating from the early Yi period was maintained.

One of the leading Western authorities on East Asia, John K. Fairbank, has suggested that the picture of political stagnation may have been due in part to the fact that so much had been borrowed from China. But Fairbank also writes that Korea remained distinctly different from China 'in historical experiences, social structure, and worldly situation. But like the Manchus when they ruled the Middle Kingdom, the Korean ruling class felt themselves to be conservators of a great tradition, not innovators.'

Fairbank goes on to write that the hereditary and nonproductive yangban class used Chinese attitudes to support a monopoly of public life narrower than that of the gentry class in China. They clung to the letter of Confucianism, tolerated no deviation from orthodoxy, and maintained private Confucian academies (*sowon*) and controlled the examination system. They controlled and restricted trade, mining, and technical innovation.

The Japanese and Manchu invasions were partly responsible for this ascendancy of the yangban. The early Yi kings, as we have seen, had attempted to rule the country directly, and dispensed with the executive powers of the State Council, relegating this body to an advisory role. However, during the Japanese invasions and after, the Korean Army's Frontier Defence Command had increasingly emerged as a *de facto* executive State Council, combining both high military and civil officials. This new council in effect administered the government for the King, so reverting to the situation which had existed in late Koryo times.

Following the Manchu invasions, this Council (now called the *Pibyonsa*) consolidated its powers and emerged as a permanent, institutionalized element of Yi government Which was to survive into the nineteenth century. The accumulation of power by the early Yi monarchs was thus quite clearly reversed, and in the abscence of a strong monarchy the yangban class was able to continue to reassert its power and privileges.

The decades following the Manchu invasions of Korea thus witnessed a new level of bureaucratic factionalism within the government. A series of feuds between 'Southerners' and 'Westerners' culminated in the triumph of the latter faction at the end of the seventeenth century. This victorious faction of 'Westerners' then divided into the *Noron* (or elder group) and the *Soron* (younger group). By the early eighteenth century, the Noron were in the ascendant, excluding all other factions from power. Yet there were usually no serious policy differences at the centre of this factionalism.

As a result of this internecine feuding, large numbers of yangban who found themselves excluded from office diverted their energies into expanding their country estates. The Confucian examination system for government personnel became increasingly irrelevant as the dominant faction within the court manipulated the results.

Under the rule of King Yongjo (1724–76) and King Chongjo (1776–1800) two successive monarchs attempted to end this bureaucratic rivalry by giving government posts to both the Noron and the Soron factions. But in a wider context this factionalism indicated the collapse of the Confucian idealism that provided much of the inspiration of the early Yi kings.

According to the Korean historian Woo-keun Han, 'although factionalism was for a time eliminated, power continued to depend upon wealth and position rather than talent, and the Confucian concepts that had contributed so much to Yi dynasty government and society no longer had any real influence on the actual practice of government'.

But there were some positive developments in economic life during Korea's time of isolation. In the aftermath of the Manchu invasions the tax system was partly rationalised in the interests of uniformity. Yet the overall tax burden demanded by the workings of the top-heavy royal administration in Seoul remained high. On the other hand, agricultural improvements meant that two-crop farming with barley and rice became common at least in southern Korea. These improvements, combined with new irrigation techniques, led to a gradual increase of population. Thus the total population of Korea is believed to have grown from over two million in 1657 to over seven million in 1753.

There was a steady growth in the size of Seoul. This was partly due to the slow development of a mercantile economy stemming from the increase in national population and wealth. Despite the formal Confucian disapproval of commercial activity, displaced yangban, losers in the factional struggle in government, increasingly entered business life in Seoul. Another development that pointed the way towards a less rigidly stratified society was the government's sale of some official posts to raise cash for the exchequer. Rich peasants also found themselves able to buy yangban estate titles as social mobility gradually increased.

Gradually, too, serfs and slaves won their freedom. In the aftermath of the Japanese and Manchu invasions, which left a devastated countryside, there was a labour shortage. Both an impoverished government and yangban class found it was cheaper to let slaves become tenants rather than to keep them. This process was underlined when in 1801 the registers of serfs or bondmen were destroyed by the government to assist the process of emancipation. As traditional Confucian society declined, so wealth rather than family became the indicator of status.

In contrast to this slow decay of Confucian society during the time of isolation, the period was one of continuing cultural achievement. During the eighteenth century the Korean law codes were revised, and there were significant developments in studies affecting Korean history and geography. A new national consciousness began to form. Another significant development was the growth of the *Sirhak* (Practical Learning) movement amongst the intelligentsia. As its name implies, the movement demanded a practical approach to administration rather than concentration on the tenets of Confucianism and on Chinese classical literature. This movement flourished in the eighteenth century.

In the visual arts there were continuing achievements in calligraphy and especially in genre painting with artists increasingly inspired by scenes drawn from everyday Korean life.

Thus Chang Son (d.1759), an especially innovative painter, depicted the Korean landscape in a variety of scenes, while Kim Hong-do (b.1740) painted scenes from the daily life of the common people. Another famous artist of this period, Sin Yunbok, painted romantic love scenes of men and women in striking colours and with decisive brushwork. While Chinese forms were still influential, the inspiration of these artists was specifically Korean.

The Coming of the West

In the seventeenth and eighteenth centuries, European influence grew slowly but steadily in the Far East. In China and even in Japan there was a growing awareness of Western scientific and technical knowledge amongst the elite.

But Korea was several hundred miles to the north of the Western trade routes which extended from the Indian Ocean to southern China at Canton and to the Dutch trading post at Nagasaki in Japan. In any case, as we have noted, it was specifically forbidden for Koreans to have contact with other nations. Moreover the Confucian governing class in Korea believed that nothing could be learnt from any other foreign country but China.

However, during the seventeenth century Western books on science and religion, translated into Chinese, began to enter Korea from the small Jesuit mission in Peking which had been founded originally by the famous missionary Matteo Ricci (d.1610). These books were brought back to Seoul by Korean envoys to the Chinese Imperial court. 'Western Learning' (*Sohak*) made no appreciable impression on the Korean elite. But during the eighteenth century the influence of Roman Catholic Christianity began to spread gradually among the people of western and southern Korea.

By the end of the century many of the inhabitants of Hwanghae province in north-western Korea were reported to be sympathetic to Catholicism. The faith was also apparently popular in the southern provinces of Chungchong and Cholla. As Catholic influence began to spread amongst the yangban classes, the government now took counter-measures. The new religion was banned in 1795, and the import of Catholic books from China forbidden.

No ordained Christian minister had entered Korea until 1795 when the Chinese Catholic priest Chou Wen-mu crossed the Yalu. Prior to about this time, Catholicism had not been actively persecuted. But with the accession of boy-king Sunjo in 1800, there came a change of policy by the court's new advisers. Catholicism was now regarded as a subversive cult. The first large-scale persecution of Catholic adherents in 1801 cost the life of the priest Chou Wen-mu. Catholicism was also regarded as a foreign creed which threatened the state, for about this time an appeal by a Korean Catholic for French naval assistance was intercepted by the authorities. The faith was soon driven underground, but continued to flourish, as so often in the past, despite persecution. French priests were sent to Korea from China, and in 1831 Korea was detached from the Catholic bishopric of Peking and made a see in its own right. A renewed wave of persecution soon followed in 1839 when three French priests were executed.

By 1850 there were about 11,000 Catholics in Korea, and by 1865 this number had doubled. A central element in this prolonged persecution, which lasted until 1873, was the official belief that Catholicism was associated with the foreign intervention that had cost Korea so much in the past. This concern was underlined by contemporary events which now ripped apart the old Confucian order in East Asia. Essentially these developments, which were to affect Korea profoundly, were caused by the inevitable collision between the dynamic, merchantile Western powers and the closed societies of China, Japan and Korea.

By the treaty of Nanking (29 August 1842) which ended the Opium War the British were awarded Hong Kong and the opening of five Chinese 'treaty ports' to British trade and residence. A supplementary treaty in 1843 put British subjects in the treaty ports under consular protection, so giving them extraterritorial status, a provision that was developed in all subsequent Sino-Western treaties. For the Celestial Empire this was a humiliating end to the Opium War which was to cast a long shadow over subsequent events in the Far East.

In 1844 Chinese treaties with America and France consolidated the initial Western penetration of China. These and subsequent treaties which China, Japan and finally Korea made with the Western powers all incorporated a 'most-favoured-nation' clause which automatically gave to each Western signatory those privileges which might later be given to another power. So a whole system of 'treaty law' came into existence in the Far East which underwrote Western commercial penetration.

After China, Japan was the next ancient state of the East Asia to be 'opened'. Ever since the turn of the century, British and American clippers had sailed close to its forbidden shores, but all attempts to initiate trading relations had failed. At last, during 1853, Commodore Matthew Perry, U.S.N., entered Tokyo Bay with a small but very powerful naval task force. The shogunate was unable to resist and the ensuing Treaty of Kanagawa (31 March 1854) opened two Japanese ports to American trade. The Japanese also conceded a most-favoured-nation clause.

A parallel treaty was signed later in 1854 between the Japanese and the British, and the following year with the Russian Empire. Another treaty was later signed with the Dutch and in 1858 these four powers, together with France, signed a further round of commercial treaties with Japan, 'The Treaties with the Five Powers'. After over two centuries of isolation Japan had been opened to the West.

In the wake of the Japanese treaties, Western penetration of China was now carried considerably further by Anglo-French operations in China during 1856–60. Initially, after several years of tension Anglo-French military action in north China had ended in treaties signed between the two powers and China at Tienstin in June 1858. The concessions won by Britain and France were also awarded in similar treaties signed by American and Russian envoys. These treaties also provided for permanent Western missions in Peking which went far towards ending China's ancient assumption of superiority over the Western barbarians.

The Chinese were dilatory in implementing the 1858 treaties. The issue was now put beyond doubt when formidable Anglo-French forces returned to north China in 1860 and fought their way into Peking in October of that year. The Emperor fled beyond the great Wall and his brother, Prince Kung, signed new treaties with new concessions to the powers which in effect opened the whole of China to international trade. America and Russia shared these concessions under the 'most-favoured-nation' clause.

Of particular significance for Korea were the quite separate Sino-Russian accords of 1858 and 1860 which began the large-scale dismemberment of China. By the Treaty of Aigun (May 1858), the Chinese conveyed to the Russian Empire the extensive Manchu lands north of the Amur River bordering the Pacific. The large Manchu Maritime Province between the Ussuri River and the Pacific, with its great strategic potential, was placed under Joint Sino-Russian administration.

Two years later the Sino-Russian Treaty of Peking (November

1860) gave the Maritime Province in its entirety to the Russian Empire which now had an eleven-mile border with Korea along the estuary of the Tumen River. A hundred miles to the east the Russians had already founded the port of Vladivostok ('Rule of the East') in the summer of 1860.

These historic events, and the increasing activity of Western vessels off the Korean coast, now led to international speculation as to which Western nation would be the first to open the last of the closed societies of East Asia. But the initial Korean reaction to the opening of China and Japan was to draw closer than ever into its isolation.

Revolt and Limited Reform

Like China and Japan in the 1850s and 1860s, the old order in Korea faced an internal as well as an external challenge. In China the Taiping rebellion, a highly nationalist reform movement, part Chinese, part Christian in its intellectual origins, took over large parts of South China between 1850 and 1864 when it was finally defeated by the Imperial government. In Japan, as we shall see below, a group of south-western clans with Imperial connivance, overthrew the Tokugawa Shogunate following a short civil war during 1867–68.

Internal developments in Korea were distinct from both China and Japan. During the early 1860s a new religious cult made its appearance which provided the inspiration for serious peasant revolt in southern Korea during 1862–64. The cult was not only a protest against poverty and bad government, but as its name of *Tonghak* ('Eastern Learning') indicated, it was a reaction against the gradual spread in Korea of 'Western Learning' now increasingly identified with Catholicism. The founder of the Tonghak creed was Ch'oe Che-u (b.1824), the son of an impoverished yangban family from Kyongsang province in south-east Korea.

It appears that Choe was partly inspired by the Taiping rebellion in China, and also by news of the concessions forced from the Emperor by the Anglo-French operations of 1856–60. Choe claimed to have received a divine message during 1860 to create a new religion which would restore the East to primacy with the West.

The roots of this utopian cult lay in a mixture of Buddhism, Confucianism, and Taoism with a distinct element of shamamism, the indigenous Korean animistic religion still rooted in the peasant classes, which of course pre-dated Buddhism and Confucianism. Understandably the Tonghak creed had a special appeal for peasants and tenant farmers at the lower end of the social scale; agricultural discontent in Korea was endemic following a series of natural disasters in the earlier part of the century.

The Tonghak movement claimed to be strongly anti-Catholic. But the authorities distrusted the clearly subversive elements in the creed; Choe was captured, tried and executed at Taegu, in his native province, during 1864. But he left behind him many followers and the movement continued to spread, underground, throughout Korea. In a wider context, the Tonghak movement, like the Catholicism it opposed, indicated the continuing disintegration of traditional Korean Confucian society with its emphasis on a changeless hierarchy.

But the challenge posed by the Tonghak movement was met by determined counter-measures on the part of the authorities. With the death of King Ch'olchong in 1864, the boy-king Yi Myong-bok came to the throne. King Kojong, to give him his posthumous title, was to rule until 1907, and was the penultimate Yi monarch. But his youth meant that his father, Yi Ha-ung (d.1898) was appointed Regent. He was to be known by his title of Taewongun ('Lord of the Great Court').

The Taewongun was one of the most forceful characters in later Korean history, and he was to rule in the name of his son for the next decade until 1873. He was determined to meet both the internal challenge of the Tonghak and the Catholics and the external threat of the Western powers by a strictly applied policy of conservative reform. This policy aimed at restoring traditional Confucian society. There was thus a distinct element of idealism in the Taewongun's approach.

In accordance with his policy, the Taewongun took measures to strengthen the royal powers. He also tried to eliminate yangban factionalism, the curse of Korean politics, by closing most of the private Confucian academies, the *sowon* to which we have referred. The Taewongun also embarked on a process of legal reform as part of his policy of improving the central administration.

Another aspect of the Taewongun's reforms was the building of a small modern army, and the creation of new coastal defences for use against the barbarians. The corollary of this policy was of course increased taxation. There was also renewed, severe, and prolonged persecution of Catholics.

Initially, the Taewongun's exclusionist policy seemed to work. In 1866 the American trading vessel, *General Sherman*, tried to enter the Taedong estuary on the north-western Korean coast which leads to Pyongyang. The ship was sunk with all hands. That same year, the execution of French Catholic priests brought a small French fleet to the mouth of the Han River. French troops landed on Kanghwa Island and even occupied Kanghwa town as a resprisal, but these intruders were beaten off.

During 1867–68, American warships off the Korean west coast tried to discover the fate of the *General Sherman*, but without avail. In 1871, the American Minister to China was sent to the Han estuary with five warships. American troops then occupied the Kanghwa Island forts, not without resistance and a number of casualties on both sides. But the Koreans refused to negotiate, and the American expedition withdrew. The Taewongun continued, meanwhile, with the anti-Catholic persecutions, and evidently believed that these limited successes against the Western barbarians justified his policy of continuing isolation.

This was a mistaken view, for the Western powers in the Far East were preoccupied with developing their newly-won concessions in China and Japan. Korea was secondary to these interests. A more significant miscalculation was to ignore developments in Japan after the successful revolt against the Shogunate during 1867–68.

In early 1868, the samurai and nobles now in the ascendant formally 'restored' the powers of the young Emperor Mutsuhito. He took the name *Meiji* ('Enlightened Rule') for his reign and moved the capital from Kyoto to Edo, which was now renamed *Tokyo* ('Eastern Capital'). Under the policies of the Meiji restoration, Japan embarked on a systematic and far-reaching modernization of its government, economic structure, and armed forces, drawing on the best-available Western models. Meiji institutions generally were to show a great ability to adapt.

This policy meant of course that Japan was now increasingly able to resist Western political and economic pressure. It seems likely that only a parallel policy could have saved Korea from subsequent foreign intervention.

As early as 1870 the new Meiji administration in Tokyo attempted to open diplomatic relations with Korea. But this attempt was ignored by the Taewongun who characteristically disliked the passing of the Shogunate. Two years later in 1872 a Japanese delegation appeared at Tongnae, near Pusan, but was refused official permission to proceed to Seoul. Evidently the Taewongun, and the Yi bureaucracy, believed the Japanese could be denied admission to Korea.

During 1873 the Taewongun was removed from office and King Kojong took over his full powers. But the former Regent's exclusionist policies remained. Thus once again in 1875 a Japanese delegation sent to Tongnae was rebuffed. But Meiji Japan, slowly growing in self-confidence, was determined to enter Korea. The Hermit Kingdom's long period of self-imposed isolation was now at an end.

Chapter Five:
The Opening of Korea

Following the Western example, the Japanese decided in late 1875 to back their demands for trading relations with Korea by a show of force. A Japanese battleship and another warship sailed up the Korean east coast from Pusan to the vicinity of the northern harbour of Wonsan, and then returned to the west coast. The Japanese warships then anchored off the port of Inchon, which lies on the Yellow Sea about eighteen miles west of Seoul, and which was then still known by its old name of Chemulpo.

The Kanghwa Treaty

A small Japanese contingent then landed on nearby Kanghwa Island, the traditional refuge of the Korean court, there was a skirmish, and the Japanese withdrew. But the Japanese soon notified the Koreans that negotiations must now begin. After considerable hesitation by the Koreans, talks then started on Kanghwa Island. Eventually on 26 February 1876, a commercial treaty based on Western models was signed. The accord opened three Korean ports for Japanese trade, Pusan, Wonsan, and Inchon. The treaty also provided for an exchange of diplomatic missions and gave extraterritorial rights to the Japanese in Korea. Japanese diplomats were allowed freedom of travel.

The Kanghwa treaty also stipulated that Korea 'being an independent state enjoys the same sovereign rights as Japan'. This statement meant of course that Japan was attempting to remove Korea from its traditional tributary relationship with China as a means of facilitating Japanese freedom of action, both commercially and politically. But the Chinese, on the other hand, were determined to retain their interests and their influence within Korea. An important element in this contest, inherent in the opening of Korea, was the rivalry between the traditionalists (or conservatives) and the modernizers (or reformers) in Korea as the country now began to react to the foreign influences so long proscribed.

Traditionalists and Modernizers

Although Japanese trade now began to enter Korea through Pusan there was still strong opposition to the Kanghwa treaty from the traditionalist elite within Korea. Wonsan was only opened to Japan in 1880 and Inchon in 1883. Meanwhile, the Chinese advised the Korean court to embark on treaty relations with the Western powers as a means of countering Japanese and Russian pressure. The Chinese also hoped to forestall external pressure on Korea by sponsoring a limited amount of modernization, parallel to that being attempted in China itself.

In line with the Chinese policy of playing off the foreign barbarians against each other, Korea signed a treaty of 'friendship, commerce and navigation' with the United States on 22 May 1882. A similar treaty was signed with Great Britain the following month. The customs terms were not considered favourable enough by the British Foreign Office and a revised Korean-British treaty was later signed on 26 November 1883. A Korean Treaty with the German Empire was signed the same day. Other treaties followed with Italy and Russia (1884) and France (1886).

These treaties recognised Korean independence. But the contradiction remained between Korea's tributary role in Confucian system and the precise sovereign status accorded the country under Western international law. Yet most Western countries recognised that there was something special in the Chinese-Korean relationship. Subsequent to the American-Korean treaty, for example, the United States agreed to accept a letter from the Korean King stating that the treaty had been made with Chinese consent; and initially, most of the first Western legations in Seoul were placed under the jurisdiction of the parent missions in Peking.

Western diplomats, traders, missionaries, writers and other visitors now began to enter Korea in increasing numbers. The concept of modernizing reform (*Kaewha*) began to gain adherents within Korea. Initially this concept meant a willingness to acquire Western knowledge and technology. Thus during the 1880s the telegraph, electricity and other Western inventions and services entered Korea. Newspapers were published, and modern postal services arrived. Western-type schools were established, and literacy increased.

Kaewha soon came to encompass as well the modification of Korean institutions to the new ways. During the early 1880s the leading modernizers, who came to be known as the Independence Party, seemed to favour Japan as an example in view of that country's greater efficiency in promoting internal reform than China. The reformers began to object to the increasing Chinese influence in Korea, and especially in the Korean Court.

China in the Ascendant

Despite the challenge posed by Japan and the Western powers, China was able to remain the predominant power in Korea from the early 1880s to 1894. There were several reasons why this was so. In general, Confucian intellectual influences and sympathy with the old order remained strong. Traditional Korean dislike of foreigners was another element. In particular, King Kojong's queen was a conservative influence who backed Chinese policies in general. She came from the powerful Min family and was, however, known as 'Queen Min'. The Korean court was thus on the whole against radical change and certainly not sympathetic to those modernizers who looked across the Korea Strait to Japan.

Events also played into Chinese hands. A brief, but violent army revolt in Seoul in July 1882 precipitated the despatch of a Chinese presence to Korea that was to last for over a decade. During this rebellion, which was motivated by anti-foreign nationalist sentiment as well as by concern over official corruption involving Queen Min's relatives, the Japanese legation in Seoul was attacked; high court officials were also killed. Queen Min was forced to flee the capital.

Both Chinese and Japanese forces were sent to Seoul to restore order, but the Chinese detachments were the bigger. In compensation, Japan was given new trading privileges, but China now began to actively supervise Korean political and economic affairs.

Chinese policy in Korea was overseen by an able statesman, Li Hung-chang, while the Chinese garrison in Seoul was commanded by an efficient, autocratic general, Yuan Shih-k'ai. A new Sino-Korean trading agreement, signed late in 1882, reaffirmed the traditional Chinese suzerainty over Korea. This traditional relationship gave the Chinese great latitude in their activities in Korea. But as we have seen, the relationship was not based on a treaty or legal agreement in the Western sense. Rather, it was based on a Confucian family understanding between China and Korea that reached back to the beginnings of the Korean kingdom.

The Korean court thus became (and remained) a focus of pro-Chinese traditionalism. Yet the very ascendancy of the Chinese faction spurred the modernizers to greater efforts. They were helped to a certain degree by the growing foreign missionary element in Korea. Contact with these foreigners widened the reformers' ambitions, and also introduced them to the latest Western ideas.

Kim Ok-kyun, the leader of the Independents, meanwhile visited Japan during late 1882. he soon came to believe that only the forcible removal of Queen Min and her faction would ensure the success of the lndependents and their modernizing policies. Kim may also have believed that such action would correspond to the Meiji revolution of 1868 in Japan. At any rate, for their own reasons, the Japanese supported Kim in his plans.

During early December 1884, the Independents launched their *coup d'etat*. King Kojong was seized, a number of royal officials were killed, and a new modernizing government proclaimed. The *coup* was backed to the hilt by Japanese troops in Seoul, clearly as a result of pre-arrangement. But the larger contingents of Chinese troops under General Yuan reacted swiftly and crushed the insurrection. Kim Ok-kyun and the Japanese Minister in Seoul barely escaped to a Japanese ship in Inchon.

Eventually, the differences between China and Japan were patched up, for the time being. Japanese and Chinese representatives, meeting at Tientsin in 1885, agreed to withdraw their military forces from Korea, and to inform each other before returning their to that country. However General Yuan Shih-k'ai remained in Seoul as the grandly-styled Supervisor for Foreign Affairs in Korea'.

Some civil and military reforms were instituted under Chinese sponsorship and Chinese economic presence in Korea flourished at the expense of the Japanese. But decisive reforms and systematic modernization remained unlikely as long as the

Korean court remained attached to the traditional Chinese connection.

Great Power Rivalries in Korea

Although the Chinese ascendancy in Seoul after the abortive coup of December 1884 seemed reassuring to the traditionalists the long-term prospects for continuing Korean independence were not good.

The country's prolonged isolation and now the traditionalist resistance to reform weakened the possiblility of effective resistance to outside pressure. The conflict between Westernizing reformers and the Confucian establishment in the 1880s recalled the self-destructive factionalism of earlier Korean history. Increasingly, these factions came to be allied to outside forces, a process which quite overtly threatened Korean independence.

During the 1880s, it also became clear that Korea was increasingly at the mercy of the great-power rivalries that were now coming to a climax in the Far East. To be sure, American and British diplomats and business interests were soon evident in Seoul after the signing of the commercial treaties in the early 1880s. But strategic rather than commercial interests were now to dictate the course of Korean history for the next two decades. Initially events pointed towards a showdown between China and Japan over Korea.

On paper, the Chinese position in Korea seemed strong. The traditional cutural links, geographical proximity, and a forceful representative in Seoul in the person of General Yuan Shih-k'ai all seemed to point towards renewed Chinese paramountcy for the forseeable future.

Yet the Chinese position in Korea was weaker than it seemed. Japanese agreement with China over a mutual troop withdrawal in 1885 was based on a conscious decision of national policy in Tokyo to avoid a foreign war pending the creation of a strong military establishment. German instructors were attached to the Japanese army while British counterparts supervised the creation of a modern navy, soon to prove itself second to none in the Far East.

In essence the Japanese believed that the headlong modernizing process in their country gave them a growing military capability that would soon offset China's traditional advantages in any conflict over Korea. Japanese diplomatic and commercial pressure continued unabated in Korea and Korean modernizers still looked to Japan.

Japan's growing strength was only part of the pattern of international rivalry that now increasingly centred on Korea. During the negotiations of the Russian-Korean commercial treaty in 1884, St. Petersburg had indicated that it was willing to modernize the Korean Army in exchange for a warm-water port in southern Korea near Pusan. The Russians were also interested in obtaining facilities at Wonsan, on the north-eastern coast. Underlying the Russian drive for a warm-water port in Korea was the fact that Vladivostok was ice-bound for three or four months annually.

As a precaution against Russian naval activity in Korean waters, the Royal Navy occupied Komun Island, off the Korean south coast, in 1885. This was a strategically placed anchorage, known as Port Hamilton, which gave control of the Korea Strait. Eventually, the British withdrew their ships during 1887 following Russian assurances that occupation of Korea territory was not considered. A tombstone recording the death of two British sailors in 1886 remains on Komun Island to commemorate this fleeting episode.

The failure of the Russians to gain any significant advantage in Korea following their commercial treaty in 1884 indicated their general strategic weakness in the Far East. The enormous distances which separated Vladivostok from European Russia, combined with inferior Russian naval resources in relation to the Western powers, precluded the effective projection of St. Petersburg's ambitions in the region.

During 1886 the Czar Alexander III decided to redress the strategic balance by the construction of a 6,000 mile Trans-Siberian railway from Moscow to Vladivostok. The railway, when completed, would enable the Russian Empire to send large numbers of troops to the Far East. St. Petersburg would thus be able to pursue more effectively its policies in China and Korea, and to offset Japan's growing strength. Construction of the railway began from both ends in 1891. It was hoped to complete the immense project in little over a decade. Meanwhile, the primary rivalry over Korea remained that between China and Japan.

Sino-Japanese War, 1894–95

Domestic events within Korea now brought this simmering Sino-Japanese rivalry to a head. Although the founder of the

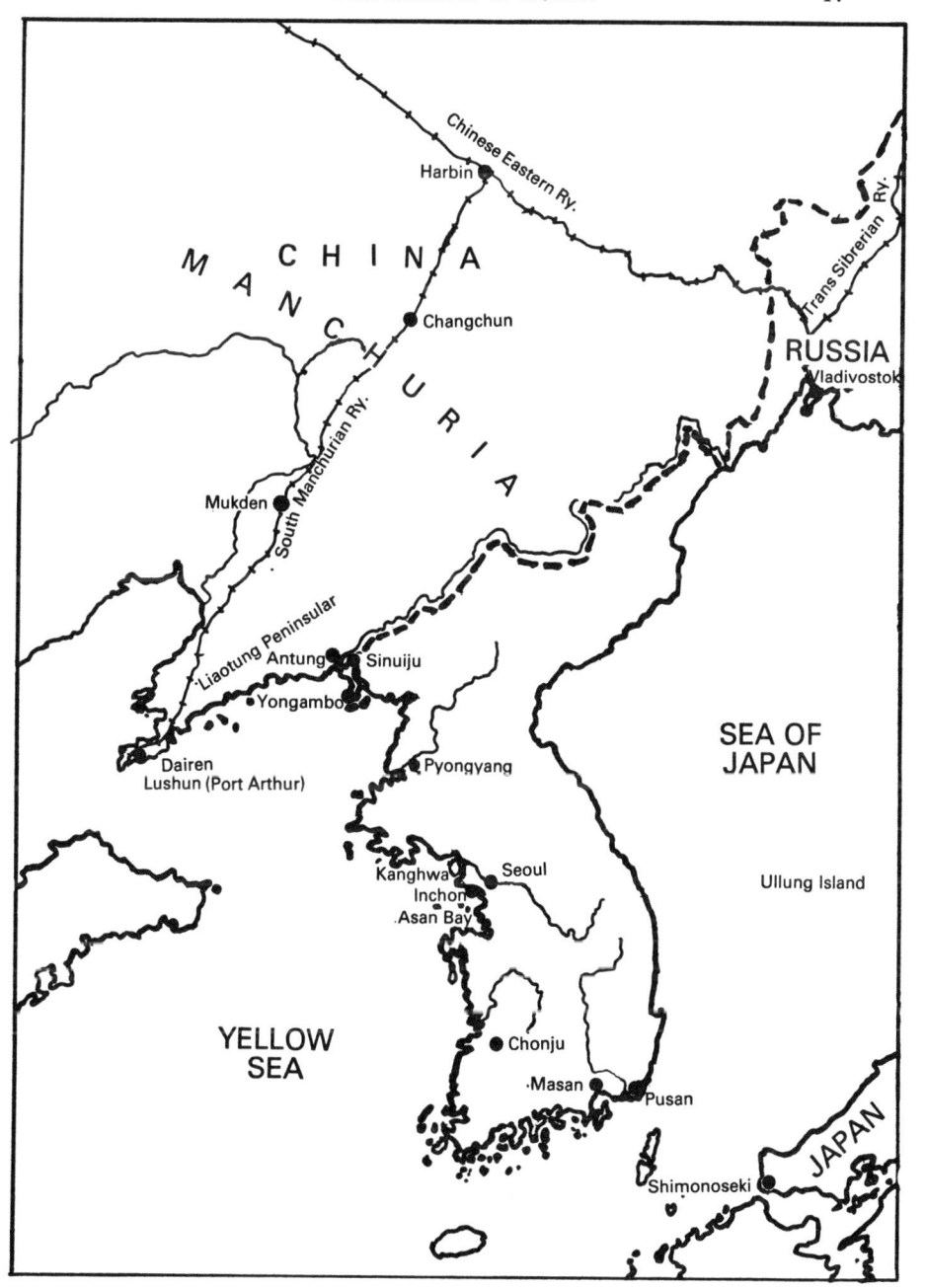

Sino-Japanese Russo-Japanese conflicts.

Tonghak creed, Ch'oe Che-u, had been executed in 1864, his doctrines lived on. His followers continued to meet in the hills of southern Korea. As a result of continuing rural poverty and deprivation the Tonghak leaders presented a petition to King Kojong in early 1893. The petition was rejected and the Tonghak followers were told to return home. The road to peaceful reform seemed closed.

Endemic rural discontent now broke into open rebellion, and by the spring of 1894 the three southern provinces of Cholla, Kyongsang, and Chungchong were affected. At the end of May 1894 Chonju, the provincial capital of Cholla, fell to the insurgents. The Tonghak now put forward demands for sweeping reforms.

Although the Korean military were able to recapture Chonju, King Kojong asked for Chinese assistance to crush the rebellion in the south. This was done against advice, yet it was a traditional request for a Korean monarch who looked instinctively to Peking in times of national danger. But this time a request for Chinese assistance was to lead to a chain of events which would end for ever Korea's formal dependency on China.

Following this Korean request to Peking, Chinese warships and troop transports were sent to Inchon and to Asan Bay on the Korean west coast. The Japanese also sent troops to Inchon, ostensibly to protect their legation in Seoul. China responded with further troop reinforcements, and so did the Japanese, who did not of course recognise China's claim to suzerainty over Korea. Japan also claimed that it had the right to send her troops to Korea under the Sino-Japanese accord reached at Tienstin in 1885.

Initially both sides seemed to act pre-emptively in fear of the other. But as the stakes were raised, the Chinese apparently came to believe that the military advantage was theirs. The Chinese were further disposed to act following the Japanese sinking of the British steamer *Kowshing* which was ferrying Chinese troops to Korea. The outcome of the Tonghak rebellion was now relegated to second place as the issue became one of which power would win this historic confrontation over Korea.

The Japanese proposed that the Korean government should institute fundamental reforms under Sino-Japanese supervision a course of action that would certainly terminate Chinese influence in Korea. When the Koreans refused to consider this plan, the Japanese military occupied the Kyongbok Palace in Seoul on

23 July 1894, so capturing King Kojong and his court. Queen Min, the symbol of the court's pro-Chinese policy, was forced out of Seoul and so was the Chinese General, Yuan Shih k'ai.

Japan now acted with great speed and decision. On 25 July, without declaring hostilities, the Japanese navy attacked Chinese ships at Asan Bay. Japanese troops marched south from Seoul to defeat the Chinese at Kongju. China and Japan then declared war on 1 August. The Japanese also forced the Korean court to declare war against China. King Kongjo, in Japanese hands, signed a number of accords which in effect gave Japan a free military hand in Korea for the duration of hostilities.

To the south of Seoul, Japanese and royal Korean units now quickly crushed the Tonghak rebels. But the Japanese main force in Korea struck north to Pyongyang, defeating the Chinese. The Japanese then swept on northwards, crossed the Yalu, and advanced into southern Manchuria, taking the Liaotung peninsula, and with it the modern fortress of Port Arthur (Lushun), which fell in November 1894.

The key to these Japanese victories – which changed the world's perception of Japan – lay in Japan's naval supremacy, for Chinese resupply in Korea was by sea. Overall, the Chinese had about 65 warships to Japan's 32, so that the advantage seemed to lie with the Ching fleet. When the opposing fleets met off the mouth of the Yalu in the Yellow Sea on 17 September 1894 each side deployed 12 ships. But the Japanese had faster vessels, better gunnery and more effective tactics. Four Chinese warships were sunk, while the Japanese suffered no losses. Thereafter Japan dominated Korean waters.

Following these Japanese successes, the Chinese Empire had no alternative but to sue for peace. China then made many concessions in the Treaty of Shimonoseki, signed in that Japanese port on 17 April 1895.

The Chinese were forced to give Formosa and the Pescadores to Japan and also ceded the Liaotung peninsula and Port Arthur. This naval base, named after the French military engineer, William Arthur, who had fortified the Chinese seaport of Lushun in the early 1880s, dominated the Yellow Sea. The Chinese also agreed to negotiate a new commercial treaty with Japan. In the event, this trading accord gave the Japanese all the Western privileges in China, and yet further concessions.

As for Korea, the Chinese finally relinquished all their historic

tributary claims, for the Treaty of Shimonoseki stipulated that
'China recognises definitively the full and complete independence and autonomy of Korea, and in consequence the payment of tribute and the performance of ceremonies and formalities by Korea to China, in derogation of such independence and autonomy, shall wholly cease for the future.'
Korea was now formally independent, a sovereign state in the full meaning of the term as understood in Western international law. But this new status was an ambivalent achievement, for the Treaty of Shimonoseki only ushered in a new and even more bitter struggle between Japan and Russia for supremacy in Korea.

Chapter Six:
Japan and Russia in Korea
1895–1910

Although Japan's great victory over China brought her general Western recognition as one of the leading nations in the Far East, it also aroused conflicting attitudes amongst the powers. In the United States and Great Britain there had been admiration for Japanese military efficiency (and pride in the way that Japan had learnt from the West). The Czarist government, however, was concerned that the overwhelming Japanese success might result in a check to Russia's own ambitions in Manchuria and Korea. Russian diplomacy was extremely active in the Far East at this time; the continuing construction of the Trans-Siberian railway emphasised Russian interest in the region.

In line with this concern over Japan's victory and in the immediate aftermath of the Treaty of Shimonosehi in April 1895, St. Petersburg now organised a Russian-French-German diplomatic intervention. This *démarche* forced Japan to abandon the Liaotung peninsula and with it Port Arthur. As the Russians were apparently ready to back the 'advice' of the 'Triple Intervention' by military means, Japan had no alternative but to abandon the territory involved in exchange for a large additional indemnity from China. It was a necessary but humiliating retreat that was not forgotten in Tokyo.

Following the Triple Intervention, Korea quickly became the cockpit of Russo-Japanese rivalry in the Far East. Japan now discovered that despite the withdrawal of China from Korea and the emergence of a legally independent Korean state in the Western sense, she was confronted in Korea with a far more determined and powerful adversary than China. In addition, Japanese influence in Korean domestic politics was soon to suffer a serious reverse in favour of the Russians.

To be sure, in the immediate aftermath of the Japanese seizure of the Korean court in July 1894 the prospects for advancing Japanese influence seemed good. A new Korean Reform Council passed a number of fundamental reforms which were approved by the Japanese. A governmental structure with eight ministries, headed by a Prime Minister, was created. A new examination syllabus for state service was devised which superseded the old Confucian models. The local government system was re-cast.

The Korean court also tried to reform the chaotic Korean financial system by setting up a centralized Ministry of Finance to integrate the many local taxation systems which existed in the country. A new coinage was issued. The customary privileges of the yangban class were abolished, as were the traditional four classes of Korean society, to which we have already referred. There was a reorganization of the police, the judiciary, and the small Korean army. Concurrently, the Christian missionaries in Korea, especially the Protestants, continued to expand their educational programmes. A new, self-conscious Korean nationalism began to emerge out of the old, traditional isolationism.

Queen Min Murdered

On paper, the infrastructure of a modern state began to appear in Korea. When the new cabinet took over at the end of 1894, a fourteen-point 'Great Plan', a summary of over two hundred reform measures, was promulgated. This *de facto* Constitution stressed that Korea was a fully independent state, that the Royal court and the government were to be separate, and that reformed law codes were to be issued. During January 1895 King Kojong and his family went to Chongmyo, the Royal Ancestral Shrine of the Yi kings in Seoul, to announce the reforms to his ancestors.

The new reform programme was formally completed by April 1895. But implementation was naturally difficult in view of the speed with which the programme had been promulgated. The new measures also met resistance because they were associated with the Japanese. In the van of the opposition to the reforms was Queen Min, the champion of the traditionalists.

Once again, external events began to affect developments within Korea. Following the 'Triple Intervention' by the powers which had forced the Japanese to abandon Port Arthur, the Korean court now began to turn to the Russians, as in the past they had turned to the Chinese, to counteract Japanese influence. Queen Min was naturally active in these intrigues. Gradually, pro-Japanese ministers were eased out of the new administration by the influence of the court.

The Japanese in Seoul, through the person of their new Minister, Miura Goro, now overplayed their hand. It will be recalled that in July 1894, at the opening of the Sino-Japanese war, the Japanese had taken over the Korean court, forcing Queen Min out of Seoul. This time the Japanese evidently decided to eliminate Queen Min, the centre of anti-Japanese opposition, for good.

On 8 October 1895 a party of Japanese agents and soldiers accompanied by disaffected Koreans from a military training unit, stormed the royal Kyongbok Palace and killed Queen Min. Her body was burnt in the Palace grounds. King Kojong was seized and some royal officials were killed.

The Japanese evidently hoped to restore a government more sympathetic to their policies but had miscalculated. There was a storm of international protest, and the Japanese government dissociated itself from the deed. Miura and some of his associates were later tried but released for what was officially termed lack of evidence. There was mounting unrest throughout Korea during the winter of 1895–96 and eventually the Russian Minister arranged for over 200 armed Russian sailors to come to Seoul from a Russian warship anchored at Inchon. Ostensibly these men were extra guards for the Russian legation.

On 11 February 1896, through connivance with court officials, and protected by the Russians, King Kojong fled from the Kyongbok Palace to the Russian legation in Seoul. The pro-Japanese Korean premier was killed by a mob, and the Japanese were deterred from further action by the knowledge that an attack on the Russian legation could be construed as an act of war. A new pro-Russian government was formed.

The Japanese soon accepted the *fait accompli* and agreed with the Russian Minister in Seoul to jointly limit their forces in the Korean capital. It was also agreed that the King could live where he wished, and choose whatever ministers he wanted. Russian influence was now completely in the ascendant. An agreement between the Russian and Korean governments in May 1896 arranged for Russian military and financial advisers to be sent to Korea. Further Russian troops were to be sent, if necessary.

Japan remained in a strong economic position in Korea, and bided her time. For the present, however, King Kojong, and with him Korean sovereignty, was under Russian protection. The Japanese had suffered a serious political reverse.

The Independence Club

Although the physical security of the Korean court was improved by its transfer to the Russian legation in Seoul, its prestige suffered. A further source of weakness lay in the numerous foreign concessions that were increasingly handed out by the Korean government. These concessions granted rights for the development of minerals, timber and other commodities. The Russians pressed for the concession of Choryong Island near Pusan, while the Japanese obtained extensive rights to build a railway from Pusan, through Seoul, to Uiju on the Yalu. American, British and French interests were also involved in these concessions.

In these circumstances there was a renewed growth of the modernizing reform movement which now attracted increasing support. In particular, the movement began to crystallize around the person of So Chae-p'il, who had been one of the leaders of the abortive *coup* of December 1884.

So Chae-p'il had escaped to the United States, where he had acquired both American citizenship and a degree in medicine. he took the Western name of 'Philip Jaisohn'. In early 1896 Jaisohn returned to Korea and founded the Independence Club (*Tongnip Hyophoe*), which was a reformist political grouping. He also founded a newspaper, *The Independent* (*Tongnip Shinmun*) which was published three times weekly in English and in the indigenous Korean script, *Hangul*. Jaisohn considered that the intensive promotion of Hangul was an integral part of the reform movement.

The first issue of *The Independent*, published in Seoul on 7 April 1896, proclaimed that its platform was 'Korea for the Koreans, clean politics, the cementing of foreign friendships . . .' *The Independent* also called for the speedy translation of foreign texts into Korean so that Korean youth might have access 'to the great things of history, science, art and religion without having to acquire a foreign tongue. . . .'

The Independent continued to promote Korean literacy, and also a variety of reform causes. It criticised corruption and maladministration. The newspaper was written in a clear, forceful style, and its circulation soon rose from 300 to over 3,000. Meanwhile, the Independence Club organized mass meetings and called for a continuing policy of government reform. There was a strong emphasis on popular education. One of the many supporters of the Independence Club was a young Korean patriot called Yi Sung-man, later known as Syngman Rhee (1875–1965), who after many vicissitudes in the cause of Korean nationalism eventually became the first President of the Republic of Korea in 1948.

During 1897 the Independence movement became increasingly concerned with the great-power threat to Korea, and in particular with the number of foreign concessions which had been granted. Philip Jaisohn called for the King to leave the Russian legation. On 20 February 1897 King Kojong left Russian protection and established his court in the Kyongun royal palace; his security was assured for this palace stood near the foreign legations in Seoul. After Kojong's eventual abdication in 1907, the Kyongun was renamed in his honour the Toksu Palace (The Palace of the Virtuous Longevity).

As part of the growing awakening in which the reform movement was playing such an important part, it was decided to change the King's title to Emperor. The word *king* meant in Chinese a ruler subordinate to the Chinese Emperor, The title of the Japanese Emperor made him semantically the equal of his counterpart in Peking. Accordingly King Kojong was crowned Emperor of Korea on 12 October 1897.

The new royal title had little practical effect on the number of important concessions still being awarded to the Russians. In the far north of Korea the Russians were awarded valuable timber concessions along the Yalu. Further concessions were given to them on Ullung Island (Dagelet) in the Sea of Japan. During early 1898 a Russian bank appeared in Seoul, and it was rumoured that this institution would henceforth supervise the operations of the Korean treasury.

There were vigorous protests over these developments and the Russian bank was closed. Russian military advisers who had been sent to Korea in 1896 were also withdrawn. The Russians were unable to obtain the concession of Choryong Island which would have given them the control of Pusan harbour.

Originally, the Korean government had supported the new reform movement. But as the reformers criticised increasingly the vested interests of the conservative Korean court, the Independence Club became an embarrassment. First, Philip Jaisohn was forced to leave Korea. Then, after a series of street demonstrations and clashes later in 1898, the Independence Club was dissolved and some of its leaders arrested. Others fled from Korea. *The Independent* was closed down. The reform movement was suppressed.

The reformers had thus failed in many of their objectives. They were essentially an urban reform group, and had failed to develop a following in the countryside where rural discontent was unabated. But the memory of the Independence Club, and of *The Independent*, lived on to inspire later, twentieth century Korean nationalists.

Another important legacy of the Independence Club was the gradually increasing use of Hangul. Eventually, in 1907, the National Language Research Institute was established, and soon the sole use of Chinese in official documents was replaced by a mixture of selected Chinese characters and Hangul. Books and other publications began to use this new mixed system.

There was also continuing research on the Korean language, which scholars increasingly saw as the basis of the national spirit and the national tradition. Thus despite the Japanese annexation of Korea in 1910, a new Korean literary movement began to develop after this date.

Russo-Japanese War

During the late 1890s, the rivalry between Japan and Russia over Korea acquired a new momentum. Initially, both powers had made a half-hearted attempt at reconciliation. In June 1896, for example, both countries had agreed at St. Petersburg – during the prolonged coronation ceremonies of Czar Nicholas II – that if it became necessary for either to reinforce their troops in Korea the other country would be informed.

The Japanese had also suggested at this time, the partition of Korea into spheres of influence along the 38th Parallel, a demarcation line that would appear again in Korean history. But the Russian foreign minister, Alexei Lobanoff, refused. This was only natural given the Russian interest in the warm-water anchorages of southern Korea, a zone which would fall to Japan under this proposed partition.

The Russians were indifferent to a comprehensive settlement

with Japan over Korea because they calculated that the regional balance of power was moving in their favour. During the Czarist coronation period referred to above, Russia signed a secret alliance with China with far-reaching consequences. By this agreement Russia was allowed to build a 1,000-mile long railway, across Manchuria from Lupin in Siberia towards Vladivostok. This railway, to be known as the Chinese Eastern Railway, provided a short cut for the main Trans-Siberian line which necessarily swung north above the Amur River Manchurian frontier on its way to Vladivostok.

This initial Russian penetration of Manchuria was followed in March 1898 by the Russian lease of the Liaotung peninsula together with Port Arthur and the commercial harbour of Ta-Lien or Dairen. St. Petersburg also gained Chinese permission to build a 700-mile spur of the Chinese Eastern Railway southwestwards from Harbin to Port Arthur. From the South Manchurian Railway, as this spur was known, branch lines could quickly be constructed to the Korean border.

In April 1898 the Japanese gave tacit recognition to the Russian lease of Port Arthur in exchange for a free hand in Korea. But the Russian concessions on the Korean island of Ullung (Dagelet), in the Sea of Japan, and the Russian attempt to obtain facilities on Choryong Island, near Pusan, remained major irritants. The Russians also had ambitions of gaining a naval base near Masan, thirty miles west of Pusan. It became impossible for Japan to ignore the strategic implications of Russian aspirations in Korea.

The balance seemed to tip even further against Japan in the aftermath of the Boxer rebellion in north China during 1900–01. An international army was sent to Peking to suppress this anti-foreign rising; under the pretext of guarding their railway concessions the Russians despatched over 150,000 troops to Manchuria. These forces remained in the area despite an agreement with the Chinese in early 1902 to withdraw. A year later, in the early months of 1903, Russian forces crossed the lower Yalu estuary and occupied Korean territory at Yongampo. This was done without any authorization or concession from the Korean government.

By this time the balance of power had begun to swing in Japan's favour. The Japanese army and navy had been significantly expanded since 1895 and the Japanese economy continued to thrive. The Anglo-Japanese treaty of 30 January 1902 was also of great significance. The treaty tended to isolate Russia in the Far East, gave Japan a great-power ally, and implicitly demonstrated that the Western maritime powers were concerned over Russian objectives in Manchuria and Korea. The treaty specifically recognised that Korea lay within the Japanese sphere of influence.

As the first Russian troop reinforcements for Manchuria came over the newly-opened Trans-Siberian railway in early 1903 it became obvious that the long-prophesied confrontation between Russia and Japan was at hand. Formal negotiations between the two adversaries opened in August 1903 as both sides stepped up their preparations for war.

While the Russians demanded exclusive control of Manchuria, they were prepared to give Japan a free hand south of the 39th Parallel in Korea. Japan counter-proposed with a plan for a neutral zone along the Korean-Manchurian border so completely excluding Russian influence from Korea. The two positions over Korea could not be reconciled and there was a complete impasse.

Japan now turned from diplomacy to war, breaking off negotiations on 6 February 1904. Two days later Japanese warships attacked the Russian fleet in Port Arthur; hostilities were declared on the 10th. *The Times* of London considered that 'The Japanese Navy has opened the war by an act of daring which is destined to take a place of honour in naval annals.'

With great speed, Japan also transported an expeditionary force to Inchon. Seoul was occupied, and the Korean government forced to give Japan complete freedom of military action in Korea. All Russian concessions in Korea were taken over by Japan. The Japanese also took over all telegraph lines within Korea, and appointed advisers to all Korean ministries. Meanwhile, Russian scouting parties from Manchuria were probing deep into northern Korea.

From Inchon Japanese forces marched northwards to the Yalu and onwards into Manchuria to besiege Port Arthur which eventually surrendered with its large garrison in January 1905. The loss of this great fortress was of course a major setback for the Russians. The fall of Port Arthur was soon followed by the Japanese defeat of the main Russian Far Eastern armies at Mukden, southern Manchuria, after a prolonged 17-day battle during February and March 1905. At sea the Russian Baltic Fleet, which had been sent round the world, was almost entirely sunk in Japan's classic naval victory near Tsushima Island in the Korea Strait on 27 May 1905.

These historic victories made Japan a world power and gave her a regional ascendancy in North East Asia that was to last for forty years. The fate of Korea for the next four decades was also decided by these Japanese successes and the Treaty of Portsmouth, New Hampshire (5 September 1905) which ratified Japan's victory.

By this treaty Japan acquired the Russian lease of Port Arthur, Dairen, and the Liaotung peninsula. Japan was also awarded the Russian-built South Manchurian Railway from Port Arthur northwards to Changchun, which cemented the Japanese hold on southern Manchuria. Japan also won southern Sakhalin, the Russian island to the north of the Japanese home island of Hokkaido.

The Treaty of Portsmouth formally gave Japan a free hand in Korea, for the accord specifically acknowledged that Russia accepted Japan's 'paramount political, military and economic interest in Korea'.

It was in this way that the Russo-Japanese rivalry over Korea was finally resolved. Only five years of token independence now remained to Korea before final, formal annexation by Japan.

The Road to Annexation

During the Russo-Japanese war, Japan had assumed military control in Korea. The Japanese were particularly sensitive about the main railway and its associated telegraph system which ran from Pusan in south-east Korea through Seoul to Pyongyang and the Yalu. Along this line men and supplies were sent from the homeland to sustain Japan's armies in Manchuria. A major link in the system was the 3,000 foot long Yalu highway bridge, built in 1900, which joined Sinuiju in Korea with Antung in Manchuria.

Korea was thus strategically indispensable to the maintenance of the new Japanese civil and military presence in Manchuria following Russia's defeat. It became of great importance to the Japanese government to legitimise Japan's ever-growing interests in Korea, both internationally and with the weak Korean government. Thus even before the Portsmouth treaty of September 1905, Japan obtained American and British recognition of its vital interests in Korea.

On 29 July 1905, during a visit to Tokyo, the American Secretary of State, William H. Taft, concluded a secret agreement with the Japanese Premier, Count Katsura. In this agreement, the United States approved Japan's 'suzerainty over Korea' in exchange for a pledge that Japan did not harbour any designs against the Philippines. It will be remembered that these islands had fallen to the United States after the Spanish-American war of 1898.

A few days later on 12 August 1905, the Anglo-Japanese Treaty of Alliance was renewed. In exchange for an understanding that Japan would not in any way threaten Singapore, Great Britain recognised Japan's 'paramount' political, military and economic interests in Korea. For the Western powers generally, a Japanese-controlled Korea was preferable to Russian influence in that country. Together with the Treaty of Portsmouth, therefore, these Japanese agreements with Britain and America ended the period of intense international rivalry in East Asia and restored a balance of power.

Japan also moved quickly to obtain official Korean recognition of its dominant presence within the peninsula. A draft Protectorate Treaty was presented to the Korean government during October 1905. This proposed treaty delegated Korea's foreign relations to Japanese control, so precluding any independent Korean diplomatic initiatives. A Japanese Resident-General in Seoul would supervise the protectorate; Japanese regional commissioners, acting under the Resident-General, would be placed in the Korean provinces. The Korean Emperor, Kojong, would have his safety guaranteed by the Japanese and would continue to reign; but much of the essence of Korean sovereignty would pass to Japan.

The Protectorate Treaty was debated by a Korean government surrounded by troops from the Japanese garrison in Seoul, and was eventually signed by both sides on 17 November 1905. The veteran Meiji statesman, Ito Hirobumi, became the first Japanese Resident-General. He was responsible to the Japanese Emperor and had the authority to use Japanese troops to enforce his powers. Apart from one battalion for the Korean Emperor's security, the Korean army was dissolved. Korea thus became a Japanese protectorate.

As might be expected the Protectorate Treaty aroused much opposition in Korea. The Japanese military presence was underlined by the increasing number of Japanese colonists and settlers who flocked to Korea and who were now allowed to buy land. The Emperor Kojong made an attempt to alert world opinion to this gradual process of Japanese colonization. In early 1907 the Emperor sent a secret mission to the Second International Peace Conference held at The Hague in the Netherlands. Although the mission failed to obtain an official hearing there was a strong Japanese response. Kojong was forced to abdicate in July 1907 and was succeeded by the Crown Prince, the last monarch of the Yi dynasty, who was later given the posthumous title of Sunjong. In a further effort to strengthen their position in Korea the Japanese imposed the 'New Agreement' on an already subservient Korean government. The Japanese Resident-General took fresh powers, senior Japanese officials were inserted into the Korean government, and the Korean Army was finally abolished.

These new Japanese measures were implemented against a background of widespread Korean resistance. Armed clashes and attacks on Japanese garrisons and communications developed into guerrilla operations on a national scale. Many Korean villages were destroyed and there were of course many Korean casualties. But as the Korean insurgents found it hard to obtain arms, resistance was gradually beaten down between 1907 and 1910. In Japan, meanwhile, there were demands for the outright annexation of Korea.

Yet as Korean independence came to an end in these unhappy circumstances, the indigenous process of cultural and educational renaissance continued. John K. Fairbank has written that 'it was particularly tragic that the Korean people, having come at last into contact with the modern world, should be so soon subjugated by Asia's first leader in modernization, Japan.... Korean nationhood was thus suppressed at the very time when conservative *yangban* . . . reformist students, disbanded soldiers, and impoverished peasants, rebelling alike against foreign rule, were developing a common sentiment of nationalism. . . .' Future events were to show that this new spirit of Korean nationalism was to flourish steadily under Japanese rule.

The final act of the annexation process began with the assassination of Ito Hirobumi by a young Korean patriot at Harbin, Manchuria, in October 1909. Shortly before Ito had resigned in favour of Sone Atasuke as the Japanese Resident-General in Korea. But with Ito's death a former Japanese War Minister, General Terauchi Masatake, was now made Resident-General in

Korea. In early 1910 General Terauchi placed the Japanese civil police in Korea under the control of the military police. A draft Annexation Treaty was presented to an intimidated Korean government.

Eventually the Korean-Japanese Annexation Treaty was signed on 22 August 1910. It provided for all treaties between Japan and other countries to apply to Korea; all treaties signed by Korea were to be voided. The Korean Emperor Sunjong was reduced to the rank of King and pensioned off. Korea was to be ruled by a new Japanese agency, the Chosen Government-General, which took its name from the ancient name of Korea.

On 29 August 1910 the Annexation Treaty came into force, and on that day both the rule of the Yi dynasty and Korean independence came to an end. Korea was now to remain a Japanese colony until the moment of Japan's defeat in the Second World War.

Chapter Seven:
Japanese Rule 1910–1945

Many East Asian countries were affected by the colonial experience. But Korea was unique in that it was formally ruled from August 1910 to August 1945 by an Asian neighbour with which cultural and historical links had always been close. As we have seen earlier in our story it was through Korea that Chinese writing, religion and art forms reached Japan. But in general these cultural contacts counted for little during the period of Japanese rule which paradoxically was a period of both cultural repression and administrative innovation.

Following the Annexation Treaty of August 1910 the new Chosen Government-General acted quickly to impose its authority. The chief security agency of Japanese rule remained the military police (or gendarmerie) which as we have seen had authority over the civil police. But since about 1906 a division of Japanese regular troops had been stationed in Korea, a force that was increased to two divisions in 1915.

The gendarmerie, which recruited Koreans, operated throughout the country. The Japanese army, meanwhile, suppressed the remaining Korean guerrilla bands in the northern part of the country. But these partisans were never completely eliminated until towards the end of the Japanese rule, for they made good use of local knowledge and also of the Chinese and Russian borders for their protection.

In general the Japanese were to claim that their rule brought efficiency as well as reform to the Korean administration. The Government-General functioned as an autonomous organization under the Colonial Ministry until 1942 when Korea was administered as part of Japan under the Home Ministry. Ultimately all major decrees had to be sanctioned by the Emperor and the Imperial Diet in Tokyo held oversight on policy matters including finance. But within these parameters the Governor-General had broad executive powers both civil and military. He appointed all officials except his chief assistant, the Administrative Director, who was appointed by the Imperial Government.

Japanese Administration and Economic Policy

The more general activities of Japanese government in Korea were carried out by a small number of Ministries such as those dealing with Finance, Home Affairs, Justice, Agriculture and Industry. The Governor-General's Administrative Director headed a powerful executive Secretariat which was comprised of more specialized bureaux or sections. These included Police, Railways, the Land Survey, Trading Monopolies and so on. A Japanese local government system was established from the province level down through prefectures to townships and villages. All senior and middle-level officials were invariably Japanese.

Japanese government in Korea was therefore comprehensive, but historians of their rule have noted that Japanese administration was not simply a matter of law and order. There was a distinct element of cultural regimentation, for as an ancient people the Koreans saw their language and history as rallying points against foreign rule. Thus Japanese was enforced as the language of government and education, a Japanese press was set up in each Korean province, and the Japanese renamed some Korean cities and towns. The Korean press and publishing were carefully censored. All Korean political groupings were banned. Through these and other measures, the Japanese attempted to enforce a policy of cultural assimilation between Japan and Korea.

During the first two decades of Japanese rule, until about 1931, the primary objective of economic policy lay in the development of the agricultural sector. Japanese settlers flocked to Korea, and the Japanese-owned Oriental Development Company was in the van of an almost classic example of colonial exploitation.

Initially, the Japanese encountered a significant problem in their attempts to expand Korean agriculture as as source of cheap food for the homeland. Traditional Korean farming was inefficient, and usually organized on a local basis. Large areas of land were loosely attached to the estates of the former Korean royal family or to senior yangban estates. There were further ill-defined areas of common land. The Japanese therefore initiated, in the first years of their rule, a comprehensive land survey on a national scale. The survey attempted to define the precise ownership of Korean land with a view to development in the interests of the new rulers of Korea.

Many Korean peasants, as well as small tenant farmers, who tended their land by custom either failed to register or could not prove title in the Western sense. Large areas of land thus lapsed by law to the Government-General which now came to own about five per cent of cultivated land. Other land was conveyed to the Government in lieu of unpaid taxes. The Japanese administration of Korea thus became a major landlord in its own right. Some of this land was leased to Japanese individuals but the Government-General also used the Oriental Development Company as its agent in developing its newly-acquired estates.

Consolidation of forfeited land in this way made for a certain degree of efficiency. The Japanese pursued modern measures of agricultural improvement, sponsoring irrigation and drainage schemes, and the intensive use of fertilisers. The administrative framework of Korean agriculture was modernized, and thus land came to be used more efficiently. Production of rice and other cereals rose significantly, but at the cost of driving many impoverished Koreans from the land to the cities and towns. Other Koreans emigrated to Manchuria.

By the early 1930s it had been calculated that Korean rice production had increased by about one third since 1910. But about one half of this total was being exported to Japan, so that Korean *per capita* consumption of rice had declined by over forty per cent over the same period, allowing for the increase in the Korean population. This process of enforced decline in the rice consumption, and hence of the basic standard of living, was one of the major complaints against Japanese rule in Korea. Another charge against the economic policies of the Government-General was its creation of official trading monopolies which closed down Korean firms, so precluding the development of Korean capital.

On the other hand, there was a considerable and systematic expansion of public works under Japanese rule. New roads, railways, bridges, harbours, schools and hospitals were built, often for military or strategic reasons. Communications were improved. Public health measures on a significant level were introduced. Between 1910 and 1945 the Korean population doubled. After 1931, once again for strategic reasons which we shall note below, a certain amount of industrial development took place in Korea. In many ways, Korea was transformed during the thirty-five years of Japanese rule.

From the earliest days of Japanese administration, national aspirations for lost independence counted for more than any purely economic balance sheet. Both countries shared a Confucian heritage. but imposed change and modernization were suspect because they were associated with alien rule.

The Korean Independence Movement

On 1 March 1919, there were nation-wide mass demonstrations in support of Korean independence. For several years before this date, exiled Koreans in China and Manchuria, Korean students in Japan, and patriots within Korea itself had been discussing a mass protest against Japanese rule. Inside Korea, the movement was supported by Buddhist organizations as well as by the Chondo-gyo ('The Society of the Heavenly Way'), the successor to the Tonghak movement of the late nineteenth century.

In particular, the independence movement was also inspired by the right of national self-determination proclaimed in President Woodrow Wilson's 'Fourteen Points' for a just settlement of the First World War. The movement was thus broadly based and fully conscious of events in the Western world. The new Korean nationalism, rather than looking backwards to the Confucian monarchy, thus envisaged a modern, independent democratic state.

Early in 1919 a Declaration of Korean Independence was drafted and secretly circulated throughout Korea. The movement was sponsored on the national level by 33 leading Koreans, and by local supporters in other parts of the country. On 1 March 1919, the 33 leaders read the 'Declaration' in Seoul. The Declaration was also publicly read throughout Korea . . . 'We herewith proclaim the independence of Korea . . . in witness of the equality of all nations , and we pass it on to our posterity as their inherent right. . . . The result of annexation, brought about against the will of the Korean people, is that the Japanese are concerned only for their own gain. . . .' Two million people throughout Korea are believed to have taken part in the subsequent demonstrations.

These mass demonstrations were of course suppressed with great severity which is still recalled; but the 1 March protest involved Koreans of all classes and viewpoints and thus intensified a common awareness of shared nationality. The demonstrations, which showed to world opinion the nature of Japanese rule in Korea, also resulted in some practical reforms. The Japanese created a Central Advisory Council, composed of Koreans, and also set up a parallel system of provincial and local advisory councils. Some members of these councils were elected on a restricted franchise. The military gendarmerie was replaced by a civilian police. Controls over the Korean press and publishing were relaxed. These limited reforms also reflected a period of liberalism in Japan; some upper class and affluent Koreans were won over to the government in this way.

Koreans In Exile

However, the fundamental nature of Japanese colonial rule remained unchanged. Hence the demonstrations of 1 March 1919 signified the beginning of a new struggle for Korean independence, not only within Korea but also abroad. Perhaps the most visible result of the movement was the establishment of a Korean Provisional Government-in-exile in the French concession of Shanghai on 18 September 1919. This government was formed by representatives from Korean groups in Manchuria, Siberia and China.

The first President of the Provisional Government was the veteran nationalist Syngman Rhee, whose prestige was probably higher than any other Korean exile. Following the suppression of the Independence Club in 1898, Rhee had been imprisoned for seven years by the Korean government. On his release, he had gone to America where he had studied at Harvard and received a doctorate from Princeton in 1910. Rhee had then returned to Korea in the early years of Japanese rule, but had understandably gone into exile again. He now made his home in Hawaii, where there was a Korean community, until the 1930s.

Like so many exiled political groups, the Korean Provisional Government was soon splintered by irreconcilable policy differences. One faction advocated direct military action against Japan, while another favoured long-term propaganda aimed at the Korean homeland. Syngman Rhee, as befitted his American background, favoured political work and lobbying in the United States, which was now emerging as Japan's main strategic rival in the Pacific area.

During the early 1920s, therefore, Rhee set up in Washington the Korean Commission, which was in effect a shadow legation of the Provisional Government. Rhee soon became estranged from the operations of the exiled Government, which now came under the leadership of another well-known Korean expatriate, Kim Ku. Rhee continued to regard himself as President of the Provisional Government. He continued to work in his own way for Korean independence in Hawaii and in the United States.

The exiles who supported the generally conservative Korean Provisional Government represented only part of the Korean community abroad. Koreans in Siberia had formed Communist and Socialist groups as early as 1918–19 under the influence of the Russian Revolution. In January 1921, a Korean Communist Party was formed in Shanghai; but Lenin soon decided that the Communist International (or Comintern) could not recognise a Korean Party which was based outside Korea. As a result, Korean communist groups from Siberia, Shanghai and Tokyo established a new, underground Korean Communist Party in Seoul in April 1925. The party was affiliated to the Comintern, and thus part of the international Communist movement.

The Party was bedevilled by disunity and by the activity of the Japanese police from its very inception. In December 1928 the Comintern dissolved the party for factionalism and ineffectiveness. A few Korean Communists remained to work underground until 1945, but most of the leadership escaped to Siberia, Manchuria, or China. From 1927 to about 1931, an alliance of Communists and Korean Nationalists existed in the 'New Korea Society' (the *Shinganhoe*). But this group too was eventually dissolved because of its own disunity and the intense surveillance of the police. Thus by the early 1930s the internal Korean independence movement had been neutralised or liquidated by the Japanese.

Despite these setbacks within Korea, the cause of Korean independence continued to flourish in radically new settings. Some of the Korean Communists who had fled to China entered the Chinese Communist Party and eventually, after 1935, reached Mao Tse-tung's Yenan headquarters in north China. Here these Koreans later formed a Korean Independence League and also a small Korean Volunteer Army of several hundred men which fought alongside the Chinese Communists against the Japanese until 1945.

Other Korean Communists in Manchuria also fought with the

Chinese Communists in the 1930s. These Koreans operated both in eastern Manchuria and across the international border in north-east Korea. Eventually the Japanese military pushed these insurgents into Soviet Siberia in 1941. One of these Korean guerrillas was named Kim Sung Chu, who took the name of Kim Il Sung, a celebrated anti-Japanese fighter of an earlier generation. Kim Il Sung's precise links with the Soviets after 1941 have never been elucidated, but what is certain is that he returned to Korea with the Soviet Army in 1945. He then began an entirely new chapter in Korean history as the Soviet-backed leader of Communist North Korea.

While these different cadres of Korean Communists fought with Mao's armies, the Korean Provisional Government under Kim Ku as its President, remained in Shanghai until the Japanese invasion of China in 1937. The Provisional Government then fled in stages before the Japanese to Chungking, deep in the Chinese interior, which was Chiang Kai-shek's wartime capital. Here in Chungking, Kim Ku formed a Korean unit to fight with the Chinese Nationalists; the Korean Provisional Government declared war against Japan after the Pearl Harbor attack of 7 December 1941. But as we shall see, official recognition by the United States, or indeed any other country, eluded these Koreans in Nationalist China.

Syngman Rhee, meanwhile, had continued to work for Korean independence without much success. He had tried, in vain, to present the case for independence to the League of Nations in Geneva in 1932 when that body discussed the Japanese seizure of Manchuria. Rhee had then made several lecture tours in the United States. Eventually, late in the 1930s, Rhee left Hawaii to live in Washington, and to wait for what he considered would be the inevitable war between Japan and the United States. From then until 1945 Syngman Rhee was to term himself the Chairman of the Korean Commission in the United States. But this rather grand title carried little if any influence in Washington.

We can thus see from these events that the wide ideological, personal and geographical differences within the Korean Independence movement precluded the formation of an unified, effective government-in-exile. During the 1930s, moreover, Korea had become ever more integrated within the strategic and economic administration of the Japanese Empire as the Rising Sun spread into the whole of Manchuria, north China, and then deep into China proper.

Thus by the late 1930s, the one belief shared by the far-flung members of the different Korean independence movements was the conviction that only the military defeat of Imperial Japan would bring freedom to Korea.

Japanese Rule: The Final Phase

In September 1931 following an incident at Mukden between Chinese and Japanese troops, Japan began the occupation of the whole of Manchuria. The following year the puppet state of Manchukuo was set up: the Japanese soon moved into the neighbouring Chinese province of Jehol. These were successive steps in an expansionist drive that was to lead Japan into full-scale conflict in China by 1937. After a further four years of ever-increasing tension in the Far East, Japan went to war with the United States and the British Empire in December 1941.

These historic events had a very important effect on Korea. After 1931 the relative relaxation of controls that had characterised Japanese policy in Korea during the 1920s was reversed as Japan began to put her continental possessions on a war footing. Increasing emphasis was given to strategic industrial investment in both Korea and Manchuria. The stress on agricultural development in Korea, which had characterised the first two decades of Japanese rule, was downgraded. A new priority was given to improving communications, and especially those between Korea and Manchuria. In line with this latter policy during 1934 a new doubletracked railway bridge was built over the Yalu between Sinuiju and Antung in Manchuria, a link which was claimed to be the longest railway bridge in the Japanese Empire.

As an integral part of this programme, the mining of coal, iron and other non-ferrous minerals found in northern Korea was stepped up. Some metal processing and chemical plants were built, mostly in north-east Korea where the ports of Hungnam and Chongjin gave easy access by sea to Japan, so cutting production and transportation overheads. A small iron and steel industry was developed in northern Korea as well as facilities for manufacturing machine tools. Light industry was promoted around Seoul and Pyongyang.

From 1931 to 1941, manufacturing as a share of the total Korean national product increased from 20 per cent to 40 per cent. During the period of Japanese rule as a whole, the agricultural labour force dropped from 90 per cent of the total in 1910 to about 70 per cent in the early 1940s.

The showpiece of Japanese industrial development in Korea was the hydroelectric industry which was planned to mobilize the potential energy resources of Korea's northern rivers. Large facilities were built at Changjin (in Japanese, Chosin), north of Hungnam, and at nearby Pujon (Fusen). At Suiho on the Yalu River, about sixty miles upstream from Sinuiju, Japanese engineers constructed the 3,000 foot long Supung dam with a large power house on the Korean side of the river. The Suiho plant provided power for much of Korea and also for the industrial zone of southern Manchuria.

This partial Japanese industrialization of Korea in the 1930s has to be seen in its historical context. Following the launching of the 'China Incident. in 1937, the industrial targets of the Korean economy were controlled as part of the 'Japan-Korea-Manchuria Resources Mobilization Plan'. The Imperial Japanese Planning Board set the targets for Korea, and the whole concept of continental development under Japanese aegis was rationalised in late 1938 when Japan proclaimed the 'New Order in East Asia'. The region was to become self-sufficient, and Western influences excluded. When Japan turned south during 1940–41, the concept of the 'New Order' was naturally succeeded by that of the 'Greater East Asia Co-Prosperity Sphere'.

Korea's role in this hegemonistic strategy was central. By the late 1930s the peninsula was becoming a virtual Japanese military base both by reason of its growing industrial resources and its strategic geographical position between Japan and Manchuria.

The industrial, manpower and natural assets of Korea were increasingly seen as elements in a war economy which after 1941 was now organised on a totalitarian basis. All Korean industrial production not needed for Japanese military purposes was curtailed. The corollary was that Korean agriculture was even further downgraded as Korea became increasingly integrated into the Japanese war economy. Koreans were conscripted into the Japanese army and after 1939 drafted for forced labour as well.

As part of this integration process the administrative links between the two countries became ever-closer. After thirty years of autonomous administration within the Japanese Empire, the coming of the Pacific War in December 1941 meant that Korea was now completely subordinated in its government to Japan.

During 1942 it was decreed that Korea would be governed by the Japanese Home Affairs Ministry with the administration in Seoul acting as its agent. The following year, the police system was reorganised. By 1945 there were over 300,000 Japanese troops garrisoned in Korea. Korea was thus ruled as part of Japan.

In the wake of this administrative integration, the process of enforced cultural assimilation between the two countries came to its climax. The last two Korean-language newspapers had been closed in 1940, and it was even decreed in the final years of Japan's rule that Koreans should take Japanese personal names. In early 1945 the Japanese announced a plan for the election of 10 Korean representatives to the Upper House of the Diet in Tokyo, and for the election of 16 Korean representatives to the Lower House. This was the culmination of the wartime integration process termed 'Japan and Korea One Body' (*Naisen Ittai*).

This plan for integrating the two countries on the legislative level was of course never implemented. By early 1945 Japan's military position was already desperate. When the two atomic bombs were dropped on Hiroshima and Nagasaki on 6 and 9 August 1945 total defeat was imminent. With the Imperial Rescript announcing Japan's capitulation on 15 August 1945 Korea was freed from Japanese rule under terms of the Cairo and Potsdam declarations which Japan had accepted with its surrender.

In retrospect the period of Japanese rule is one of complicated paradox. Loss of Korean independence was accompanied by an intensive modernization process in some key sectors of the Korean economy. Undeniable economic exploitation by Japan, especially in the agricultural sector, was balanced by the deliberate creation, often for strategic reasons, of the public works and communications infrastructure of a modern country.

For the same strategic reasons the Korean economy was partly industrialised after 1931. When Japan acknowledged defeat in August 1945 Korea was further along the road towards modernization than any other Asian country apart from Japan itself, but the cost to Koreans had been heavy.

Perhaps the greatest paradox of all lay in the circumstances that surrounded the ending of Japan's rule in Korea. For at the very moment of capitulation Korea was partitioned for the first time since the emergence of the Silla Kingdom.

Chapter Eight:
Korea Divided

Japan's defeat in the Pacific War ended her rule in Korea. After the Pearl Harbor attack of 7 December 1941 the allies were completely preoccupied with the military problems of stemming Japan's tide of conquests, which had spread to the borders of India and to the Solomon Islands in the south-west Pacific. It was only in 1943, as the Japanese advances were contained, that the allied leaders began to consider the entire question of dismantling the Japanese Empire.

During March 1943, President Franklin Roosevelt and Anthony Eden, the British Foreign Secretary, discussed in Washington the disposition of Manchuria, Formosa, Korea and other Japanese acquisitions. The two men agreed that after Japan's defeat, Korea should be governed under an international trusteeship, and that the trustees might be the United States, the Soviet Union and China. The concept of a trusteeship reflected Roosevelt's belief that the colonial people of the Far East, when freed, would need a period of education in democratic institutions.

From the beginning of these discussions by the allied leaders on Korea's future, there was no question of giving recognition to any exiled Korean group. When Chiang Kai-shek's Chinese Nationalist Government suggested to Washington as early as April 1942, that America might recognise the Korean Provisional Government (in Chungking), the State Department declined. The United States considered that there was a lack of unity amongst Korean nationalist groups, and that the following of the Korean Provisional Government, even among exiled Koreans, was limited.

Syngman Rhee's wartime lobbying in Washington on behalf of

the Korean Provisional Government was thus to no avail. After an appeal to President Harry Truman in June 1945, Rhee was told that American policy was to avoid taking action which might 'compromise the right of the Korean people to choose the ultimate form and personnel of the government which they may wish to choose'.

In view of later events, it should be remembered that until the very last days of hostilities with Japan. there was no intention of dividing Korea. Whatever the post-war form of Korean government or trusteeship that was envisaged-, in the wartime conferences and meetings, Korea was seen as one country.

From Cairo to Potsdam

Roosevelt's idea of a postwar Korean trusteeship was again present during the conference with Churchill and Chiang Kai-shek at Cairo (23–27 November 1943). The three leaders agreed that Manchuria and Formosa should be returned to China with Japan's defeat, and that Korea should become independent. The draft communique promised Korean independence 'at the earliest possible moment', but Roosevelt personally altered these words to read that independence would be granted 'at the proper moment'. Churchill revised this particular phrase to 'in due course'.

The final draft of the Cairo Declaration then stated that 'The aforesaid three great powers, mindful of the enslavement of the people of Korea, are determined that in due course Korea shall become free and independent'. The Declaration, agreed by the three leaders on 26 November 1943, was then released to the world on 1 December.

From Cairo, Roosevelt and Churchill proceeded to the Teheran Conference. Here Roosevelt told Stalin that the Koreans needed 'some period of apprenticeship before full independence might be attained, perhaps forty years'. Stalin agreed, and there the matter dropped. But on 12 January 1944, Roosevelt returned to the idea during a secret session of the Pacific War Council held in the White House. The President was Chairman of this body composed of members of the United Nations fighting in the Pacific. Reporting on the conferences at Cairo and Teheran, Roosevelt again stated that following Japan's defeat, Korea should be placed 'under a forty-year tutelage'.

Over a year later during the Yalta conference of February

1945, Roosevelt reverted to the subject of the Korean trusteeship during his meeting with Stalin on 8 February. The President suggested that the trusteeship might be composed of the United States, the Soviet Union, and China and that the period involved might be 'twenty to thirty years'. Stalin considered 'the shorter the period the better', and said that a British representative might also be considered. In reply to Stalin's query, Roosevelt replied that no foreign troops should be stationed in Korea. Stalin approved of this reply which ended the discussion on Korea.

In very general terms Roosevelt's suggestion of a postwar trusteeship may have been a politic attempt at ensuring Korean independence. Given Soviet proximity to Korea the Russians were perfectly capable of occupying the country with or without allied agreement at the close of the war. In this context the Yalta agreement on Japan was highly significant. By this agreement, signed by Roosevelt, Churchill and Stalin, on 11 February 1945, Soviet participation in the Pacific War was promised in exchange for Russia's pre-1905 rights in Port Arthur, Dairen, and over the Manchurian railways. The agreement also implied that with Japan's defeat, and with the restoration of a strong Russian presence in Manchuria, the traditional Russian interest in Korea would be rekindled.

Following Roosevelt's death on 12 April 1945, the personal agreement between him and Stalin over Korea was reaffirmed when Harry Hopkins visited Moscow at President Truman's request late in May 1945. Stalin then agreed to a short-term, four power trusteeship for Korea. The country's independence would be guaranteed; there was no detailed discussion.

After the Hopkins visit to Moscow, preparations went ahead for the great-power conference at Potsdam in mid-July. Meanwhile, there was growing suspicion of Soviet motives in Washington. In particular, the new President and his advisers, as has often been related, were distrustful in particular of Russian behaviour in Poland. There were increasing doubts whether the United States and the Soviet Union could work together in the post-war world, whether in Europe or in the Far East.

On 30 May 1945, Hopkins had reported from Moscow that 'Stalin expects that Russia will share in the actual occupation of Japan and wants an agreement with us and the British as to zones of occupation'. This was a new request with probable implications for the future of Korea as well as Japan. Yet with no plans for American occupation of Korea, there hardly seemed an alternative to the tentative outlines of the Korean trusteeship agreement as a means of preserving Korean independence after Japan's defeat. But irrespective of post-war planning, events were now to dictate developments in Korea.

The primary discussions at the Potsdam Conference (17 July – 2 August 1945) centred on the future of Germany and the associated European peace settlement. There was no discussion between the 'Big Three' on the post-war settlement in Korea. Neither was the question of a Korean trusteeship discussed on the Foreign Ministers' level.

For the American and British leaders at Potsdam the negotiations with Stalin were eclipsed by the news of the successful test-firing of the first atomic weapon in New Mexico. The brief, initial report of this event reached the American delegation late on 16 July. Subsequent reports only added to the impression of the overwhelming power of the new bomb. After intensive discussion with his advisers and with Churchill, President Truman approved a directive on 24 July which sanctioned the dropping of the atomic bomb on Japan in early August.

On 26 July, the Potsdam Declaration was issued to Japan in the name of Truman, Churchill, and Chiang Kai-shek. This ultimatum called for the unconditional surrender of Japan on pain of 'complete and utter destruction'. Japanese sovereignty would then be confined to the four home islands. Article 8 of the Potsdam Declaration stated that 'the terms of the Cairo Declaration shall be carried out. . . .' This meant that Japanese rule over Korea would end at the moment of Tokyo's acceptance of the Potsdam Declaration. Two days later, the Imperial Government in Tokyo stated that it would 'ignore' the Potsdam Declaration: planning now went ahead in the Marianas for the atomic strike against Japan. The Pacific War seemed likely to end far sooner than anyone had hitherto dreamt.

Military Planning

The chief preoccupation of the American military at Potsdam lay with the problem of defeating Japan. President Truman had already given provisional approval for the invasion of Japan, 'Operation Olympic', on 18 June. Final approval of the great invasion, scheduled for November 1945, was of course delayed pending the outcome of the first atomic test.

Military planning for the defeat of Japan went ahead quite independently of the atomic project. Thus on 24 July, during a meeting of the Combined (Anglo-American) Chiefs of Staff with their Soviet counter-parts, the Russians stated that they would be ready to begin operations against Japan in the second half of August. On 26 July, the American and Soviet Chiefs discussed naval and air operations in the Korean-Manchurian area. They agreed on an operational demarcation line that ran through Cape Boltina on the north-east coast of Korea. American forces would operate south of this line, Russian forces to the north. There was no discussion of any invasion or of any occupation zones in Korea.

Nevertheless, the impending atomic strike against Japan inevitably began to affect American strategic calculations. At the opening of the Potsdam Conference, Stalin had stated that the Soviet Union would not be ready to move against Japan until about 15 August. While President Truman's chief reason for using the atomic bomb was to save American casualties, it seems probable that the President and his advisers hoped that an early Japanese surrender would preclude Soviet entry into the Pacific War. This might prevent unilateral Russian occupation of Korea and Manchuria, which was certainly possible otherwise.

It was prudent for the United States to make plans for the military occupation of part of Korea. Thus one day during the Potsdam Conference, General George C. Marshall, the U.S. Army Chief of Staff, called in Lt. General John Hull, Chief of the Operations Division, and a member of the American delegation, and told him to prepare to move forces into Korea.

General Hull and his planning staff then studied a map of Korea and thought that at least two Korean ports should be part of any proposed American zone. They thus drew a line north of Seoul that included within this proposed zone both Inchon and Pusan. The line that was drawn by the planners at Potsdam was near to the 38th Parallel, but not on it. Subsequently, on 25 July 1945 Marshall informed President Truman that the U.S. could put a division ashore at Pusan within a short time after the end of hostilities with Japan. But Marshall also considered that the Russians would be able to occupy the port of Chongjin in north-east Korea.

The subsequent speed of the Russian advance into northern Korea in August 1945 shows that the Soviets too were engaged in military contingency planning involving Korea at this time.

In this way, as Japanese rule over Korea entered its last weeks, so the differing interests of the wartime allies began to assert themselves over that strategic peninsula.

Decision at the Pentagon

With the end of the Potsdam Conference, Japan's defeat became imminent. On 6 and 9 August 1945, atomic bombs were dropped on Hiroshima and Nagasaki respectively. On 8 August, the Soviet Union declared war against Japan and subscribed to the Potsdam Declaration. Moscow was now committed to the promise of Korean independence.

Following the Russian declaration of war, on 9 August Soviet military operations on a huge scale began against the Japanese Empire. Three Soviet army groups invaded Manchuria. Southern Sakhalin was invaded from ports in the Siberian Maritime Province. Another invasion force for the Kurile Islands was mobilised at Petropavlovsk.

The Soviets moved quickly into Korea from their bases in the Vladivostok area. On 10 August, the first Russians landed at the port of Unggi, in the far north-east of Korea. This landing was followed by another at Chongjin, about fifty miles south, on 13 August. By 16 August Soviet troops were in Wonsan, a major port, and about two hundred miles south of Chongjin. The nearest American forces, meanwhile, were in Okinawa, 600 miles from Korea and scheduled for occupation duties in Japan.

Stalin's declaration of war against Japan, and the swift advance of Soviet forces in the new war theatre, now meant that the United States had to move very quickly to preempt the Soviet overrunning of Korea. While Japan's sudden capitulation had been envisaged ever since the Potsdam Conference, it was not expected that the Soviet armies would move until mid-August at the earliest.

On 10 August, the Japanese government asked Washington for surrender terms. Immediately Secretary of State James F. Byrnes instructed the State-War-Navy Co-ordinating Committee (SWNCC)to prepare plans for a joint American-Soviet occupation of Korea which would divide the peninsula 'with the line as far north as possible'. The SWNCC was a high-level planning group which had been considering plans for the surrender and occupation of Japan since the Potsdam Conference.

That same day, 10 August 1945, planners in the Operations

Division of the American War Department in the Pentagon began drafting 'General Order No. 1' which would be issued by the allies to the Japanese government after its formal surrender. This was a document of great importance for the first paragraph of the General Order would specify which commands, and which nations, would accept the surrender of the far-flung Japanese forces throughout the entire Far Eastern and Pacific theatres of war.

The actual drafting of General Order No. 1 was the responsibility of the Policy Section of the Strategy and Policy Group of the Operations Division, headed by Colonel Charles H. Bonesteel. He was assisted by another Colonel, Dean Rusk, then on active service in the Pentagon and later Secretary of State under Presidents Kennedy and Johnson.

Late on 10 August, Colonel Bonesteel was given thirty minutes to draft Paragraph 1 of the General Order for the SWNCC which was in overnight session. In accordance with their instructions, Bonesteel and Rusk had to find a line in Korea which was as far north as they thought the Soviets would accept, bearing in mind that the Russians could occupy all Korea before the Americans arrived. At first the two men thought of using Korean provincial boundaries; but time was urgent, and the only map available was a small-scale office map of the Far East on the wall of Bonesteel's office.

The two colonels noted that the 38th Parallel passed north of Seoul and almost divided Korea into two halves. They thus decided to use this line as the Soviet-American boundary in Korea for the draft of General Order No. 1. South of this line, the Americans would receive the Japanese surrender. to the north, Russians would take the surrender.

Dean Rusk was later to recall (in 1950) that 'we recommended the 38th Parallel . . . because we felt it was important to include the capital of Korea in the area of responsibility of American troops'. The two planners also recommended that until the Japanese surrender was complete, the American commander was to have civil affairs (or Governmental) responsibility south of the 38th Parallel.

Another recommendation of the two Pentagon planners was that once the ceremonies of Japanese surrender were over, the two zonal administrations in Korea should be combined to form a single all-Korean administration. This unified administration should then be placed under a Joint council formed of the commanders of the United States, Soviet, and other forces making up the Korean occupation. The planners had thus not only devised a means of dividing Korea for the purpose of accepting the Japanese surrender; they had also drafted a charter for an American military government south of the 38th Parallel. But a permanent division of Korea was not of course envisaged.

But as well as administrative convenience in coping with the Japanese surrender, there were strategic factors underlying the choice of a Korean demarcation line 'as far north as possible'. The 38th Parallel prevented the occupation of all Korea by fast-moving Russian forces; it would augment the security of Japan which was scheduled to come under long-term allied occupation; and presumably it would put the United States in a good position to negotiate a Korean trusteeship.

Once the draft General Order No. 1 was completed during the night of 10–11 August, it was quickly cleared through the chain of command passing upwards through the SWNCC the Joint Chiefs of Staff, and the Secretaries of State, War, and the Navy until the document arrived on President Truman's desk on 15 August.

Japan's Surrender

It was a momentous day. Late on 14 August, the Japanese Emperor had signed the Imperial Rescript accepting the Potsdam Declaration. The recorded announcement by the Emperor, of Japan's surrender, was then broadcast at noon, Tokyo time, on 15 August. So ended Japanese rule in Korea under the provisions of the Cairo and Potsdam declarations.

General Order No. 1 was now quickly signed by President Truman on the same day, 15 August. The President asked that copies of the document be sent for clearance to the British, Soviet and Chinese governments. These governments raised no objection to the provision of the 38th Parallel as a means of facilitating the Japanese surrender in Korea. But Stalin's reply asked for a Soviet occupation zone in the northern Japanese home island of Hokkaido. This request was refused by President Truman. A copy of General Order No. 1 was also sent to General MacArthur in Manila. He had assumed the post of Supreme Commander for the Allied Powers in Japan on that same day, 15 August 1945, VJ day. As Supreme Commander MacArthur would sign the Instrument of Japanese Surrender for the allies, issue General Order No. 1, and then preside over the occupation of Japan.

MacArthur would thus issue the General Order as Supreme Commander. But in his other capactity as Commanding General, U.S. Army Forces, Pacific, it was also MacArthur's duty to appoint a subordinate officer to receive the Japanese surrender in Korea south of the 38th Parallel, and to govern South Korea for the United States. Accordingly on 27 August, MacArthur designated Lt. General John R. Hodge as Commander, United States Army Forces in Korea. General Hodge was commander of the U.S. XXIV Corps in Okinawa which was now scheduled as the American occupation force in South Korea.

Less than a week later, on 2 September 1945, General MacArthur received the formal surrender of the Japanese government and the Imperial General Staff on the quarter-deck of the U.S.S. *Missouri* anchored in Tokyo Bay. General Order No. 1 was then issued to the Japanese government, over which MacArthur now had full powers. The division of Korea was thus at hand.

Russians and Americans in Korea

During and after the processing of General Order No. 1 in Washington, the Soviet Army had continued with its advance into Korea. On 24 August, troops from Col. General I. M. Chistiakov's 25th Army entered Pyongyang, the largest city in northern Korea. Soviet units then moved south to the 38th Parallel in the Kaesong vicinity in the west and in the Chunchon area in the central mountains. A few individual Russians filtered over the Parallel, but there was no crossing in unit strength.

The arrival of American troops in Korea was delayed because of the priority given to shipping for Japan. But on 4 September 1945 an advance party from XXIV Corps landed at Kimpo Airfield across the Han River from Seoul. The main body of the Corps arrived by ship at Inchon on 8 September. The following day General Hodge took the surrender of the Japanese administration in Korea below the 38th Parallel in a ceremony at Seoul.

On 7 September MacArthur issued a proclamation to the Koreans in the new American occupation zone. He told them that the purpose of the occupation was to enforce the Instrument of Japanese Surrender and he guaranteed personal and religious freedom. MacArthur referred to the allied promise of Korean independence 'in due course' and he stated that south of the 38th Parallel 'all powers of government' would be exercised under his authority. In line with MacArthur's proclamation American military government was now formally established in Seoul on 12 September 1945.

In difficult circumstances the wartime allies had taken two decisions on Korea. They had agreed on a post-war trusteeship and also on a temporary partition to enforce the Japanese surrender.

The trusteeship proposals were now to be revived, once the process of Japanese capitulation was over. Trusteeship was to prove unacceptable to Korean opinion which wanted immediate independence. Of much more historic significance was the division of Korea, conceived as an expedient in an almost tragic conjunction with the country's liberation from Japan. By September 1945 this division was a reality; it has lasted ever since.

Chapter Nine:
The Two Koreas

The first months of Korean liberation were a confused period. Yet even before the close of 1945, the future pattern of political developments within Korea began to emerge quite clearly. During the interregnum between the Japanese capitulation and the arrival of American troops in the South, some Korean politicians had set up a 'Korean People's Republic' which was proclaimed in Seoul on 6 September 1945. The left-wing People's Republic claimed national jurisdiction and operated through a system of subsidiary committees on an all-Korean basis, including the Soviet zone.

But as we have seen, it was American national policy that initially no Korean group would be recognised as having exclusive jurisdiction. Following the formal creation of the 'United States Army Military Government in Korea' (USAMGIK) on 12 September 1945 as the sole legal authority south of the 38th Parallel, the People's Republic was treated as one of the many political parties that were already emerging in South Korea.

Exiles Return

With Japan's surrender, the exiled Korean Provisional Government in Chungking had applied to return to Korea, but this request was refused by the Americans. The leaders of the Provisional Government were told, however, that they could return as individuals. As a private person, Syngman Rhee had thus arrived in Korea from the United States on 16 October. Kim Ku, the President of the Provisional Government, and other supporters in China later returned to Korea during November. They too, travelled as individuals.

Following Japan's capitulation, the American government was preoccupied with the arrangements for the creation and supervision of MacArthur's Supreme Command for the Allied Powers (SCAP) in Tokyo. It was not until 21 October 1945 that the State Department announced that since Korea was not ready for self-government, a period of trusteeship would be necessary. During this period, Koreans would 'be prepared to take over the independent administration of their country'. This of course was stated allied policy on Korea. Preparations now went ahead between Washington, London and Moscow for a Foreign Ministers' conference in Moscow in December 1945 during which the proposed Korean trusteeship would be discussed and if possible agreed.

In South Korea the trusteeship idea was opposed across the political spectrum. Most leading politicians of both right and left announced their support of the Korean Provisional Government. It was hoped that this Government would be recognised by the allies as a transitional regime and that all-Korean elections would then be held to create a Korean national government. The 38th Parallel, so it was hoped, would then be removed by the occupying forces.

This was the programme announced by the Central Conference for the Acceleration of Korean Independence, formed under Syngman Rhee's chairmanship, on 25 October 1945. The left-wing 'People's Republic' and other leftist groups, including the Korean Communist Party which had been reformed in Seoul after the arrival of the Americans, soon withdrew their support from the Central Conference. These leftist groups criticised Rhee for being under American influence.

As we have noted, in November 1945 Kim Ku, the leader of the Korean Provisional Government, returned to Seoul from Chungking. There were again renewed hopes that right and left could work together. But these hopes were soon dashed. Kim Ku very quickly broke with the leaders of the leftist People's Republic claiming that this group was undermining his support and his legitimacy. In any case on 12 December 1945, the American Military Government banned the People's Republic on grounds of its claim to provide a rival jurisdiction. So ended any attempt at a coalition between the right and the left wings of the Korean independence movement. But Syngman Rhee was gradually emerging as the leader of a conservative independence grouping.

The 38th Parallel

These hopes for early Korean independence were illusory for a number of reasons. While the politicians disagreed in Seoul, the allied powers were proceeding with their own plans for Korean trusteeship. Moreover, while Kim Ku and other Korean nationalists assumed that the 38th Parallel was a temporary demarcation line, the zonal boundary was already becoming a frontier. Although there may have been good reasons for its speedy adoption in August 1945, this arbitrary line cut across ancient provincial boundaries as well as roads, rivers, and railways, separating the agricultural south of Korea from the partly-industrialised north. At the time of the Japanese surrender, it was estimated that there were about 21 million Koreans in the southern zone, and about 9 million in the north.

The Russians had quickly sealed off their zone, setting up road blocks. But during the first few weeks of the new boundary's existence thousands of refugees, both Korean and Japanese, had crossed the Parallel to the South. By the end of October 1945, the Russians had cut rail, postal and telegraph links, as well as stopping the movement of trade and people. The 38th Parallel had become a frontier.

This division was very soon to have serious consequences both economic and political. Economically the two Korean zones were complementary. The agricultural south was dependent on the coal, fertilisers and industrial products of the north, while immemorially the rice surplus of the south had fed the mountainous north of Korea. Most of the light industry and thus most of the consumer goods production of Korea were also found in the south. The 38th Parallel thus prevented a newly-liberated Korea from taking advantage of Japanese-built industry and communications on a national basis.

Politically, too, the 38th Parallel was extremely significant. During the critical period of 1945–46, most South Korean politicians, including the veteran 'domestic' Communists who had worked underground during Japanese rule, believed as a matter of course that Seoul was all-important. It was generally believed that the traditional capital would once again become the centre of a newly-independent Korea.

Events north of the 38th Parallel were soon to show, however, that even before the end of 1945 two Koreas were in the making. Following their initial occupation, the Russians had quickly decided to govern indirectly through Korean organizations instead of relying on military government. At first the Soviet military had formed a group of provincial committees; these were consolidated into a 'Temporary Five Provinces People's Committee' on 8 October 1945, headed by a Christian Korean Nationalist, Cho Man-sik. Cho claimed an unique legitimacy because the Japanese governor of South Pyongan province had handed power to him soon after 15 August 1945.

In late October 1945 the Soviets renamed the 'Temporary Committee' the 'Five Provinces Administrative Bureau'. Cho Man-sik remained the Chairman. This was the first tentative move towards a separate zonal government in North Korea.

Of much more lasting significance was the meeting organized under Russian auspices in Pyongyang on 10 October when a 'North Korean Branch of the Korean Communist Party' was organized. According to subsequent North Korean histories, this was 'the first Korean Communist Party organization established on the principles of Marxism-Leninism'. Kim Il Sung was elected the First Secretary of the Central Bureau of this organization. Aged 33, he was a former Korean partisan leader who, as we have seen, had operated in north-east Korea and Manchuria during the 1930s.

Kim had spent the war in the Soviet Far East and is said to have landed at Wonsan in September 1945 in the uniform of a Soviet major. Following this meeting, Kim and his followers, composed of both 'Soviet Koreans' from Siberia and a personal 'partisan group' worked to extend their influence through the Communist Party in North Korea. Kim was backed by the Soviet army and there seems no reason to query the later official claim that by the end of 1945, the Party's organization was 'firmly established' throughout the Soviet zone.

Thus by the time of the Moscow conference of December 1945 there was already a polarization of Korean affairs north and south of the 38th Parallel. Two distinct political entitles were beginning to emerge.

The Moscow Agreement and The Joint Commission

The Foreign Ministers of the three wartime allies, James Byrnes, Ernest Bevin, and V. M. Molotov, now met in Moscow on 16 December 1945. The conference, which was to last ten days, dealt with many problems of the post-war world in China, Japan and elsewhere.

Agreement was reached relatively quickly on the objective of a unified administration in Korea as the forerunner of a fully independent government. The agreement, 'The Moscow Protocol on Korea', was later subscribed to by Nationalist China. The Moscow Protocol was to form the basis of all international discussion on Korea for the next two years.

The Moscow Agreement stated that a provisional Korean democratic government was to be established. It was also laid down that a Joint American-Soviet Commission, representing the two commands in Korea, should meet to assist in forming this government through consultation 'with the Korean democratic parties and social organizations'. The long-term proposals of the Joint Commission, following consultation with the Korean provisional government, should then be presented to the four powers 'for the working out of an agreement concerning a four-power trusteeship for Korea for a period of up to five years'.

The Moscow Agreement was thus quite clearly intended to implement the wartime pledge of Korean independence 'in due course'. As a preliminary to the meeting of the Joint Commission, a Joint Conference of the two commands in Korea was to meet to co-ordinate administrative matters between the two zones.

When the news of the Moscow Agreement reached Korea late in December 1945 there were violent objections to the trusteeship provisions from all parties. Immediate independence was the national goal. The trusteeship proposals were commonly seen as a virtual great-power protectorate over Korea. But early in January 1946, the Communists in both North and South Korea changed their line and accepted the Moscow Agreement together with its trusteeship proposals.

Initially, the Joint Conference on the detailed level between the two commands in Korea met in January 1946 and reached minor agreements on mail exchange and liaison which were never implemented by the Russians. The Joint Commission, the main body established by the Moscow Conference, then met in the Toksu Palace in Seoul on 20 March 1946. The Soviet delegate took the position that only those Korean political parties and social organizations favourable to the Moscow Agreement should be consulted by the Joint-Commission.

This proposal of course excluded all the democratic parties opposed to the trusteeship proposal and would have probably paved the way for a Communist-dominated provisional Korean government. On grounds of both democratic principle and of protecting their own security interests the American delegation could not accept the exclusion of groups opposed to Korean trusteeship. The Joint Commission was deadlocked and adjourned on 8 May 1946.

The drift towards the creation of two Korean states meanwhile continued. In early February 1946 Syngman Rhee organised the 'National Council for Rapid Realization of Korean Independence'. A few days later, on 14 February 1946, General Hodge set up a new zonal advisory body termed the 'Korean Representative Democratic Council'. The Council was mostly composed of right-wing politicians and Syngman Rhee was elected Chairman. There was now an increasing consolidation of the conservative parties in the American zone. The leftists replied with the creation of the 'Korean People's Democratic Front'.

In North Korea, the nationalist leader Cho Man-sik was purged in January 1946 and the 'Five Provinces' administration which he headed was abolished by the Russians. Opponents of the Moscow Agreement were attacked as American running dogs; many fled to South Korea. During February 1946, a 'Provisional People's Committee for North Korea' was set up under Kim Il Sung. This effective, Soviet-model embryonic government had a Presidium as its Cabinet and ten administrative departments as its ministries.

During August 1946, the North Korean Communists absorbed the Korean returnees from Mao Tse-tung's headquarters in Yenan in Northern China who had formed the New People's Party. This amalgamated Party was termed the North Korean Workers' Party; although Kim Il Sung was but Vice-Chairman he retained overall control through his dominance of the Party apparatus and his close links with the Soviet military. A counterpart of the new party was formed in South Korea in October 1946 and soon organised a series of violent strikes and demonstrations. Many of its leaders were arrested on the orders of the Military Government.

Throughout this critical period of 1946–47, General Hodge attempted in vain to find a democratic South Korean 'third force' which would back the Moscow trusteeship proposals and so provide a middle way between Syngman Rhee and the Communists. But when the Military Government created a South Korean Interim Legislative Assembly in October 1946, with half its members elected, Rhee's supporters easily won the elections.

Rhee now began to campaign for an interim South Korean

state pending reunification. Responding to all these pressures, the Military Government in South Korea designated its own Korean elements as the South Korean Interim Government in May 1947; the Americans retained financial control. In North Korea, a Supreme People's Assembly was inaugurated in February 1947; the term 'provisional' was removed from the title of the Provisional People's Committee formed in 1946; and headed by Kim Il Sung.

The Moscow Agreement was thus increasingly irrelevent to developments in Korea. The Joint Commission now met for a second session in Seoul in May 1947. But once again its deliberations were stalemated over the Soviet refusal to allow consultation with parties opposed to the Moscow trusteeship proposals. The Americans continued to consider that acceptance of the Soviet proposals would result in a Communist-dominated provisional government in Korea. By July 1947, the impasse was so great that when the Joint Commission adjourned the two delegations could not even agree on a joint report.

There were several reasons for the failure of the Joint Commission. By mid-1947, as we have noted, separate institutions cast in the political image of the two rival occupying powers were already emerging north and south of the 38th Parallel. It was becoming ever more difficult to envisage an unified, independent Korean government.

Secondly, by mid-1947, the wartime alliance between the Western powers and the Soviet Union was dead; on a whole range of issues a global confrontation was emerging between Washington and Moscow. Korea was bound to be affected by the coming of the cold war. As so often in the past, the national aspirations of the Korean people were in conflict with the strategic importance of the peninsula.

Lastly, there can be little doubt that the Soviet Union was not disposed to accept an united and democratic Korean government which was the wish of most Koreans. The Soviet intention to exercise a continuing control over at least North Korea was thus a very important element in the division of Korea.

On the other hand, if all Korean parties had been able to agree on an independence programme in the first few months of the occupation, the Soviets might have accepted an all-Korean administration. In somewhat differing circumstances Moscow accepted an Austrian government in 1945 while retaining zonal control of part of that country. But what slim chance existed of such a solution in Korea must have been dissipated by the disunity of the Korean parties.

The United Nations and Korea

Faced with the breakdown of the Moscow Agreement on Korea, the United States in the late summer of 1947 decided to turn over the Korean issue to the United Nations. But first Washington tried to make one last attempt to resolve the Korean problem by a direct approach to Moscow.

On 26 August 1947, the United States suggested to Moscow that four-power conversations be held to solve the Korean issue on the basis of free, all-Korean elections held in both zonal commands and supervised by the UN. Britain and China were prepared to accept this proposal. The Soviet Union held that it lay outside the provision of the Moscow Agreement and hence rejected the American suggestion.

The United States now felt free to go with the Korean problem to the UN. On 17 September 1947, Secretary of State George C. Marshall, speaking before the General Assembly, stated that 'because of the inability of the two powers to reach agreement' the United States was now laying the question of Korean independence before the world body. Six days later the General Assembly voted to place the Korean question on its current agenda. Throughout the subsequent deliberations on Korea, the Soviet delegate at the UN insisted that the Korean question did not lie within United Nations jurisdiction.

On 14 November 1947 the United Nations now passed a far-reaching United States resolution on Korea. The resolution provided for a Temporary UN Commission on Korea (UNCTOK) to observe free, all-Korean elections which should be held prior to 31 March 1948. Following the elections a Korean National Assembly and a National Government should be created. The armed forces of the occupying powers should then be withdrawn within 90 days of the establishment of the Korean national government. As a preliminary, UNCTOK should have the right 'to travel, observe and consult throughout Korea'.

Following the creation of UNCTOK the Soviet zonal command in North Korea refused recognition and admittance to the Commission. The North Korean Communists also strongly attacked the UN resolution of November 1947. As a result, the

UN Interim Committee decided in February 1948 that if national elections were impossible, elections should still be held in South Korea.

This decision by the UN led to opposition from the right and the left in South Korea on the grounds that the partition of the country as a whole would be perpetuated. Syngman Rhee and his followers, however, by now the most influential political force south of the 38th Parallel, argued that a separate South Korean government was imperative as a protection against the Soviet-armed North Korean Communists.

Rhee's long-term objective remained Korean unity. But he and his influential supporters pointed to the creation of a North Korean regular army in February 1948. There was no such equivalent force in the South. For the time being, Rhee argued, a divided Korea was better than one under Communism.

On 10 May 1948, UN-supervised elections were held throughout South Korea. The following month the UN Commission called this vote 'a valid expression of the free will of the electorate in those parts of Korea which were accessible to the Commission and in which the inhabitants constituted approximately two-thirds of the people of all Korea'.

Events now led quickly to the formal creation of two separate states in South and North Korea. The elected representatives in South Korea formed a National Assembly, adopted a presidential constitution, and then voted for Syngman Rhee as the first President of the Republic of Korea (ROK). The new Republic was then formally inaugurated on 15 August 1948 with ceremonies in Seoul attended by General MacArthur. American Military Government ended that day, and General Hodge soon left Korea. But for the time being, American troops remained.

North of the 38th Parallel, another Korean state was being created in the summer of 1948. On 3 September a Supreme People's Assembly met to ratify a national constitution, and on 9 September the Democratic People's Republic of Korea (DPRK) was proclaimed in Pyongyang. The following day, Kim Il Sung took office as Prime Minister. The Soviet Union and its allies soon recognised North Korea. Meanwhile, on 12 December 1948 the UN General Assembly adopted a resolution which clearly legitimised the Republic of Korea. The resolution stated that 'there has been established a lawful government (the Government of the Republic of Korea) having effective control and jurisdiction over that part of Korea where the Temporary Commission was able to observe and consult . . . and that this is the only such Government in Korea'. The resolution also recommended that all occupying forces be withdrawn from Korea, and that a permanent UN Commission on Korea (UNCOK) be forthwith established to bring about Korean unification.

Following this resolution, in early 1949 the United States, Great Britain, and other Western countries recognised the Republic of Korea. By 1949, therefore, two opposed Korean states, both claiming sole jurisdiction over Korea, faced each other across the 38th Parallel. The *de facto* partition of Korea in 1945 as a military expedient had four years later developed into an internationally-recognised division. Korean unity seemed further away than ever.

Prelude to the Korean War

The period between the formation of the two Korean states in 1948 and the Communist invasion of South Korea in June 1950 was a time of great and growing tension in Korea.

But it was also a period of uncertainty generally in the Far East as the Chinese Communist victories over the Nationalist armies of Chiang Kai-shek culminated in the proclamation of the Chinese People's Republic on 1 October 1949. In Japan, as the emphasis of the Occupation changed from reform to reconstruction, there were increasing signs that the United States and its allies hoped to rebuild the country as a bulwark of democracy in the region. Diplomatic preparations went ahead slowly for a Japanese peace treaty which would restore Japan to a place in the international community.

All these developments helped to divert attention from Korea. Yet the tension in that country was real enough. Both north and south of the 38th Parallel the two opposing governments continued to assert they were the rightful rulers of all Korea. There were escalating border incidents along the Parallel. President Syngman Rhee threatened to 'March North' as a means of achieving Korean unification, but this rhetoric was unreal given the essential military weakness of South Korea.

On the other hand, within weeks of its founding, the ROK successfully countered a series of Communist-led rebellions in southern Korea. During October and November 1948 subverted South Korean constabulary forces rebelled on Cheju Island, at Yosu and Sunchon in the far south, and even in Taegu City. But these revolts were decisively suppressed, public opinion rallied to the government, and the South Korean security forces went on to develop effective counter-insurgency tactics against the remaining Communist guerrillas. The option of unification by insurgency seemed closed to the Communists. Yet the gradually improving internal security situation in the South may have prompted Pyongyang to consider more drastic means of achieving its ends.

There was also gradual economic progress in South Korea after independence, progress helped by American economic assistance. By early 1950, the level of industrial production had increased by about 80 per cent over the admittedly low figure of 1947; the ROK was reported as making good progress towards self-sufficiency in food production. Land reform begun under the American Military Government was continued after independence. As a result of this economic progress, even a Soviet source reported in late 1949 that the insurgency had 'markedly subsided'.

Nevertheless, later events were to show that the North Korean regime of Kim Il Sung was to plan actively for the military unification of Korea during 1949–50. The overall security situation for South Korea was not good because American troops had been completely withdrawn from South Korea during 1949.

Two years previously, in late 1947, the American Joint Chiefs of Staff had told President Truman that the United States had 'little interest' in maintaining a defence structure in Korea. Budgetary restrictions and the conviction that Korea would be relinquished in a global war played their part in this withdrawal process which was approved by President Truman.

During June 1949, the Joint Chiefs in a further assessment considered, somewhat surprisingly, that Korea had 'little strategic value' for the United States. Military commitment there, the Joint Chiefs believed, was ill-advised. The last remaining American troops were then withdrawn from Korea at the end of June 1949, and MacArthur ceased to have any formal military responsibility for the ROK

The American withdrawal from South Korea was compounded by a famous, and perhaps ill-advised speech by Secretary of State Dean Acheson in January 1950. Acheson considered that the American 'defence perimeter' in the Western Pacific ran from the Aleutians through Japan and Okinawa to the Philippines, so excluding South Korea. Areas outside the perimeter, said Acheson, would have to rely on self-defence and the United Nations.

This speech, combined with the American troop withdrawal from South Korea, may well have encouraged the North Korean leaders to pursue their invasion plan. According to the later memoirs of Nikita Khrushchev, *Khrushchev Remembers* (1971), Kim Il Sung conceived the plan of invading South Korea during 1949, and journeyed twice to Moscow to obtain Stalin's approval and promise of military aid. Kim did indeed visit the Soviet capital several times in 1949.

But the precise timing may have been left, in circumstances still unclear, to Premier Kim. A successful invasion of South Korea would solve the unification problem on Communist terms. It would also present the Soviet Union with considerably strategic gains in North East Asia. There can thus be little doubt that Moscow both knew of, and provided the resources to North Korea for the invasion of the ROK.

Accordingly, during the winter of 1949–50 large shipments of Soviet military equipment including tanks, heavy and medium artillery, and Yak fighter aircraft, were made to North Korea. There were deliveries of petroleum, oil and lubricants, indispensable for the waging of modern warfare. The [North] Korean People's Army was consolidated into a formidable, highly trained force of about 135,000 men, deploying eight infantry and one armoured regiment, together with several independent units.

Each infantry division possessed its own organic artillery, and there were altogether about 150 T-34 tanks. Combat aircraft numbered about 170. This was a small but highly effective Soviet-style army which was opposed in June 1950 by only six lightly-armed South Korean divisions which had no armour, aircraft or heavy artillery.

As a modern, fully armed North Korean Army was created during 1949–50, so Pyongyang stepped up its political warfare against the South. In June 1949, the separate communist parties in North and South Korea were integrated into a single Korean Workers' Party (KWP) under the chairmanship of Kim Il Sung. At the same time, the newly-formed 'Democratic Front for the Unification of the Fatherland' began a prolonged campaign for the 'peaceful unification' of Korea. But in his New Year address of 1950, Kim Il Sung called on South Koreans to destroy their government, and to support the guerrillas 'both morally and materially'.

In early June 1950, as North Korean troops took up their attack positions north of the 38th Parallel, the Democratic Front began a new campaign, calling for all-Korean elections to bring about peacefully an 'unified supreme legislative organ'. The call was repeated in an appeal by the North Korean Supreme People's Assembly on 19 June 1950. The timing for such action by Pyongyang must have seemed propitious given the setback to Rhee's supporters in the ROK assembly elections of 30 May.

North Korea's 'peaceful unification' proposals were probably part of a carefully organised deception campaign designed to mask the military build-up north of the 38th Parallel. In the event, the North Korean invasion was to achieve tactical as well as strategic surprise. But the secrecy of North Korea's preparations, and its 'peaceful unification' campaign were not the only reasons for this surprise.

As we have noted, Korea had been downgraded in American strategic priorities; the North Korean threat was seen in Seoul as well as in Washington in terms of political warfare and guerrilla insurgency. According to Secretary of State Dean Acheson's testimony in 1951, while all agencies of the American government believed that North Korea had the capability of invading the South, 'they were all in agreement that its launching in the summer of 1950 did not appear imminent'. It was a grave miscalculation of North Korean intentions.

Five years of cumulative tension between the two Koreas now came to a head in late June 1950. At about 0400 hours, in the pre-dawn dusk of 25 June 1950, the Korean People's Army opened its offensive against South Korea. After a co-ordinated artillery barrage, Communist tanks and infantry moved south over the 38th Parallel at a number of points. A few hours later, the American ambassador in Seoul, John J. Muccio, signalled Washington that the North Korean operations constituted 'an all-out offensive against the Republic of Korea'. So began one of the most significant events in Korean history.

Chapter Ten: Korea at War

As news of the North Korean Invasion spread throughout the world's capitals on Sunday 25 June 1950 the Korean People's Army (KPA) continued with its 'all-out offensive'.

Following the pre-dawn artillery barrage at key points all along the 38th Parallel at least seven North Korean infantry divisions as well as other units were in action. The North Korean infantry was supported by tanks from the KPA's armoured regiment which was upgraded to divisional status a few days after the outbreak of war. The North Koreans had achieved complete tactical and strategic surprise.

The invaders struck in four main thrusts southwards. In the west an infantry division assisted by armoured elements advanced through Kaesong and crossed the Imjin heading for Seoul. The main North Korean thrust, once again backed by tanks, came down the historic Uijongbu corridor heading for Seoul. In the central mountains Chunchon was threatened while another Communist force moved down the Korean east coast. North Korean independent assault units made amphibious landings on the east coast ahead of the infantry.

During 25 June North Korean Yak fighters attached railway stations and petrol storage tanks in the Seoul area, as well as the installations at Kimpo International Airfield, which lies between Seoul and Inchon. This formidable invasion was opposed by four lightly-armed South Korean divisions which lacked heavy artillery, armour and air cover.

On 25 June Kim Il Sung broadcast to the Korean people. He said that as North Korean territory in the Haeju area, west of Kaesong, had been attacked by South Korean forces North Korea had gone over to the counter-offensive. The following day

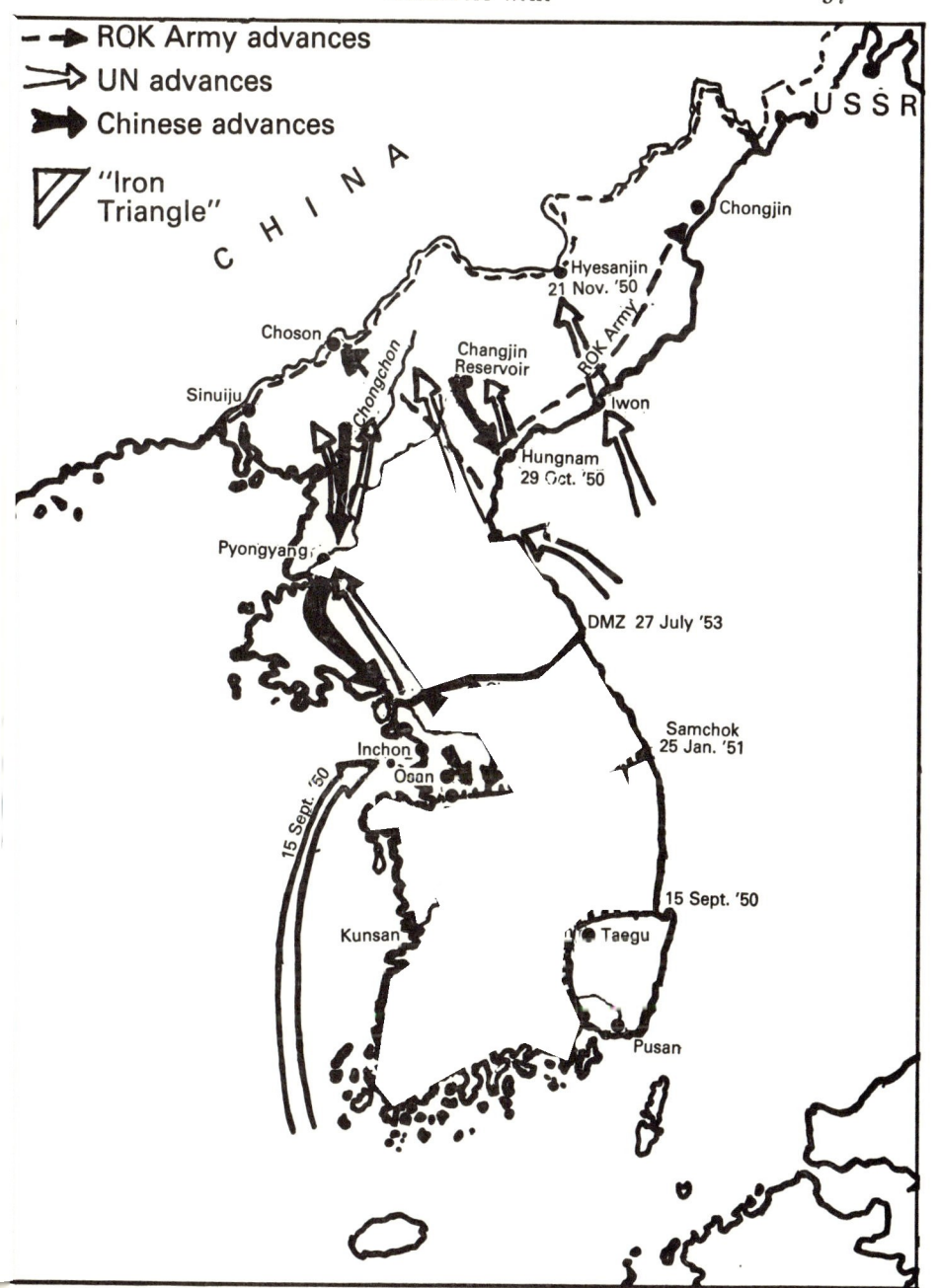

Korean War 1950–1953.

Kim Il Sung again broadcast stating that the Syngman Rhee regime must be liquidated and that North Korea 'must complete the unification of the motherland and create a single, independent democratic state'. Kim went on, 'The war which we are forced to wage is a just war for the unification and independence of the motherland. . . .'

On Monday, 26 June, the UN Commission on Korea in Seoul cabled the UN Secretary-General, Trygve Lie, at the then UN HQ at Flushing Meadows, New York. The Commission reported that the North Koreans were carrying out a 'well-planned, concerted and full-scale invasion of South Korea, second, that the South Korean forces were deployed on a wholly defensive basis in all sectors of the Parallel, and third, that they were taken by surprise as they had no reason to believe from intelligence sources that invasion was imminent'.

The North Korean advance continued all along the front and on 28 June Communist tanks entered Seoul. The North Koreans then prepared to cross the Han River and continued their advance southwards.

Truman's Korean Decision

Despite the initial shock and consternation caused by the first news of the invasion, the United Nations and the American government reacted swiftly to the news from Korea which reached Washington late on the evening of Saturday 24 June. (Korean time is thirteen hours ahead of Washington Eastern Summer Time.)

On 25 June, the UN Security Council passed the first of three resolutions on Korea which would place the world organization's full authority behind the defence of South Korea. Throughout this critical period the Soviet delegate on the Security Council, who of course possessed a veto, was absent over the UN's refusal to recognize the new Communist regime in Peking. In its first resolution the Security Council called for a cease-fire, the withdrawal of North Korean forces to the 38th Parallel, and for all UN members to render 'every assistance' to the UN in the execution of the resolution.

As the North Korean advance continued, the Security Council again met on 27 June and called on the UN members 'to furnish such assistance to the Republic of Korea as may be necessary to repel the armed attack and to restore international peace and security in the area'.

Already on 25 June President Truman and his senior civilian and military advisers, including Secretary of State Acheson and the Joint Chiefs of Staff, had begun to authorise a number of measures to help South Korea. During this first meeting it was decided to send arms and ammunition from Japan to South Korea, as well as a military survey team. The Seventh Fleet was ordered north from the Philippines towards Japan.

The following day, Monday, 26 June, saw a further deterioration of the situation in Korea. After another meeting of Truman and his advisers on that day, the President authorised the use of American naval and air assistance to the ROK. Ships of the Seventh Fleet were ordered to Formosan waters to prevent a Chinese Communist invasion of the island and to stop Chinese Nationalist action against the mainland from their Formosan sanctuary. The United States was acting cautiously because Soviet intentions in the Far East were unknown.

But as the crisis deepened, further action was necessary. On 29 June MacArthur had flown from Tokyo to Suwon, about twenty miles south of Seoul, to see for himself the growing disintegration of the ROK Army. The General decided that he would now have to ask permission from Washington to use American ground forces from Japan to stop the North Koreans. Quite independently, that same day, Truman told MacArthur to use American combat troops from Japan to defend the Pusan area in south-east Korea. MacArthur was also authorized to use his naval and air forces north of the 38th Parallel.

In all these developments MacArthur's role was central. From his GHQ in the Dai-Ichi building in Tokyo MacArthur, as we have seen, ruled over Japan as Supreme Commander for the Allied Powers. But he was also the American Commander-in-Chief, Far East, directing a great unified command with half a dozen subordinate commands including the Far East Air Forces (FEAF), Naval Forces, Far East (NAVFE), and the Eighth Army, the occupation force in Japan. MacArthur also held the post of Commanding General, US Army Forces, Far East.

These proconsular offices combined with MacArthur's prestige as a former Army Chief of Staff and the architect of many historic victories in the Pacific War meant that the General was now to dominate events in Korea for the next ten months.

On Friday 30 June 1950, as the North Koreans continued to advance virtually unchecked President Truman made his irrevocable Korean decision. In response to MacArthur's urgent request, Truman at first authorized the General to send a Regimental Combat Team to Korea. A few hours later the President told him to use all combat troops under his command if necessary. This meant that MacArthur was free to use in Korea all four divisions of the Eighth Army based in Japan. A naval blockade of all Korean waters was also ordered.

In pursuance of these orders the first American combat troops from the 24th Infantry Division in Japan were sent by air to Pusan on 1 July 1950. These troops then began moving northwards by rail to meet the North Koreans wbo were now across the Han River and advancing southwards through Suwon. The Korean crisis had become the Korean War.

Why had American policy been so suddenly reversed over Korea? As we have related, the country's strategic importance had been discounted on the highest level and American troops withdrawn from the ROK in 1949. But the sudden, brazen North Korean invasion had presented both the United States and the United Nations with a challenge that could not be spurned.

Clearly, the broad strategic threat to Japan concerned the United States. This threat was underlined by the collapse of the ROK Army which made the complete occupation of South Korea by the Communists a virtual certainty unless the United States intervened. The North Korean aggression also reminded President Truman and his advisers – and many of his allies in Western Europe – of the events which had led to the Second World War. The credibility of the American guarantee to the Atlantic alliance was thus involved as well as the effectiveness of the United Nations. The line therefore had to be held in Korea, and it was seen to be right as well as necessary to defend the ROK.

'We let it be known,' Mr. Truman later wrote in his *Memoirs*, 'that we considered the Korean situation vital as a symbol of the strength and determination of the West.' Truman also wrote in his Memoirs that the decision to intervene in Korea was 'the toughest decision' of his entire presidency.

The United Nations Command

Following Truman's 'toughest decision' two further measures were taken which gave the defence of South Korea the complete sanction of the UN and which then placed the ROK armed forces under MacArthur's command.

On 7 July 1950 in a third major policy resolution affecting

Korea the UN Security Council recommended that UN members providing military assistance under the previous resolutions should make their forces available to an 'Unified Command' under the United States. The US was requested to designate the commander of such forces and the Security Council authorized the Unified Command 'to use the United Nations flag in the course of operations against North Korean forces concurrently with the flags of the nations participating'.

The United States was thus named as the executive agent of the United Nations in Korea. Periodic reports were forwarded by the American government to the Security Council. Accordingly on 8 July President Truman designated General MacArthur as Commander-in-Chief of the United Nations Command (UNC). The chain of command through the President, the Secretary of Defence, and the Joint Chiefs of Staff to MacArthur was unaltered.

Eventually some sixteen nations were to send forces to the UNC, another five sent medical units, and altogether forty members of the UN offered aid in one form or another to the UNC. Although materially this aid was small in relation to the main burden carried by the United States these lesser UN contingents emphasised the collective, idealistic nature of the UN mission in Korea.

Following the creation of the UNC President Syngman Rhee signed a letter to MacArthur as UN Commander on 14 July 1950 placing under him all the South Korean armed forces. Henceforth the commander of the Eighth US Army in Korea issued his orders to the ROK forces as requests to the Chief of Staff of the South Korean army. This arrangement worked well and continued throughout the Korean War and long afterwards.

The Soviet response to the US and UN commitment to South Korea was contained in a long diplomatic note to the American government on 4 July 1950. Moscow claimed that the Korean fighting was an internal affair and thus the Security Council had no jurisdiction. Moreover, the Security Council decisions on Korea were illegal as they had been taken in the absence of the Soviet delegate, who was of course a permanent member of the Council.

Speaking in the house of Commons the following day the British Premier Clement Attlee stoutly defended the UN action against what he evidently regarded as North Korean aggression. Attlee stated that under international law every country had the right of self defence, which was also sanctioned under Article 51 of the UN Charter. 'The broad principle is that all states may be endangered if the aggressor is allowed to get away with the fruits of aggression in any part of the world.' Attlee also noted that a practice had developed in the Security Council that if a permanent member was absent this did not invalidate a Council resolution. The USSR had in the past accepted this custom.

Jacob Malik, the Soviet delegate to the UN, returned to the Security Council in early August after an absence that had clearly not served Soviet interests . On 4 August Malik described the fighting in Korea as 'an internal civil war', a phrase that was to characterise Soviet propaganda on the subject for the remainder of the Korean War.

But by the time Malik spoke in these terms the UN Command was already firmly established. Nevertheless the overriding problem facing MacArthur was whether his forces could stay in Korea at all.

Defending the Pusan Perimeter

Throughout July 1950, the North Koreans continued with their often headlong advance towards Pusan. There seemed good grounds for the expectation by the invaders that all of South Korea would be conquered by 15 August, the date assigned by Kim Il Sung.

The two companies of American troops from the 24th Infantry Division which had landed at Pusan on 1 July moved north through Taegu and Taejon. Immediately north of Osan, about forty miles below Seoul, the Americans set up a good blocking position on the main highway south on 5 July. But the North Korean T-34 tanks with their formidable 85mm cannon pushed their way through while the Communist infantry expertly outflanked their foes by filtering over the hills. This was the foretaste of many such actions in the following weeks as small, outnumbered groups of Americans were thrown piecemeal into the fight. The North Korean T-34/85 meanwhile proved to be the cutting edge of the Communist offensive.

After Osan, the Communist advance began to lose some of its momentum as more units from the 24th Division entered the fray. But by mid-July the North Koreans were on the Kum River. They then began to encircle Taejon which fell on 20 July after a tough, heroic defence in which the divisional commander, Major General William Dean, was lost as a prisoner.

Following commitment of the 24th Division, the US 25th Division was sent from Japan to Korea in mid-July, followed by the 1st Cavalry Division (also infantry). Some armour and artillery followed. On 13 July the Army commander in Japan, Lieutenant General Walton H. Walker arrived in Korea and set up the headquarters of the Eighth US Army in Korea (EUSAK) at Taegu. The HQ of the ROK Army was also established at this ancient city in south-east Korea.

By late July 1950 the North Koreans were advancing on four fronts towards Pusan. In the east a Communist column moved down the difficult coastal road, harassed by US naval gunfire. To the west, three Communist divisions pushed through the passes of the Sobaek mountains separating the upper waters of the Han River from the Naktong valley which leads to the far south of Korea. Another North Korean force of tanks and infantry struck into south-west Korea from Kunsan on the west coast, occupied the port of Mokpo, and then wheeled east with the intention of outflanking American forces moving north from Pusan. The main Communist thrust continued south-eastwards along the Korean arterial highway leading from Taejon to Kumchon and the Naktong River.

Despite American reinforcements and the arrival of a veteran army commander who had fought in the European war, the North Koreans by the close of July 1950 were approaching the Naktong River. This formed the main defensive line of the Pusan Perimeter. The perimeter was a rectangle about eighty miles from north to south and about fifty miles wide. The northern front was defended by the ROK Army; the north-south river line was mostly held by the Americans.

Defence of the Pusan Perimeter was vital to the UN cause. Pusan was the only harbour in South Korea which had the modern facilities to handle American personnel, supplies and heavy equipment sent from Japan. The harbour could take over 20 deep-sea freighters at one time while large landing craft, including LSTs (Landing Ship Tank), could be run aground on Pusan's sheltered beaches. There was also a good airfield. On 1 August, General Walker ordered all his forces to retreat behind the Naktong River to the hastily prepared defences of the Pusan Perimeter. All bridges over the Naktong were then blown.

During the heavy fighting over the next six weeks, Walker proved himself a master of defensive fighting as he shuffled his scanty reserves from sector to sector. The North Korean offensive retained its momentum, but Walker was helped by the arrival of reinforcements in the nick of time. A fourth American division, 2nd Infantry, arrived from the US at the end of July, followed by a brigade of the 1st Marine Division sent direct from San Diego. Walker also received over 300 heavy tanks during August, mostly M-26 Pershings. These tanks were not used usually in armoured engagements but rather to give vital artillery support to hard-pressed UN infantry.

Walker needed every man, gun, and tank that could reach him. At first the chief threat to the perimeter came from the southwest where North Korean spearheads advanced towards Masan, only 30 miles from Pusan. During early August a combined force from the 25th Division and the Marines checked the Communists in this sector. By mid-August the threat switched to the central Naktong front where the North Koreans crossed the river in an area known as the Naktong Bulge and where the invaders were stopped again, but only after very heavy fighting. According to the official Marine Corps account of this episode, the contest in the Naktong Bulge 'ranks with the hardest fights in Marine Corps history'.

During the struggle for the perimeter, the US Fifth Air Force, its fighter aircraft often flying from Japanese bases, gave vital tactical air support to the infantry. Light (B-26s) and medium (B-29s) bombers from the FEAF struck at the roads and railways far behind the front which carried North Korean men and supplies to the Naktong. General Walker went on record as stating that but for his air support his forces would not have been able to stay in Korea. But the tenacity of the American and South Korean infantry was also indispensable.

Following their failure in the Naktong Bulge, the North Koreans mustered their forces to the north of Taegu, driving southwards through the mountains immediately east of the Naktong. Walker once again switched his reserves and once again the Communists were held. But by early September 1950 the main defence line in the northern sector had been forced back to a line running east from Taegu to Pohang-dong on the coast.

In early September 1950 the North Koreans launched their most ambitious offensive against the Pusan Perimeter with co-ordinated attacks against Masan, the Naktong Bulge, Taegu, and the northern front. Despite air interdiction of their supply lines, the North Koreans were still able to bring men and supplies to the front.

This was the climax of the fighting around the Pusan Perimeter. In the south Masan was threatened, and North Korean tanks crossed the river in the Naktong Bulge sector. Other Communist units seized the walled city of Kasan in the north which gave artillery observation into Taegu. Waegwan on the northwest of the perimeter was lost; Walker despatched the newly-arrived British 27th Brigade to this sector. From Pusan refugees were already beginning to depart by fishing boat for the Tsushima islands.

This was Walton Walker's finest moment. The Texan general rallied his troops and checked the North Koreans in all sectors. But as far as the wider strategy it was obvious that a balance existed between the attackers and the defenders of the Pusan Perimeter.

For some weeks, therefore, MacArthur in Tokyo had been planning an ambitious amphibious landing far behind the North Korean lines at Inchon. This landing, MacArthur believed, would envelop the North Koreans and destroy their army. While Walker and his men checked the all-out Communist offensive aimed at taking Pusan, the ships of MacArthur's landing force were already leaving Japan for Inchon.

Victory at Inchon

MacArthur had first conceived of an amphibious landing at Inchon behind the North Korean lines during his flying visit to Suwon on 29 June. As the North Korean advance continued during July 1950 the General became more than ever convinced that as the Inchon-Seoul area was the communications centre of Korea a landing here would completely disrupt the Communist supply and logistic system. The North Koreans would be enveloped and faced with a two-front war. There was the added attraction that the early recapture of Seoul would provide a major political success for the United Nations cause. If successful, MacArthur envisaged that the Inchon landing could result in the destruction of the North Korean army.

A preliminary plan for landing the 1st Cavalry Division at Inchon on 20 July was abandoned and the division was sent instead to Pusan. But the prospects for the Inchon operation brightened as the Joint Chiefs of Staff in Washington promised MacArthur three regiments of the crack 1st Marine Division. The 5th Regiment of this division had been despatched to Pusan in mid-July (where it was termed the 1st Provisional Marine Brigade), but later the 1st Marines and then the 7th Marines were promised MacArthur. Two Marine regiments would thus be available for the Inchon landing now scheduled for 15 September, and a third regiment, the 7th, would arrive shortly afterwards.

During August 1950 as Walker's troops fought desperately to hold the Pusan perimeter intensive planning went ahead in MacArthur's GHQ for the Inchon landing, now known as Operation *Chromite*. A Special Planning Staff was set up. In addition to the 1st Marine Division, the 7th Infantry Division in Japan was also scheduled for the landing. Both divisions would comprise the newly-formed X Corps which was formally activated on 26 August under the command of Major General Edward Almond, MacArthur's Chief of Staff.

The overall mission of X Corps was to seize Wolmi-do, the small island controlling Inchon harbour, land at Inchon City, occupy Kimpo International Airfield, and finally to recapture Seoul. The X corps would then form a blocking position south of Seoul as Walker's men broke out from the Pusan Perimeter. The North Koreans would be trapped in a giant pincer movement.

In charge of the actual assault on Inchon was Rear-Admiral James Doyle, the American Pacific Fleet's Amphibious Group Commander. he was responsible to Vice-Admiral A. D. Struble, the 7th Fleet Commander, who was in overall command of the naval armada which was being assembled to take 70,000 men to Inchon.

It took all MacArthur's exceptional prestige and authority to win acceptance for the landing from the Joint Chiefs of Staff in Washington and from the Naval staff in Tokyo. An amphibious assault on Inchon had many disadvantages for the only sea approach was through the narrow Flying Fish channel which was surrounded by extensive mud flats at low tide. There was also a very large tidal range at Inchon which narrowed the choice for the landing to but a few dates if full advantage was to be taken of the seasonal high tides necessary to bring in LSTs. In view of the military crisis at Pusan, the landing had to be on 15 September.

Central to the operation was the initial assault on the Inchon harbour wall preceding high tide on 15 September. Here the Marines would have to climb over the wall on ladders carried in their landing craft. Once ashore there were further dangers as the hills of Inchon City looked down on the landing zone.

After a series of inter-service meetings, MacArthur presented his final plan to the service commanders in his Tokyo GHQ on 23 August 1950. Present were two of the Joint Chiefs, General J. Lawton Collins for the US Army, and Admiral Forrest Sherman, the Chief of Naval Operations. MacArthur eloquently defended his plan, and compared it to Wolfe's historic plan at Quebec when the attackers had climbed the impossible Heights of Abraham to the south of the city to bring them victory. Inchon too, MacArthur said, would be an impossible victory which would crush the North Koreans. Eventually the Joint Chiefs were won over and final preparations went ahead for Operation *Chromite*.

As heavy fighting continued on the Pusan Perimeter, the first ships left Japan for Inchon on 5 September. Altogether there were 260 ships in Struble's armada including vessels from Britain, Canada, Australia, New Zealand, France and Holland. MacArthur had also conjured up over thirty Japanese-manned LSTs. He himself left Sasebo for Inchon on 13 September in the Admiral Doyle's flagship, the *Mount McKinley*.

On the morning of 15 September the assault force entered Flying Fish channel following several days intensive naval bombardment of Inchon. Shortly after 0600 hours a battalion of the 5th Marine Regiment landed successfully on Wolmi Island in Inchon harbour. The tide ebbed and flowed, Inchon was again shelled, and at 1730 hours shortly before high tide as planned the 5th Marines landed on the Inchon harbour wall. The 1st Marines, meanwhile, landed south of the city. By midnight most of Inchon had been taken with very few casualties. Next day the advance began on Kimpo Airfield and Seoul.

The North Koreans had been surprised and MacArthur's great gamble had won. As reinforcements flowed into Inchon, the X Corps now advanced to Seoul which fell after heavy fighting on 28 September. Far to the south the Eighth Army broke out of the Pusan Perimeter as the North Korean forces began to disintegrate. On 26 September forces from the Eighth Army and X Corps met at Osan, where nearly three months previously the North Koreans had first clashed with the Americans.

The Korean People's Army was largely encircled and almost destroyed by these events. Probably not more than 30,000 effectives managed to flee north across the 38th Parallel at the end of September 1950. Hundreds of Soviet-built artillery pieces were captured, and eventually survey teams located nearly 240 knocked-out T-34s south of the 38th Parallel. MacArthur's GHQ was soon to claim 200,000 North Korean casualties and 135,000 Communist prisoners.

The whole course of the war was now changed by new directives from Washington which authorised MacArthur to move north of the 38th Parallel. The tables had been completely turned on Kim Il Sung as MacArthur's command prepared to cross the Parallel and unify Korea in the name of the United Nations.

MacArthur Crosses the 38th Parallel

The crushing defeat of the People's Army had left the UN Command free to advance into North Korea. But as a result of Inchon the political objectives of the United Nations also changed. Prior to MacArthur's victory, the aims of the UN Command had been to restore the 38th Parallel as the border between the two Koreas. Military victory in Korea meant that the United Nations now envisaged the creation of an united, democratic Korea which had been the objective of successive UN resolutions since late 1947.

During the fighting on the Pusan Perimeter clear policy statements on the future of Korea had not been possible by either the Truman administration or the United Nations. But with the success of the Inchon landing it seemed as if the military issue had been decided. Thus on 27 September 1950 the Joint Chiefs in Washington told MacArthur in a directive that his military objective was 'the destruction of the North Korean armed forces'. To attain this objective MacArthur was authorized to conduct amphibious and airborne operations north of the 38th Parallel provided there was no entry, or threat of entry by Chinese or Soviet forces. Only South Korean troops were to be used near the Soviet or Chinese borders.

As MacArthur had been convinced for some weeks that a crossing of the 38th Parallel was necessary to destroy the KPA, he had asked his staff to prepare an operational plan for the occupation of North Korea. This plan was then forwarded to Washington on 28 September. It envisaged an advance northwards by the Eighth Army to Pyongyang, while the X Corps would be redeployed by sea and landed at Wonsan in north-east Korea. The Corps would then drive westwards to link with the Eighth Army so sealing off the peninsula. The Eighth Army offensive would begin shortly after 15 October.

This outline was approved by the Joint Chiefs and the President on 29 September. Truman's Secretary of Defence, the former US Army Chief of Staff and Secretary of State, George C. Marshall, sent a personal message to MacArthur at the same time assuring him that 'we want you to feel unhampered strategically and tactically to proceed north of the 38th Parallel'. MacArthur then broadcast a call to the North Korean Commander-in-Chief from Tokyo on 1 October demanding his unconditional surrender. There was no reply. The invasion of North Korea was now inevitable.

MacArthur had already decided to retain personal control of Almond's X Corps instead of placing it under the Eighth Army command. He reasoned that this was the best way of fulfilling his mission in North Korea as the spinal Taebaek mountains split the region into two naturally separate theatres. The Marine Division was then evacuated from the Seoul area through Inchon, while the 7th Infantry Division was sent by land to Pusan. The east coast landing at Wonsan was scheduled for 20 October.

As the military planning went ahead for the advance into North Korea, the political consensus was reached during interallied consultations in Washington and in the United Nations. By late September 1950 it was agreed that an eight-nation resolution should be introduced by the United Kingdom into the UN General Assembly which would call for Korean unification followed by free elections. The allies could not work through the Security Council as the Soviet delegate had returned. But the general drift of opinion amongst the allies was indicated by Ernest Bevin's reported statement in New York (on 29 September) that there should be 'no artificial perpetuation' of division of Korea.

By early October, military developments in Korea were already outpacing the deliberations of the politicians. On 1 October troops from the ROK I Corps crossed the 38th Parallel on the Korean east coast road and continued advancing northwards towards Wonsan. Simultaneously there was a series of warnings and threats from Peking that China would not tolerate an American advance across the 38th Parallel. Late on 2 October, the Chinese Foreign Minister, Chou En-lai, told the Indian ambassador that while South Korean entry into the North was not significant, American intrusion would be resisted by China. These warnings were largely dismissed as bluff or blackmail by the allies.

On 7 October, the UN General Assembly gave a clear mandate for the projected advance into North Korea. The Assembly voted for a resolution stating that 'all appropriate steps' were to be taken to restore stability in Korea and that UN-supervised free elections were then to be held 'for the establishing of a united, independent and democratic government in the sovereign state of Korea'. The UN Commission on Korea was to be replaced by the UN Commission for the Unification and Rehabilitation of Korea (UNCURK).

The first patrols of the Eighth Army crossed the 38th Parallel north of Kaesong the same day. On the 9th a general advance began northwards towards Pyongyang, and MacArthur was told by the Joint Chiefs of Staff that he could advance into North Korea as long as 'in your judgement action by forces under your control offers a reasonable chance of success'. This of course gave MacArthur great latitude. Unlike his earlier directive of 27 September, he was still free to continue operations even in the event of external intervention.

It was soon to become clear that these hurried decisions following Inchon were to change and prolong the entire course of the war in Korea. But for a very few weeks after Inchon it was a common assumption that not only had a great victory been won but that the war was coming to its end.

Enter the Chinese

Following the UN resolution of 7 October, MacArthur's command swept into North Korea. On the western front Walton Walker's Eighth Army pushed northwards through Sariwon to Pyongyang which fell on 19 October. The ROK II Corps kept in step by advancing through the central mountains and entering Pyongyang from the east. Wonsan on the east coast had already fallen to the South Korean I Corps after a swift progress northwards along the coastal road. Meanwhile, Kim Il Sung and his associates had fled from Pyongyang to Sinuiju on the Yalu.

On 15 October President Truman had conferred with MacArthur on Wake Island. The General had assured the President that there was 'very little' chance of Chinese intervention and that in any case his air forces could inflict the 'greatest slaughter' on any Chinese troops entering Korea. On 20 October MacArthur visited Pyongyang where he told reporters that 'the war is very definitely coming to an end shortly'.

Following his return to Tokyo from Wake Island MacArthur issued new orders to expedite the conquest of North Korea. Instead of linking up along the Korean 'waist' between Wonsan and Pyongyang, the Eighth Army and X Corps were to advance north separately to a new restraining line about 60 miles south of the Yalu. Beyond that line only South Korean troops would operate. But on 24 October MacArthur abandoned all restraints. His field commanders were ordered 'to drive forward with all speed and full utilization of their forces'.

From Pyongyang Walker's forces moved quickly north to the Chongchon River which was crossed on 24 October. On the left flank advance units of the US I Corps turned north-west from the Chongchon bridges at Sinanju and by 1 November these forces were about 18 miles south of the Yalu. Kim Il Sung and the North Korean government had by now moved inland to Kanggye in the central mountains about 100 miles to the east. On the opposite flank of the Eighth Army an unit from the ROK II Corps had headed north from the Chongchon and reached the Yalu at Chosan on 26 October. These were the only forces under Walker's command to reach the Yalu.

Far to the east of the Eighth Army across the Taebaek mountains the landing of Almond's X Corps at Wonsan had been delayed by mines until 25 October. Then the US 1st Marine Division began to go ashore. On 29 October the US 7th Infantry Division began landing at Iwon, over a hundred miles north from Wonsan.

The Marines were then deployed to Hungnam, north of Wonsan, and from here were ordered north again to the Changjin Reservoir preparatory to the final advance to the Yalu. From Iwon, units of the 7th Division pushed into the wild mountains of north-east Korea heading for Hyesanjin on the Yalu (which was taken on 21 November). The South Korean I Corps continued to move along the coast towards Chongjin and the Soviet border. For a few days at the end of October it seemed as if total victory was in the grasp of the UN Command and the whole of North Korea would by quickly occupied.

But at the very moment of apparent triumph there were portents of Chinese intervention in Korea. In the western Eighth Army sector South Korean troops were ambushed on 25–26 October by Chinese units at Unsan and Onjong north of the Chongchon River. The US 1st Cavalry Division was ordered up to the front but in early November a regiment of this division was virtually destroyed by the Chinese at Unsan. The Eighth Army then withdrew to bridgeheads over the Chongchon. From 1 November onwards Chinese MIG-15 fighters from Manchurian bases attacked UN aircraft south of the Yalu, another portent of Chinese intervention.

The Chinese were also active in the X Corps sector where from 25 October South Koreans advancing northwards from Hungnam towards the Changjin Reservoir were under their fire. In early November American Marines also fought the Chinese near Sudong in this sector. Then, as on the western front, the Chinese faded into the hills. But within a few days the arrival of the harsh Korean winter brought plummeting temperatures, so making field reconnaissance increasingly difficult.

Precise evaluation of the Chinese threat was thus difficult. But there was no doubt that organised elements of the Chinese People's Liberation Army had entered Korea. These Chinese troops were henceforth known to the UN Command as the Chinese Communist Forces (CCF). In Tokyo MacArthur minimised the Chinese capability. .His Intelligence staff put Chinese effectives in Korea as not more than about 70,000 men. But on 6 November MacArthur was forced to tell Washington that Chinese men and supplies were 'pouring across all bridges over the Yalu from Manchuria'. The river was soon frozen all along its length, so air interdiction of the bridges joining Manchuria and Korea was pointless. Nevertheless, MacArthur ordered continuing preparations for an 'end-of-the-war' offensive at the close of November.

In fact the course of the Korean War had already changed. On 8 October 1950, the day following the UN resolution on Korean unification, Mao Tse-tung had ordered large-scale Chinese military intervention in Korea.

In line with Mao's directive between 15 October and 1 November some 180,000 Chinese troops entered north-west Korea, many of them over the great international bridges at Antung and Manpojin. These troops concentrated in front of the Eighth Army in the mountains between the Yalu and the Chongchon. A further 120,000 Chinese troops crossed the Yalu between 1 November and 15 November. These forces deployed mostly in the area to the north of the Changjin Reservoir where they prepared to destroy the 1st Marine Division. The forces in the western sector comprised the XIII Army Group from Marshal Lin Piao's Fourth Field Army; those to the east comprised the IX

Army Group from Marshal Chen Yi's Third Field Army. This initial Chinese intervention was controlled by a headquarters staff at Mukden, Manchuria.

Altogether the 300,000 men of the CCF in Korea by mid-November 1950 comprised ten numbered Chinese armies, each army made up of three divisions of 10,000 men, and thus equivalent to a Western army corps. The Chinese lacked air and heavy artillery support and their communications were rudimentary. Yet the Chinese troops were self-sufficient, each man carried with him food and ammunition for about six days, and perhaps most important of all the major movement across the Yalu had escaped the attention of the UN Command. But cautiously, on 11 November, Peking stated that Chinese People's Volunteers (CPV) were now fighting in Korea.

According to S. L. A. Marshall's memorable account of these events in *The River and the Gauntlet* (1953), 'both the movement and the concentration had gone undetected. The enemy columns moved only at night, preserved an absolute camouflage discipline during their daytime rests and remained hidden to view under village rooftops after reaching the chosen ground. Air observation saw nothing of this mass movement. Civilian refugees brought no word of it. . . .'

As confident of success as he was before Inchon, MacArthur now ordered the final offensive to conclude his mission in Korea. Walker's Eighth Army was to attack north from the Chongchon to the Yalu on 24 November; the Marines were to advance northwards from the Changjin Reservoir three days later. MacArthur then flew to Sinanju on the Chongchon on 24 November 1950, conferred with Walker, and stated that the war would be over by Christmas.

But the Chinese were also on the move in the mountains south of the Yalu. By 26 November a massive Chinese counter-offensive had halted Walker's advance towards the Yalu; on the X Corps front the Marines at Changjin were soon attacked and faced encirclement by greatly superior Chinese forces.

In a special communique on 28 November as his divided command began its long retreat from the whole of North Korea MacArthur informed the United Nations that 'Chinese continental forces' were in action in North Korea . . . 'Consequently, we face an entirely new war.'

Chapter Eleven: Trial of Strength

Following the launching of the major Chinese offensive in northern Korea on 25 November 1950 rapid retreat was now imperative to save the United Nations Command. After a conference at MacArthur's headquarters in Tokyo attended by Walker and Almond on the night of 28–29 November the orders were given. Walker's Eighth Army was told to make all necessary withdrawals to prevent its outflanking; Almond's X Corps was to contract into a bridgehead area at Hungnam.

The Great Retreat

Both elements of the UN Command faced great danger. On the Eighth Army right flank the Chinese had destroyed the ROK II Corps and the US 2nd Infantry Division was severely mauled as it withdrew through the Kunuri Pass, south of the Chongchon, towards Sunchon and Pyongyang. The Eighth Army then abandoned Pyongyang on 5 December, disengaged rapidly from contact with the Chinese, and ten days later stood along the 38th Parallel.

To the east in the X Corps zone the 1st Marine Division, surrounded by seven Chinese divisions, had begun to withdraw from the western side of the Changjin Reservoir on 1 December. Leaving Hagaru-ri at the southern tip of the Reservoir on the 6th, the column of 14,000 men with their equipment fought their way through to the south. By 12 December they were safe in Hungnam.

At this port a major evacuation of X Corps from northeast Korea was under way. MacArthur had ordered that the Corps was to be re-deployed by sea to Pusan and then consolidated under the control of the Eighth Army, so ending the divided command. On 24 December the last men from X Corps left Hungnam and the harbour installations were demolished. The UN Command had relinquished North Korea.

As the Chinese host advanced south towards the 38th Parallel the military crisis in Korea was accompanied by a political crisis amongst the UN allies. The Chinese incursion deep into Korea carried far greater risks than that of the original North Korean attack over the 38th Parallel for miscalculation now could easily escalate into general war. As it quickly became clear that the Chinese objective was the destruction of the UN Command, MacArthur was told by Washington on 4 December to withdraw into beach-heads in southern Korea if necessary.

At the same time, General J. Lawton Collins, the Army Chief of Staff, was ordered to Tokyo and Korea. After a visit to the front, Collins reported that the UN Command could hold in Korea, a prescient .observation. But MacArthur in a series of public statements hinted that the best solution might be to carry the war to China.

On 30 November President Truman had seemed to imply in a press conference that the atomic bomb might be used in Korea. This was not the case, but as a result of the general alarm in Western Europe that followed, the British Prime Minister, Clement Attlee, flew to Washington for talks with Truman that began on 4 December. After prolonged discussions that went on for four days the two leading UN allies reached understandings that were largely to govern the future course of the war in Korea.

It was agreed that while the long-term United Nations objective remained the unification of Korea this goal was to be sought by 'peaceful means'. There was tacit agreement also that, following the Chinese intervention, an honourable cease-fire based on a division of Korea was the most appropriate course. Meanwhile, American and British troops would fight on in Korea until forced out. It was also agreed that both countries would launch a major rearmament programme. The original United Nations military objective in Korea was thus restored by the Truman–Attlee talks; defence of the integrity of South Korea.

This was the darkest moment of the Korean War for the UN allies. As the Chinese re-grouped north of the 38th Parallel for a further offensive their capabilities were unknown to the UN Command. On 23 December Walton Walker was killed in a road accident north of Seoul. He was replaced as Eighth Army commander by Lieutenant General Matthew B. Ridgway, the Deputy

Army Chief of Staff for Operations who had been closely involved in the higher direction of the war. Ridgway flew immediately to the Far East, conferred with MacArthur in Tokyo on Christmas Day, and went on to Taegu to assume command of the Eighth Army.

Following Ridgway's arrival in Korea, the Chinese launched a new mass offensive on 31 December which was evidently designed to sweep the UN Command out of Korea. The main CCF drive was pointed southwards down the Uijongbu corridor towards Seoul but the Chinese were also active in the central mountains along the Chunchon–Hongchon–Wonju axis. Here the Communists clearly hoped to envelop the main forces of the Eighth Army to the west. To the east of Chunchon, North Korean units filtered south on a wide front in appalling weather through the wastes of the Taebaek Mountains.

Ridgway now gave the order on 3 January 1951 for the Eighth Army to withdraw south of the Han and abandon Seoul which fell the next day. The UN Command fell back to 'Line D', the Pyongtaek–Samchok line across the peninsula which lay about seventy miles south of the Parallel. In the central mountains Wonju fell to the Chinese yet only after heavy resistance by American troops which inflicted great casualties on the attackers.

But the CCF offensive was already faltering. The inadequate Chinese supply system made it difficult for their forces to sustain their offensives for more than five or six days. So the great retreat of nearly 300 miles by the UN Command was already coming to an end.

Ridgway's Counter Offensive

As the UN Command's resistance began to grow, an exchange of messages between President Truman, the Joint Chiefs of Staff and MacArthur clarified the UN mission in Korea. On 30 December MacArthur had been told to defend 'successive positions' in Korea bearing in mind the safety of his troops and the need to defend Japan. MacArthur doubted whether his Command could stay in Korea. He suggested the bombing and blockade of China combined with the use of Chinese Nationalist troops from Formosa both in Korea and in diversionary attacks on the Chinese mainland.

This proposed extension of the war to China was turned down in Washington and on 12 January the Joint Chiefs again told MacArthur to stay in Korea as long as possible and to inflict maximum casualities on the Chinese. It was of great importance to the United Nations and the United States, the Joint Chiefs stated, that the UN Command should only evacuate Korea if forced to do so. This message was followed and reinforced by a personal message from Truman to MacArthur. Concurrently, General Lawton Collins was again sent to Korea with the Air Chief of Staff, General Hoyt S. Vandenberg.

Once again, as in the dark days of the Pusan Perimeter, all high-level policy depended on the military situation in Korea. However, like Ridgway, Collins and Vandenberg were encouraged by the stiffening resistance to the Chinese and Collins reported to Washington on 17 January that the Eighth Army was in good shape and prepared 'to punish severely any mass attack'.

On 15 January 1951 a successful Eighth Army probe northwards on the western front through Osan towards Suwon discovered only Chinese screening forces south of the Han. Ten days later on 25 January the Eighth Army went over to the counteroffensive with the line of the lower Han as its objective but with acquisition of real estate secondary to the infliction of heavy casualties on the Chinese.

For the next two months the Chinese were slowly pushed back beyond the Han River. In mid-February a new Chinese offensive on the central front aimed at Wonju was shattered by the Eighth Army around Chipyong-ni. The northwards advance continued and Seoul was recaptured on 14 March, changing hands for the fourth and last time in the war. By the end of that month the Eighth Army once again stood on the 38th Parallel. A slow advance then began to seize commanding terrain north of the Parallel with the Army's western flank anchored on the Imjin River.

There were several reasons for this recovery by the Eighth Army which changed the course of the war. First, perhaps, was the determined personality of General Ridgway, a seasoned airborne commander in the European war, whose leadership transformed morale and efficiency after the Chinese victories. The general insisted that his Command could defeat the Chinese, stressed strict military discipline, and ordered the detailed coordination of all his units to prevent outflanking by the enemy.

Secondly, as the Ridgway counter offensive pushed northwards, the Eighth Army inflicted enormous casualties on the lightly armed Communist troops through a systematic use of artillery, air power and every form of firepower generally. In this new war of attrition the UN Command's heavy firepower soon established an ascendancy over Chinese manpower. Moreover, as MacArthur pointed out at this time, the Chinese advance south of Seoul in January 1951 meant that their stretched supply lines were vulnerable to the weather and to air attack. The logistic situation of the Communists was completely reversed from the period of the UN advance to the Yalu. It was becoming apparent that the vicinity of the 38th Parallel represented a natural strategic division of Korea.

Nevertheless, by early April 1951 it was clear that the Chinese were about to launch a major spring offensive in Korea. From beyond the Yalu Chinese reinforcements poured south into the staging area of the 'Iron Triangle' on the central front. This zone lay slightly north of the 38th Parallel bounded by the three towns of Chorwon, Kumhwa, and Pyonggang (not Pyongyang).

The Communists also reorganised their command system in a way that was to last for the remainder of the war. Officially Kim Il Sung commanded all Communist troops in Korea through a Combined North Korean–Chinese GHQ near Pyongyang. But the real direction of the Communist armies in Korea lay in the hands of General Peng Teh-huai, a Long March veteran, from his headquarters at Mukden. General Peng had his own lines of command and control to the Chinese forces south of the Yalu, and was known as the 'Commander of the Chinese People's Volunteers'.

Another indication of the increasing tempo of the war came on 12 April when forty-eight B-29s, escorted by seventy-two fighters, struck at the key road and rail bridges which linked Sinuiju with Antung in Manchuria. The UN Command aircraft were attacked by scores of MIG fighters from recently-built bases in the Antung area and three B-29s were shot down. Nine MIGs were also downed. From now on increasingly large formations of MIGs crossed the Yalu to engage UN aircraft. While in early 1951 monthly sightings of MIGs by UN Command pilots numbered 300 to 400, by October the figure had risen to 3,000. For both sides the political and military stakes in Korea were now considerable.

MacArthur's Recall: Chinese Spring Offensive

As the Chinese armies north of the 38th Parallel prepared for their spring offensive MacArthur continued to press publicly his programme of extending the war to mainland China. During visits to Korea in both February and March he had issued statements which implied the only alternative to stalemate in Korea was to carry the war to what he had already termed 'the privileged sanctuary of Manchuria'.

This view was of course in direct conflict with the Truman Administration's policy of containing aggression in Korea around the 38th Parallel. The Administration also regarded the defence of Western Europe as its chief priority, together with the preservation of the alliance that underwrote the UN Command. All this would be sacrificed, so it was believed in Washington, by unilateral action against China.

In line with this policy, and as the UN Command reached the 38th Parallel in March 1951, Truman prepared to issue a peace initiative that had been agreed by the allies. But on 24 March MacArthur ruined this plan by releasing a 'military appraisal' of the Korean situation which threatened action against China's 'coastal areas and interior bases' unless Peking negotiated with the UN. This virtual personal ultimatum had been preceded by a letter from MacArthur to Joe Martin, the Republican Minority Leader in the House of Representatives and a bitter political foe of the President. The letter claimed that there was 'no subsitute for victory' in Korea.

When the letter was publicly released in Washington on 5 April President Truman decided that MacArthur had to be relieved as the challenge to his authority and his policy was intolerable. 'I could no longer tolerate his insubordination', Truman wrote in the detailed account of these events in his Memoirs.

The President then conferred over a period of several days with his leading advisers including Secretaries Acheson and Marshall and General Omar Bradley, the Chairman of the Joint Chiefs of Staff. These men and also the Joint Chiefs agreed with the President that MacArthur must go. Accordingly an order was drafted which relieved MacArthur of his four commands, including that of Supreme Commander in Japan, and appointed General Ridgway to succeed him. Lieutenant General James Van Fleet was chosen to command the Eighth Army in Korea. The news was released in Washington early on 11 April 1951 and reached MacArthur, regrettably at second hand, later that day Tokyo time. The MacArthur era in Japan and Korea was over.

MacArthur then left for home where he addressed Congress on 19 April. In an emotional speech he again repeated his programme of carrying the war to China and again claimed there was no substitute for victory. As a result of the historic controversy caused by his dismissal it was agreed that the Joint Senate Foreign Relations and Armed Services Committees would begin detailed hearings in early May on the Truman Administration's policy in the Ear East.

But the uproar over MacArthur's dismissal was at least partly overtaken by events in Korea. On 22 April the Chinese launched a mass offensive against the Eighth Army on the western and central fronts. Nearly half a million Communist troops were in action, most of them Chinese. Under intense pressure the Eighth Army withdrew about thirty-five miles in good order to a new defensive line across the peninsula; the streets of Seoul were filled with American artillery firing north at the Communists who were held about four miles north of the city. In the western sector, below the Imjin, the 1st battalion of the Gloucestershire Regiment from the British 29th Brigade delayed the advance of three Chinese divisions for three vital days, 22–25 April.

In line with the tactics developed by Ridgway the new commander of the Eighth Army, Van Fleet, exercised close control over all units and 'rolled with the punch'. Van Fleet's firepower also inflicted enormous casualties on the Communists whose offensive, based on inadequate logistics, trailed away by 30 April.

The Chinese armies now regrouped for the second phase of their spring offensive aimed at the eastern sector. Van Fleet ordered new minefields laid, and built up his ammunition stocks. The general also brought up his reserves so that once the forthcoming Communist offensive lost its momentum, the Eighth Army could launch its own counter-offensive which it was hoped would finally drive the enemy out of South Korea.

On 16 May five Chinese armies backed by North Korean divisions launched a major offensive along a forty-mile front southeast of the Hwachon Reservoir. Its objective was to drive southwards into the mountains of the east-central front, cut communications across the peninsula, and generally envelop the main force of the Eighth Army to the west. Moving southwards from the Inje area the Chinese achieved an initial penetration of about thirty-five miles but the trackless broken country of the Taebaek Mountains restricted their mobility and played into the hands of the defence.

After suffering unprecedented casualties from the concentrated artillery and constant air strikes of the UN Command the Chinese offensive was spent by 20 May. Ridgway now ordered

Van Fleet to begin a general counteroffensive and soon the Chinese retreat became a rout as the Communists fell back into North Korea. Platoons, companies and even battalions surrendered *en masse*, and by the end of May 1951 some 10,000 prisoners, mostly Chinese, had been captured. It was clear that the Chinese, no less than the North Koreans, were unable to beat the Eighth Army and conquer South Korea. The eastern offensive of May 1951 was the last Communist attempt to destroy the Eighth Army.

On 30 May Ridgway told the Joint Chiefs that the enemy had suffered a 'major defeat' with casualties greater than those of their first spring offensive. Ridgway considered that the military situation in Korea now offered 'optimum advantages' in support of diplomatic negotiations for an armistice.

Truce Talks Agreed

While the military preconditions for armistice negotiations had thus been created in Korea, new political objectives had been agreed in Washington. After intensive discussion between the State and Defence Departments President Truman approved a new national policy directive on 17 May 1951. This directive distinguished between the ultimate political objective of an united, democratic and independent Korea and the more immediate aims of repelling aggression and ending the fighting through a military armistice. This meant that the Republic of Korea was to be defended 'south of a northern boundary line suitable for defence and administration'.

As the Administration clarified its Korean objectives in this way, the two Senate Committees inquiring into the circumstances of MacArthur's recall proceeded with an exhaustive review of the 'Military Situation in the Far East' with particular emphasis on Korea.

During these famous 'MacArthur hearings' which lasted from 3 May to 25 June the General defended with great eloquence his programme for extending the war to China in order to win in Korea. MacArthur considered that there was 'no plan' for the war in Korea and that the defeat of Communist China by bombing, blockade, and the use of Chinese Nationalist troops would be a major victory for the United States He did not think such a programme would result in Soviet intervention and wider hostilities. Korea, asserted MacArthur, lay at the heart of the world struggle and if necessary America should 'go it alone'.

However, MacArthur's strategy was effectively countered by President Truman's lieutenants who argued in general that limited war in Korea gave the West time to rearm and that the General's programme might well result in a Third World War. Secretary of State Acheson believed that operations in Korea were a defensive success and that the idea of collective security had been vindicated. Acheson believed that 'time is on our side if we make good use of it'. Secretary of Defence Marshall argued that defending South Korea was part of a global containment policy aimed at deterring aggression. The Chinese armies in Korea were being torn apart with 'terrific casualties' and thus a basis for armistice negotiations was already being reached.

In addition the Joint Chiefs of Staff told the Senate hearings that strategically the MacArthur programme was much too risky as it might involve the United States in a prolonged war of attrition with China. It was imperative to remember that American strategic air power must be preserved for a possible confrontation with the USSR, the West's chief adversary. General Bradley summed up by saying that the MacArthur programme might involve the United States in a war with China which would be 'the wrong war, at the wrong place, at the wrong time, with the wrong enemy', a telling phrase which still rings down the years.

The MacArthur hearings thus clearly demonstrated that there were unacceptable risks involved in the General's prescription for victory in Korea. The controversy surrounding MacArthur's recall began to ebb away although the war in Korea remained a major political liability for the Truman Administration.

In anticipation of armistice talks, the Eighth Army now began to dig in and fortify the *Kansas* line which ran across the peninsula north of the 38th Parallel from the Imjin in the west to above Kansong on the east coast. A further limited advance was also made to the line *Wyoming* which curved north above Chorwon and Kumhwa at the base of the Iron Triangle. Pyonggang at the apex of the Triangle was taken on 13 June but quickly relinquished as the Chinese held the hills to the north. This marked the high-water mark of the Eighth Army's counteroffensive. Unlike the 38th Parallel the *Kansas–Wyoming* line was firmly based on terrain and water defence. In accordance with national policy Ridgway had already been ordered not to make any general advance north of this line.

During June 1951, secret and informal contacts between Moscow and Washington indicated that armistice talks in Korea were now possible. On 23 June the Soviet delegate to the UN, Jacob Malik, publicly stated in a radio address that 'the most acute problem of the present day – the problem of the armed conflict in Korea' could be solved. The truce talks would be strictly military negotiations aimed at ending the fighting; there would be no discussion of political questions such as China's seat at the UN or the future of Formosa.

In late June and early July there was an exchange of radio messages between Ridgway and the two Communist commanders (Kim Il Sung and Peng Teh-huai). It was arranged that liaison officers would meet at Kaesong to make arrangements for delegations from both sides to meet and begin negotiations for an armistice. Following this initial contact on 8 July the liaison officers agreed that the main delegations would meet at Kaesong on 10 July. Thus after more than a year's bitter fighting both sides were now prepared to negotiate on the basis of a divided Korea.

The Negotiations Proceed

On 10 July 1951 the two five-man delegations began their negotiations in a former tea-house on the outskirts of Kaesong, the ancient Koryo capital of Korea. The UN Command delegation was led by Vice-Admiral Turner Joy, the American Naval Commander, Far East; the leader of the Communist delegation was General Nam Il, the Chief of Staff of the North Korean Army, although the real authority in the delegation was a senior Chinese officer, Major General Hsieh Fang. The UN Command had established a base camp at nearby Munsan, immediately south of the Imjin, and from here Joy and his colleagues went daily by helicopter to Kaesong; staff members and newsmen travelled by road from Munsan to Kaesong.

From the beginning the talks were characterised by acrimony and it was not without difficulty that an agenda of five items was agreed on 26 July

1. Adoption of Agenda.
2. Arrangements for a demarcation line and a demilitarized zone as a basis for ending hostilities.
3. Arrangements for the composition and authority of a supervisory commission to oversee the truce.
4. Arrangements relating to prisoners of war.
5. Recommemdations to the governments of countries concerned in the war.

Following the adoption of the agenda, negotiations began on Item 2, the fixing of the demarcation line. The Communists wanted a return to the 38th Parallel, while the UN Command argued in general for the defensible contact line between the two armies. Progress was slow and there were a series of incidents around the conference site involving armed Communist soldiers. Kaesong was not in no man's land, as originally thought by the UNC, but was controlled by the Communists.

Ridgway therefore was determined to move the conference site to Panmunjom, a small hamlet controlled by neither side and which lay about five miles east of Kaesong on the high road to the lmjin and Munsan. Liaison officers from both sides had met at Panmunjom since the beginning of the truce talks. On 22 October the liaison officers agreed on the move to Panmunjom; the area was neutralised and special tents built for the delegates.

Meanwhile, the UN Command continued to wage air and sea war against North Korea. Beginning in August the Eighth Army resumed military pressiire northwards. On the eastern sector, after heavy fighting, the Bloody Ridge–Heartbreak Ridge complex west of the Punchbowl area was seized by mid-October. This commanding terrain was over twenty miles north of the 38th Parallel and provided a firm anchor for this sector of the front. The nearby heights to the north of Kumsong were also taken. In the western sector the Eighth Army moved north of the Imjin during October to the *Jamestown Line* which gave maximum defensive advantages protecting the approaches to Seoul and the main supply route north to Chorwon.

These were limited advances. On 12 November 1951, as the Korean winter set in, Ridgway ordered Van Fleet to begin an 'active defence' all along the front. Offensive operations north of this 'Main Line of Resistance' were confined to seizing outposts and other local activities. This order marked the beginning of the positional warfare that was to characterise, with few exceptions, the ground fighting for the rest of the war.

At Panmunjom, talks on Item 2 had resumed on 25 October. After hard bargaining a compromise wes reached on the opposing positions on the demarcation line. The Communists now agreed to a contact line in the middle of a four-kilometre wide demilitarized zone. But they also demanded that the agreed contact line should last for the remainder of the truce negotiations, so freezing the battlefront.

As the Communists had moved away from their insistence on

TRIAL OF STRENGTH 125

the 38th Parallel, the Joint Chiefs of Staff instructed Ridgway to accept this proposal but with the proviso that the armistice be signed within thirty days of agreement on the firing line. If no general truce could be agreed within the thirty days, the demarcation line would be the contact line between the two armies when the truce was finally agreed.

After further intensive discussion in sub-delegation this UN Command proposal for a thirty-day freeze was agreed by the full (or plenary) delegations on 27 November. But although discussion proceeded to Items 3 and 4 on the agenda, no general truce agreement was reached within the thirty days. Thus the stabilization of the front gave the Communists a breathing space to increase significantly their fortifications north of the front. For its part, the UN Command had now tacitly recognised that it would not again engage in large-scale ground operations. The UN Command had gambled on a quick armistice and lost.

During the winter of 1951–52, the negotiations continued on Items 3 and 4, arrangements to supervise the truce and those relating to POWs. After the usual slow progress, marked by charge and counter-charge of bad faith, it was eventually agreed at Panmunjom that a joint Military Armistice Commission would oversee the truce; a Neutral Nations Supervisory Commission would have access to all parts of Korea to see that agreed limmits on a post-armistice military build-up were not violated. The Supervisory Commission would report to the Military Armistice Commission. After hard bargaining on the terms of inspection by the Observer Teams assigned to the Supervisory Commission, differences between the two sides on Item 3 had been resolved by April 1952 with two exceptions.

These exceptions involved the demand by the Communist side that the Soviet Union be included as a neutral nation on the Supervisory Commission, a stipulation which the UNC could not accept. For its part, the UN Command continued to insist on post-armistice restrictions on airfield construction in Korea. This the Communists refused to sanction.

During these protracted winter negotiations at Panmunjom there was however rapid progress on the least important Item 5 during February 1952. This Item involved recommendations from the armistice conference to the countries concerned in the war. Following a draft Communist proposal the UNC delegation quickly agreed that these recommendations should include the holding of a high-level political conference within three months of the armistice. The issues then to be decided should involve the withdrawal of foreign forces from Korea and 'the peaceful settlement of the Korean question etc.'

The UN Command agreed to this vague phraseology as the recommendations left complete freedom of action to the governments involved. There was no further discussion of Item 5 which was later turned into Article 60 of the final armistice agreement.

Deadlock at Panmunjom

By April 1952 agreement had largely been reached at Panmunjom on Items 2, 3 and 5 of the agenda. But it now proved impossible for both sides to agree on Item 4, arrangements relating to Prisoners of War. This of course was an issue with great political implications for the two contestants in Korea.

Following the beginning of discussions in Item 4 in December 1951 it was soon discovered that large numbers of North Korean and Chinese prisoners did not wish to return home. Intensive screening of prisoners in hands of the UN Command revealed that of about 112,000 Korean prisoners about 76,000 wished to return to North Korea. This latter figure included some South Koreans impressed into the KPA and some pro-Communist South Korean civilian internees. Of some 20,000 Chinese prisoners only 6,400 wished to return to Communist China. Thus in round figures 83,000 out of 132,000 Communist prisoners opted for repatriation, the remainder were determined to resist repatriation.

The Communists insisted that all prisoners should be returned home, while the UN Command declared their commitment to the principle of voluntary or non-forcible prisoner repatriation. Humanitarian considerations of course made it difficult if not impossible for the UN Command to forcibly repatriate all their prisoners. But there was also considerable political and propaganda advantage in these figures at a time when the UN cause in Korea was under major propaganda attach from the Communists (see below).

Accordingly, after four months of bitter wrangling, on 28 April 1952 Admiral Joy put forward the UN Command's final position on resolving the differences between the two sides. This was a package deal with three items. Joy abandoned the UN insistence on post-armistice restrictions on airfield construction, and suggested a Neutral Nations Supervisory Commission excluding the USSR. He also suggested in the most important section of the package deal that all prisoners should be 'released and repatriated as soon as possible', with the proviso that there would be no forcible repatriation.

Within a few days the Communists agreed to drop their insistence on the USSR as a member of the Supervisory Commission in exchange for the UNC concession on airfields. But the Communists refused to budge on the prisoner issue. During May 1952 Admiral Joy left Korea and was succeeded as the chief delegate for the UNC at Panmunjom by Major General William K. Harrison. The deadlock, however, was complete and the war was now to continue for another fifteen months as a result of the impasse on prisoner repatriation.

Trial of Strength

Following the opening of the truce talks ground operations in Korea were increasingly wound down. After November 1951 defence of the Main Line of Resistance was the chief priority of the Eighth Army. From their opposing lines the two sides then fought limited engagements over such outposts as The Hook, Old Baldy or Capitol Hill. Sometimes the fighting flared up into divisional-sized operations as in October 1952. Then the Chinese failed to seize White Horse Hill (Hill 395) near Chorwon; the UN Command was unable to capture Triangle Hill (Hill 598) near Kumhwa. This hill warfare then continued on a smaller scale to the last days of the war.

If the defence had come into its own in the ground fighting in Korea, and if the truce talks were stalemated, the sea and air war intensified as the UN Command tried to bring pressure on the Communist negotiators at Panmunjom. The Communist high command, for its part, seemed secure in its new defensive strength and was evidently prepared to sit out the stalemate war which thus became a trial of strength.

Although not often publicised, the sea war in Korea was a vital part of the UN war effort. Most UN Command troops came to Korea by sea, and the amphibious operations at Inchon, Wonsan, and Hungnam in the first six months of the war had been of great importance. Like the air war, the chief burden of the sea war was carried by the United States.

As the mobile phase of the Korean War ended in the summer of 1951, large-scale amphibious operations by the UN Command were no longer envisaged. The chief emphasis of the sea war was now on blockade arid air interdiction operations from UN Navy carriers off the Korean east coast. The blockade was carried out by two separate task groups in the Yellow Sea and in the Sea of Japan. As resupply by sea for the Communist armies was now precluded so an additional burden was placed on the North Korean road and rail system. In turn, this transportation system was then attacked by strike aircraft from the US Navy's Task Force 77 in the Sea of Japan which operated during 1951–53 with up to four attack carriers. The Communist main supply route from Vladivostok to Wonsan was also vulnerable to naval gunfire and naval raiding parties as it followed the north-east coast between Songjin and Hungnam.

The UN naval forces were also used to invest the North Korean east coast ports of Wonsan, Hungnam, Songjin, so drawing Communist troops away from the front by threat of amphibious attack. In particular, a small group of islands in the outer harbour of Wonsan was occupied by UNC special forces from February 1951 to the end of the war. Other strategically-placed small islands on both the east and west coasts of Korea were also occupied for most of the war so providing valuable bases for radar and electronic warfare. The sea war in Korea thus played a major part in keeping up the pressure on North Korea.

Much more publicised was the air war against the North. In the first few months of the Korean War the UN air forces had easily established air supremacy over both friendly and enemy territory and successive enemy offensives had been blunted by the effective deployment of air power. But during the stalemate war of 1951–53 it was difficult to apply air pressure on the Communist armies for a number of reasons. The static nature of the front meant that the Communist forces were not so vulnerable as when on the offensive. In any case the air bases and strategic targets of the enemy war effort were in China and even in the USSR.

Yet despite a very strong air defence effort by Chinese MIG-15s from Manchurian bases the US Air Force was able to prevent North Korean airfields from becoming operational. From early 1951 to the eventual armistice American F-86 Sabre jets from Kimpo and Suwon fought successfully against large numbers of MIG-15s for air supremacy over north-east Korea in the area between the Yalu and the Chongchon, 'MIG alley'. According to the historian of the USAF in Korea, Robert F. Futrell, 'some of the greatest air battles of history were fought at this time'.

In addition, from June 1951 the USAF initiated a major interdiction campaign against the transportation system that joined Manchuria to the Communist armies on line. But the North Koreans were able to conscript enough local labour to repair all cuts in the road and rail system and the number of front-line Communist troops actually increased during the period of Operation *Strangle*.

After June 1952 interdiction was scaled down and the main air effort moved to special, or semi-strategic, target systems beginning with an effective attack against the giant Suiho hydroelectric plant on the Yalu. Other targets included Pyongyang. The air offensive then moved to factories and installations throughout North Korea, including some selected irrigation dams in the spring of 1953. But the UN Command's air power, for all its flexibility and ingenuity, was not able to prove decisive. The decisions to end the fighting were primarily political and originated, as we shall see below, from outside Korea.

This trial of strength in Korea between 1951 and 1953 was not only a military one. It was also a major political contest between the two sides which had world-wide ramifications. The Communists evidently saw in the stalemated truce talks an excellent propaganda instrument for accusing the UN Command of imperialist aggression and crimes against peace in Korea. Such charges at Panmunjom were then projected on an international level through the medium of the Soviet-led world peace campaign. The campaign was centred on the 1950 Stockholm peace petition which called for the 'unconditional prohibition' of atomic weapons.

Increasingly during 1952–53 this campaign to undermine the will of the UN allies to continue the fight was led by accusations that the UN Command had used germ warfare in North Korea and against China. The charges were backed by alleged confessions from captured American airmen which were later shown to have been extracted by extreme physical and mental pressure. Thus this prolonged campaign of political warfare involving the Korean conflict had many sides in rallying anti-Western sentiment on a global scale.

It played an important part, for example, in consolidating the newly established Chinese Communist regime which faced a protracted and extremely expensive war in Korea. One Chinese analysis of the Korean War (published in 1958) stressed that following the end of mobile fighting in Korea in 1951 the Chinese Volunteers 'subordinated the military struggle to the political struggle'.

But the Western allies too obtained political benefits from the Korean War in that rearmament to deter further Communist aggression became possible. American defence spending, for example, jumped from about $14 billion in 1950 to about $60 billion by 1953. During 1951 Supreme Headquarters Allied Powers Europe (SHAPE) was activated, and a new system of American strategic air bases on a world-wide scale began construction. An all-out crash programme for the construction of the hydrogen bomb and other atomic weapons was also initiated by the Truman Administration in direct response to events in Korea after June 1950.

On the diplomatic front there were significant developments as the fighting continued in Korea. In September 1951 the Japanese peace treaty was accompanied by American security pacts signed with the Philippines, Australia and New Zealand. A similar treaty with Japan came into force when Japanese sovereignty was restored in April 1952; Ridgway was then sent to command SHAPE and succeeded as UN Commander-in-Chief by General Mark Clark.

Another diplomatic event of great importance was the restoration by the allies of West German sovereignty in May 1952 (subject to agreement on the West European army). The reintegration of Japan and West Germany into the international community were clearly major achievements of Western diplomacy and but for the Korean War would have taken very much longer.

Yet despite progress over all these wider problems, the UN allies continued to face complete impasse over the prisoner issue at Panmunjom, where the truce talks were formally recessed for the winter on 8 October 1952. Speaking to the UN General Assembly later that month Secretary of State Acheson reiterated the UN Command position on prisoner repatriation and stated that the allies now faced a test of their staying power in Korea.

Acheson spoke at a time when the 1952 American presidential campaign came to a climax. During the campaign General Dwight D. Eisenhower, the Republican candidate, had pledged that he would go to Korea in an attempt to end the war. The General's election on 4 November now proved to be the first in a series of events that would end the Korean War.

Korean Armistice 27 July 1953

After a visit to Korea in early December 1952, Eisenhower decided that after his inauguration on 20 January 1953 he would expand the war unless the Communists signed an honourable truce. A few weeks after the inauguration Joseph Stalin died on 5 March 1953. There were signs of a political thaw in Moscow and Peking now began an intensive re-assessment of its Korean commitment. A more conciliatory Communist attitude was evident when a limited exchange of sick and wounded prisoners was arranged during April 1953.

But still the truce talks at Panmunjom remained stalemated in the UN Command's principle of no forcible prisoner repatriation. When the full delegation met on 26 April the Communists suggested that non-repatriates should be sent to a neutral country to await the outcome of the post-armistice political conference. This was still unacceptable to the UN Command as there was no assurance of civilian status for the prisoners.

After negotiations the break came on 7 May when Nam Il suggested a Neutral Nations Repatriation Commission (NNRC) which would take charge of the non-repatriates within Korea. This plan was based on an Indian compromise proposal in the United Nations which had been vehemently rejected by the Soviet Union, China, and North Korea the previous December. On 25 May the UN Command counter-proposed with a NNRC constituted with an Indian chairman and Indian custodial forces. After a period of not more than 180 days in custody non-repatriates would be given civilian status.

This was the UN Command's final position on Item 4. If the proposals were rejected then the UN Command would break off the talks. Simultaneously John Foster Dulles, Eisenhower's Secretary of State, let it be known through diplomatic channels that unless a truce were forthcoming the US would extend the war by attacking the Manchurian bases probably with atomic weapons. This was a threat rather than a precisely formulated intention but it may have had some influence on the Communist decision to wind up the war.

Eventually on 4 June the Communists accepted in general the UNC's plan for prisoner repatriation and after further work by staff officers the terms of reference were signed by Harrison and Nam Il on 8 June. The agreement provided for a NNRC composed of Sweden, Switzerland, Poland and Czechoslovakia with an Indian Chairman and Indian custodial forces, and with its headquarters in the vicinity of Panmunjom.

All prisoners opting for repatriation would be exchanged within 60 days of the armistice. For a further 90 days all non-repatriates would be in the custody of the NNRC and open to 'explanations' by their home government. If the post-war conference had been unable to agree on the disposition of the non-repatriates during the next 30 days, then the prisoners would be given civilian status. No prisoner would thus be detained for more than six months after the signing of the armistice. The Communists had come to terms on the prisoner issue after eighteen months of negotiations.

Arrangements now went ahead for the final signing of the armistice agreement despite a vigorous protest campaign by Syngman Rhee who objected to the effective re-partition of Korea. During June 1953 Rhee ordered the unilateral release of some 27,000 North Korean non-repatriates. It was only Eisenhower's promise of a post-war mutual defence treaty between the US and the ROK, combined with the pledge of significant military and economic aid that Rhee was brought to acquiesce in the armistice, which was not formally signed by the ROK. A punishing Chinese limited offensive against South Korean troops on the east-central front during July 1953 indicated to Rhee the effects of non-compliance with the armistice.

By late July 1953, after over three years of fighting, the completed armistice agreement of 63 clauses was ready for signing. The document provided for a re-surveyed contact line between the two armies known as the Military Demarcation Line (MDL) which stood in the centre of a four-kilometre wide Demilitarized Zone (DMZ). A Military Armistice Commission (MAC) meeting at Panmunjom would oversee the truce while a Neutral Nations Supervisory Commission (NNSC), operating in North and South Korea, would report to the MAC. A Neutral Nations Repatriation Commission (NNRC) would arrange for the disposal of prisoners in accordance with the agreement of 8 June 1953. Article 60 recommended that a post-war political conference should be held within three months of the armistice to bring about 'the peaceful settlement of the Korean question etc.'

At 1000 hours on 27 July 1953 General William K. Harrison and General Nam Il, as Senior Delegates, signed the armistice agreement in a special hall built for the occasion at Panmunjom. The armistice was effective 12 hours after signing. The nine documents, signed in triplicate in English, Korean, and Chinese were then counter-signed by Mark Clark for the UN Command at Munsan, and by Kim Il Sung and Peng Teh-huai at Kaesong and Pyongyang respectively. The Korean War was over.

As a result of the war the independence of South Korea had been preserved; the authority of the United Nations in repelling aggression had been upheld; Communist China had emerged as one of the world's great powers; the balance of power in the Far East had been successfully defended by the United States and its allies.

But the cost of the war had been heavy to all concerned. South Korean military casualties numbered over 300,000. The United States had suffered over 142,000 casualties, including over 33,000 dead. In a special report to the United Nations in August 1953 the UN Command estimated that Chinese and North Korean casualties were 'between one and a half and two million'. Unofficial estimates of civilian casualties in North and South Korea run to about a million in each country. Thus the total casualties of the Korean War probably number about four million.

No final peace settlement has ever been signed and the truce that was designed to last perhaps three months has now lasted thirty five years. But the memory of the war continues to have a very significant effect on events in Korea; many Koreans consider that they are still living in the aftermath of the Korean war.

Chapter Twelve: Post War Korea 1953–1965

With the ending of the Korean War on 27 July 1953 it was not only the political division of Korea that remained. The country was divided physically by the armistice in a way it had not been in June 1950. Korea had been re-partitioned by the armistice agreement.

The new Military Demarcation Line agreed by the two sides in the truce slashed across Korea from the Han estuary in the west to above Kansong on Korea's east coast. Mostly the MDL ran north of the 38th Parallel, but former South Korean territory west of the lower Imjin had been relinquished to North Korea. Unlike the 38th Parallel the new demarcation line was based on natural defences of water and terrain throughout its length of about 155 miles.

To the north and south of the four-kilometer wide Demilitarised Zone established by the armistice both sides by July 1953 had already built deep, complex fortifications. It need hardly be stressed that these defences have been progressively elaborated ever since the truce of 1953. The net result is that the two Koreas today are separated by the most heavily fortified border in the world.

Implementing the Truce

To facilitate the implementation of the armistice a new Joint Security Area (JSA) was set up in the Demilitarized Zone at Panmunjom shortly after the signature of the truce. Both sides agreed that a permanent detail of Joint Duty Officers from both the UNC and the Communist side would be henceforth stationed in the JSA. Secretariats for the two sides were established at

Kaesong and Munsan. These arrangements still provide the framework for the continuing meetings between the UN Command and the Communists which has made Panmunjom one of the major tourist attractions of the Far East.

The armistice had created three commissions to supervise the truce. These agencies would meet at Panmunjom. The *Military Armistice Commission*, which consisted of senior representatives of both sides, was to exercise overall supervision of the truce deploying joint observer teams in the DMZ. Before long, the observer teams usually ceased to work on a joint basis, and the main work of the MAC was to hear the accusations and counter-accusations launched over truce violations in the DMZ. Full, plenary meetings of the MAC now occur infrequently, and only to listen to details of important violations of the truce.

The second agency created by the armistice was the *Neutral Nations Supervisory Commission* which was to deploy joint teams of observers and inspectors in North and South Korea. The UNC soon considered that these observers had been obstructed by the Communist authorities in North Korea, so preventing full supervision of the armistice. During 1956 the inspection teams, consisting of Polish, Czech, Swedish and Swiss personnel, were withdrawn to Panmunjom. The Commission is still in existence and the UNC regards the Swedish and Swiss members as valued neutral observers in the DMZ.

A third truce agency was the *Neutral Nations Repatriation Commission*. This agency was to supervise the exchange of POWs, their repatriation, or the eventual dispositions of prisoners not in either of these categories. In August and September 1953, the UNC transferred directly to the Communists over 75,000 prisoners who had opted for repatriation, while the Communists returned 12,000 prisoners to the UNC. Over 22,000 Chinese and North Korean non-repatriates were then returned to the NNRC, as well as over 300 former UNC personnel, including 23 Americans and one Briton, who did not wish to return home.

Eventually, in January 1954, these non-repatriates became civilians; the former North Korean personnel entered the ROK and some 14,000 Chinese Communist personnel opted for transfer to Taiwan. The story of the Korean POWs was over, and during February 1954 the NNRC voted to dissolve itself. So ended the immediate outcome of the Korean armistice negotiations. The long-term political legacy of the Korean War now passed to the politicians of East and West.

Geneva Conference on Korea

During the later stages of the armistice negotiations at Panmunjom, the Eisenhower administration had promised Syngman Rhee an American-South Korean Mutual Defence Treaty. This was part of the price asked by Rhee for his acquiescence in the truce; the old Korean independence fighter was bitter that the fighting had ended with a renewed partition of his country and with national unity further away than ever.

Accordingly, the United States and the Republic of Korea signed a brief but comprehensive security treaty on 1 October 1953. The Secretary of State, John Foster Dulles, considered that as this treaty gave a clear unequivocal warning to the Communists it would prevent a renewal of aggression in Korea.

The Treaty provided for joint consultation if the security of either country was threatened by armed attack. It was also stipulated that the United States had the right to dispose its forces 'in and about' the territory of the Republic of Korea as determined by mutual agreement. Article III of the Treaty, its vital clause, stated that in the event of an armed attack on one of the parties 'both signatories would act to meet the common danger in accordance with its constitutional processes'. Unless terminated by either party on a year's notice, the Treaty was to remain in force 'indefinitely'. The reference to 'constitutional processes' meant that the United States Congress would necessarily be consulted if the Treaty were invoked.

During lengthy Congressional hearings on the Treaty the Senate made it clear that the United States was not obligated to help South Korea except in case of an 'external armed attack'. This reservation precluded any obligatory internal security commitment to South Korea or any American support for a provocative military move northwards by any South Korean government. This understanding by the Senate was added to the text of the Treaty which then came into force on 17 November 1954. The Treaty remains in force.

Under Article 60 of the Korean armistice, 'a political conference of a higher level of both sides' was to meet to bring about 'the peaceful settlement of the Korean question'. Hence the Geneva Conference on Korea (and Indochina) which convened in April 1954 was attended by Dulles, Eden, Molotov and Chou En-lai. North and South Korea were of course participants. The conference was also attended by almost all of the allies who had fought in the UN Command in Korea. Only South Africa was absent.

From its very outset, there was complete disagreement on Korea's future. The South Koreans and their allies advocated all-Korean free elections under UN supervision. The North Koreans and their supporters suggested that as a preliminary move towards unification there should be created an 'all-Korean Commission' with equal representation from the two Koreas. Commission decisions would be unanimous, so giving North Korea a veto. After many speeches on these opposing viewpoints, by mid-June 1954 the Geneva Conference was stalemated.

These irreconcilable differences on Korea were not unexpected. As there could be no great-power agreement, let alone agreement between North and South Korea, the Korean issue was returned to the United Nations. In December 1954 the General Assembly stated that its objectives remained 'the achievement by peaceful means of an unified, independent and democratic Korea'. Ever since, at regular intervals, the General Assembly had continued to reaffirm its Korean objectives in these words.

The Korean armistice, the American-South Korean Mutual Defence Treaty, the impasse at Geneva, and the subsequent return of the Korean issue to the United Nations all marked successive steps in the winding-up of the Korean War.

In the absence of a general peace treaty, the Korean military armistice of 27 July 1953 thus remains in force. Since that truce, the Military Armistice Commission meeting at Panmunjom, often under the gaze of visiting tourists, has continued to debate, usually acrimoniously, charge and counter-charge over the many thousands of incidents in the Korean Demilitarized Zone. Over a thousand people have been killed in these incidents along the DMZ, including about fifty Americans. But despite the continuing tension between North and South Korea the armistice still holds.

North Korea: Kim Il Sung's Ascendancy

In the post-war decade events in North and South Korea, as might be expected, took widely differing courses. It was North Korea that seemed to make the most effective recovery. Although wartime destruction had been heavy, the country possessed significant natural resources including coal, iron, and hydroelectric capacity.

There was also extensive aid from both the Soviet bloc and China. The USSR in particular built a number of industrial plants, and these included textile, chemical, mining, pharmaceutical and machine building factories. The beginnings of a tractor industry were established, and shipbuilding yards were laid down. According to North Korean figures, the industrial contribution to the GNP (Gross National Product) rose from about 42 per cent in 1953 to about 70 per cent in 1961; the proportion of urban workers rose from about 30 per cent in 1953 to over 50 per cent in 1960. North Korea was becoming a primarily industrial country.

This process was significantly helped by North Korea's directed, command economy which facilitated this process of virtually crash industrialisation. A corollary of this process, carried out on classical Stalinist lines, was the almost total collectivization of agriculture between 1953 and 1958. By this latter date, Pyongyang was claiming that North Korea was already a 'socialist' economy. Moscow was more cautious in stating that North Korea was 'building' socialism.

During this post-war decade there was a decisive consolidation of Kim Il Sung's power over the Communist Party, the government and the armed forces in North Korea. This was a process which has continuing implications for the peace and stability of both the Korean peninsula and North East Asia in general.

Before 1950, as we have noted, North Korea had been regarded as a Soviet satellite and Kim Il Sung a Soviet creation. However, with the Inchon landing of September 1950 and MacArthur's subsequent drive to the Yalu, the North Korean government was forced to retreat to the border mountains near Manchuria. But for the Chinese intervention in Korea during late 1950 Kim Il Sung's regime would have been eliminated.

It was thus Communist China that enabled Kim Il Sung to recover jurisdiction over most of North Korea during the winter of 1950–51. For the remainder of the war North Korean forces fought under what was in practice if not in form Chinese military direction, although a strong Russian advisory presence remained in North Korea. But with the armistice of July 1953 Kim Il Sung began a process of removing those, of whatever ideological persuasion, who opposed his absolute rule of the Korean Workers Party. Some of Kim's opponents had already disappeared during the chaos and dislocation of the war.

Kim's most prominent post-war victim was the veteran Korean

Communist Pak Hon-yong. He had worked underground during the later years of Japanese rule and was thus known as the most prominent leader of the 'domestic' faction of the Party. Pak had surfaced to re-found the Korean Communist Party in Seoul during September 1945, shortly after the arrival of American forces.

Following the creation of the DPRK Pak had become Foreign Minister. He is believed to have opposed, in the interests of Korean unity, the truce of July 1953 which of course was signed by Kim Il Sung. Whatever his precise offence, Pak and a number of his followers were arrested during August 1953 on charges of 'anti-State espionage activities'. The subsequent execution of Pak, together with his associates, could only have strengthened Kim Il Sung's overall position in the Party.

Three years later in 1956 came the decisive challenge for Kim Il Sung in his struggle to dominate completely the Korean Communist Party. During the summer of that year Kim's rule was apparently contested by both pro-Chinese and pro-Soviet elements in the higher levels of the Party. The pro-Chinese cadres were originally returnees from Mao's China who had been absorbed, as we have noted, by the newly-formed North Korean Workers' Party in 1946. They were consequently known as the Yenan faction. The more powerful Soviet faction was composed of Soviet-trained Koreans who had returned to Korea in 1945 and thereafter flourished during the Soviet ascendancy in North Korea prior to 1950.

During the Party in-fighting which followed this challenge, Kim so successfully routed his enemies that only the visit to Pyongyang of Anastas Mikoyan, the veteran Soviet statesman and General Peng Teh-huai, the Commander of the Chinese Communist Forces in the Korea War, prevented a blood purge similar to that of 1953.

The main pro-Soviet and pro-Chinese cadres were then allowed to leave Korea. But some remaining pro-Chinese elements, especially in the armed forces, were not finally eliminated by Kim until 1958. In expelling these Soviet and Chinese factions, Kim seems to have invoked a latent Korean nationalism in the Party.

With his victory in the Korean Workers Party sealed in this way, Kim Il Sung's personal ascendancy in North Korea was complete. From now on the most sensitive posts in the Party and State apparatus were filled by loyal members of Kim's 'Guerrilla group' of supporters. These men are also known collectively as the 'Kapsan group' from one of the chief operational areas of these former partisans in north-east Korea during the 1930s. Kim's triumph was then celebrated formally in the Fourth Party Congress of 1961, known in Party circles as the 'Congress of Victors'.

At the 1961 Party Congress, Kim Il Sung claimed that all factionalism had been eliminated from the Party and that he was leader of a pure, Koreanised Marxism-Leninism. These claims have had a significant influence on subsequent events in North Korea. As undisputed Party Chairman, Prime Minister, and Armed Forces Supreme Commander Kim had evidently created the conditions for a political role independent of both Moscow and Peking: he could no longer be accused of being a puppet of the big Communist powers.

Following the Party Congress of 1961 Kim intensified the projection of his own personal political programme of *Chuche* ('Self-Reliance') as part of a new drive aimed at the reunification of Korea under Pyongyang's auspices (for details, see Chapter 14 below). This campaign has continued ever since; there has been no significant opposition to Kim Il Sung within North Korea since the events described above.

South Korea: Syngman Rhee's Decline and Fall

Following the Korean armistice of July 1953, President Syngman Rhee continued to maintain his regime in South Korea until the end of the decade. The basis of Rhee's popularity lay of course in his past services to the Korean independence movement, and lately in his role as a stalwart leader during the Korean War.

But Rhee's patriotism and courage, which no one denied, was qualified by an increasingly autocratic temperament. During 1952, he browbeat the National Assembly into passing a constitutional amendment permitting popular election of the President. Rhee was then elected President with a decisive majority in an election claimed by opponents to have been rigged. During 1954, another constitutional ammendment was passed which allowed the President to hold office for more than two terms. Rhee was then elected for a second term in 1956, with the implication that he was a virtual life-President.

Rhee's authoritarianism and prickly nationalism made it difficult for the United States and its allies to work effectively with him. As we have seen, considerable pressure was necessary from Washington before Rhee could be brought to accept the Korean armistice agreement. Following the impasse at the Geneva conference in 1954, Rhee continued to promote within South Korea the slogan of 'March North' as an offical unification policy.

Yet Rhee, as one fully conversant with world politics, also realised that his 'March North' rhetoric was unreal, as he sometimes tacitly admitted. The South Korean forces were incapable of any northern campaign as they were dependent on American logistical support and under the orders of the United Nations Command, headed by an American four-star general. The 1953 American-South Korean defence treaty was certainly a feather in Rhee's cap. But the treaty, as we have seen, was inseparable from an understanding by the American Senate that the United States would only act in the event of 'external armed attack' against the ROK. Unilateral action, even if possible, would therefore result in catastrophe.

Rhee's personal rule and continuing preoccupation with an unreal unification policy was a significant factor in preventing the expansion of the South Korean economy in the late 1950s. The ROK President's insistence on a very large South Korean army of over 500,000 men, for example, helped to divert funds that would have been better spent on capital projects. Such large defence spending, in excess of that advised by the Americans, also fuelled inflation. In the absence of a stable currency, and also of an effective stabilization programme, the benefits of generous foreign aid to the ROK were often lost. Quite apart from military programmes, the United States supplied over $1.6 billion of civilian aid between 1953 and 1960; the UN Korean Rehabilitation Agency (UNKRA) gave another $148 million.

Rhee also objected to normalising South Korean relations with Japan. That country could have been a useful trading partner for the ROK in the decade following the Japanese peace treaty of 1951 which ended the Occupation. South Korean raw materials and Japanese manufactured goods were naturally complementary. Rhee's failure to expand the South Korean industrial sector meant that population pressure on the country's limited agricultural land remained unabated. Incentives to promote more efficient farming were not developed, so perpetuating traditional rural poverty.

Yet another factor in the stagnation of the South Korean economy lay in the numerous state-owned companies, a legacy from Japanese rule and the post-1945 American Military Government. These companies swallowed up funds that could have been used for revitalising the private economic sector. Thus although there was some significant progress in postwar reconstruction after 1953, especially in restoring roads and railways, it proved impossible under Rhee's leadership to develop a self-sustaining economy with rising exports. For the last four years of the decade, ROK exports averaged little more than $22 million annually.

Eventually the political and economic shortcomings of the Rhee administration proved intolerable. When Rhee was returned yet again in the patently rigged Presidential election of 1960, large-scale student riots broke out in Seoul on 19 April. Despite martial law and other measures, it soon became obvious that Rhee would have to go. On 27 April 1960, Syng-man Rhee resigned unconditionally as President of the Republic of Korea. He then left for Hawaii; he was never to return to Korea and died in 1965.

Interregnum: The Chang Regime

Following the fall of Syngman Rhee in April 1960, and in reaction against his personal rule, the new South Korean provisional government promulgated a series of constitutional amendments which replaced a Presidential by a Parliamentary system. The President was now to be selected by a joint session of both houses of the Assembly (and not by popular vote as had been the case since 1952).

Moreover, the President was only given nominal, ceremonial powers. By contrast, the Prime Minister, in whom executive power was now concentrated, was much more powerful. He was appointed by the President, but subject to the approval of the elected lower house of the Assembly. In this way, South Korea's new system asserted the power of the Premier and his Cabinet over the Presidency.

South Korea's 'Second Republic' came into existence after the elections of 29 July 1960, which gave a majority in both houses of the legislature to the conservative Democratic Party. This party had provided the chief opposition to the Rhee's ruling Liberal Party in the 1950s. John Chang (Chang Myon) was appointed Prime Minister, and Yun Po-sun President of the Republic of Korea. The Premier had earlier served as South Korea's first ambassador to Washington in 1949, and was elected Vice-President, in opposition to Rhee's nominee, in 1956.

The experiment in liberal parliamentary democracy which now took place in South Korea was by general consent soon rated as disastrous. Industrial production fell, inflation increased, and mass student demonstrations continued unabated. The country's finances were in disorder as a result of Rhee's rule, and public order was affected because of the unpopularity of the police who were associated with the former regime. There was a dangerous instability at the heart of the Chang government, for the Democratic Party formally split into two factions in September 1960. Some Democratic deputies now demended a strict austerity programme to deal with the financial crisis. The government became in effect a precarious coalition composed of two ruling party factions and a bloc of independents.

The general authority of the Chang government was also seriously weakened by the programme of some vocal student groups which called for a 'neutralized,' united Korea. The official unification policy of the Chang government, stressed by official spokesmen, followed successive United Nations resolutions on Korea which called for free all-Korean elections supervised by the UN. The Chang government also formally repudiated Syngman Rhee's slogan of 'March North' as a unification policy. But although the Chang administration was firmly anti-Communist, millions of South Koreans believed that the mounting unrest in South Korea during 1960–61 played into the hands of Kim Il Sung.

One well-known South Korean historian, Se-Jin Kim, writing in 1972, considered that ever since 1948 South Koreans had possessed great hopes for the democratic system. But these same people had not taken into account the many prerequisites for liberal democracy such as a strong middle class, necessity for compromise, and other well known indicators. He pointed out that even for developed Western liberal democracies, a smoothly functioning system often remains elusive.

Hence the failure of the Chang experiment in South Korea 'was a natural outcome, given the long tradition of authoritarianism and absence of opportunity or right to participate in political decision-making under the Japanese. Rhee's autocratic rule, and Chang's ineffectual leadership were contributing factors, but without undergoing the necessary developmental stages, democracy in Korea was doomed from the start.'

Events in May 1961 were now to show that the Chang government was but an interregnum between the Syngman Rhee period and a military revolution whose ends and means continue to dominate South Korean life.

South Korea's Military Revolution

On 16 May 1961, in an Army *coup* in Seoul, the South Korean military took over the government. The military Junta was led nominally by Lieutenant General Chang Do Yung, the Army Chief of Staff, but the real driving force behind the coup was Major General Park Chung Hee, a professional soldier who was brought up in the Taegu area of south-east Korea. His was to be the dominant personality in South Korea for the next eighteen years.

As a young man, Park had been commissioned in the Japanese-led army of Manchukuo. He had later served in the ROK Army during the Korean War. Press reports indicated that the *coup*, which was supported by over 90 per cent of the South Korean military, had been planned before the student riots which toppled Syngman Rhee. The military conspirators had then decided to wait and see what would happen under the Chang government. When Rhee's successors failed to deal with South Korea's mounting problems, Park and his fellow officers decided to act.

Following the *coup*, the chief organ of the military, the Supreme Council for National Reconstruction (SCNR) assumed all executive, legislative and judicial powers within the Republic of Korea. The new regime was technically legitimised when President Yun Po-sun decided to stay in office. A new Cabinet and a wide range of appointed officials including provincial governors, mayors, and judges continued to govern South Korea on a day-to-day basis. The SCNR's rule was then formally legitimised by an act passed on 6 June 1961. The following month, General Park Chung Hee took over as Chairman of the Supreme Council.

Initially, the Supreme Council took sweeping powers of detention, censorship and proscription, the latter power aimed primarily at allegedly corrupt politicians and businessmen. But the military also quickly announced that they would hand over power to an elected civilian administration once their reforms were accomplished.

It soon became evident from the statements of General Park and his colleagues that whilst they believed in democracy as an ideal, they also felt that it must be adapted to specific Korean conditions. The keynote of the military revolution was thus pragmatism to ensure the objectives of national security, economic modernization and political stability. The issue of Korean reunification, which had featured so prominently in President Rhee's administrations, was thus secondary to the attainment of these goals.

In line with the military's concern with national security, the problem of dealing with North Korean subversion was dealt with through the creation of two new security agencies shortly after the May 1961 revolution. These were the Korean Central Intelligence Agency (KCIA), a civilian agency, and a military counterpart, the Counter-Intelligence Corps (CIC). These centralized agencies replaced the numerous overlapping security-intelligence organizations that had sprung up in the ROK since 1948.

Another preoccupation of the military regime was the regeneration of ROK economy. To this end a Five Year Economic Development Plan (1962–66) was announced in July 1961. The general objective of the Plan was to break the endemic stagnation and inflation that had characterised the economy under Rhee and Chang. The specific objective was to develop an economic strategy based on export-led industrial growth.

In the long-term interest of these objectives, consumer demand was to be given, at least initially, low priority in favour of capital investment in key industries such as electric power, cement, fertilizers, and iron and steel. Agricultural investment was also given a low priority, although there were soon second thoughts on this policy.

During 1962, as the first economic plan began to go into effect, a new Constitution was drafted to provide for a national election and a return to civilian rule. The Constitution envisaged a strong, popularly-elected President, so moving the focus of government back from the Legislature and the Cabinet to the Presidency. In March 1962, President Yun Po-sun resigned, and his place was taken by General Park Chung Hee, nominated by the SCNR.

The new Constitution was approved by a national referendum in December 1962. In the Presidential elections of October 1963, General Park defeated former President Yun Po-sun. Park then resigned from the Army, and was inaugurated as President in December 1963, so completing the transition from military to civilian rule. But the military remained in the background.

There was continuing emphasis on structural reform under the new Presidency of the ROK's 'Third Republic'. A number of executive agencies reporting directly to the President were set up. These included the Board of Audit and Inspection, the Economic and Scientific Council, and an upgraded Presidential Secretariat. This Secretariat was situated in Chong Wa Dae, the Presidential Mansion in Seoul, known as the 'Blue House' from the colour of its ceramic' tiles. These powerful executive agencies continued to strengthen the office of the Presidency in relation to the rest of the South Korean government.

President Park sought to expand and develop Seoul's foreign relations with as many friendly countries as possible. But he gave special attention to normalising relations with Japan. Rhee's anti-Japanese policy, as noted, had prevented the successful establishment of South Korean diplomatic relations with Tokyo after the Japanese peace treaty of 1951.

As a result, the ROK's trade with Japan was minimal, and under Rhee's administration, political energies in South Korea were dispersed in officially-sponsored anti-Japanese sentiment. During the brief regime of John Chang, it had still proved impossible to reach agreement between Seoul and Tokyo. Further talks during the early period of military rule were abortive.

President Park moved to end this state of affairs during 1964–65. As a matter of urgency, the normalisation negotiations between Japan and South Korea, which had begun in 1952, were wound up to South Korea's satisfaction. A comprehensive treaty was signed in Tokyo in June 1965, nearly twenty years after the end of the Second World War. Besides establishing full diplomatic relations, the treaty also provided for a $500 million aid programme of grants and loans from Japan to South Korea. There was no parallel Japanese recognition of North Korea.

These transfusions of Japanese capital were to have a significant and beneficial effect on the South Korean economy in the later 1960s. In the wider regional context the normalisation of relations with Japan, and the steady growth of the South Korean economy, already evident by 1965, ended for the ROK the prolonged period of uncertainty in the aftermath of the Korean War.

Chapter Thirteen: South Korea's Economic Revolution

Following the 1961 military revolution, South Korea's new economic policy of export-led industrial growth slowly began to produce results. From less than $40 million in 1961, exports rose to about $455 million in 1968. The gold and foreign exchange reserves also climbed significantly.

Although not spectacular these were significant results for a primarily agricultural country prior to 1961. This gradual progress was noted in the international financial community; it became easier for Seoul to arrange foreign loans and investment in the world's commercial money markets. There was a new international confidence in Seoul's management of its economy.

Underlying these modest economic advances was the hard work of South Koreans combined with the ingenuity and careful planning of the South Korean government. But there were several other important elements, some internal, some external, which contributed to the continuing expansion of South Korea's industrial sector under the second Five Year Economic Development Plan (1967–71).

Elements in the Success Story

Internally, South Korea possessed a large pool of under-employed labour which could be quickly mobilised for new industrial projects. These labour-intensive projects included plants for both light and heavy industry. As part of this industrial development policy, the government raised interest rates to facilitate the accumulation of domestic capital, standardised the exchange rate, and gave tax rebates on the purchase of raw material for export industries. Domestic savings significantly increased during the 1960s. Free trade zones were also established to attract foreign capital.

South Korea's industrialization was facilitated by the existence of a highly educated population. Learning and education, as we have seen, had always been prized in Korea, there was a very high literacy rate, and aspiring South Korean managers after graduation now began to go on as a matter of course to study for advanced degrees in the West. Universities at home were steadily expanded; retired military men also provided a valuable source of managerial skill.

Externally, the normalisation treaty between Japan and the ROK in 1965 proved of great importance in stimulating the South Korean economy. The treaty, settled a number of semi-diplomatic issues between the two countries such as fishing rights, property claims, and the status of Koreans in Japan. The treaty also provided for a $500 million settlement in grants and loans which Japan promised to South Korea. The normalisation treaty was not, of course, based on friendship but rather on mutual advantage. South Korea needed Japanese capital; the Japanese government saw in the ROK a good place for successful investment which would help Japan's own surging economy. Both governments also wanted the treaty in the wider interests of regional security.

By 1967, Japanese trade with South Korea was running at about $400 million per annum. This trade steadily increased so that by 1980 Japan was South Korea's best customer after the United States. Trade between the two neighbours then totalled about $9 billion, while Japanese investment in South Korea was well over $1 billion with Japanese money found in South Korean oil refining, ship-building, electronics, and many other industries. This was regarded as a mutually beneficial development after the unhappy past relations between Japan and Korea. Japanese trade with South Korea surpassed by many times that with North Korea, which was not officially recognised by Tokyo.

Apart from Japanese grants, loans and investment, a second external factor which significantly assisted South Korea's economic take-off lay in American subsidies of nearly $1 billion during the early years of the Vietnam War, 1965–70. These subsidies were a result of Seoul's' decision to send two ROK Army divisions, with support troops, to Vietnam; three hundred thousand Korean troops were eventually rotated through Vietnam between 1965 and 1970.

It was important to the United States that the despatch of these troops did not weaken the ROK either economically or militarily. But the granting of subsidies in successive years not only compensated South Korea for the cost of her expeditionary force to Vietnam. The subsidies also stimulated further economic growth in South Korea. Certainly by the late 1960s economic aid from America to South Korea was being phased out, and a normal trading relationship now ensued between the two countries.

Expanding Economy

The above were some of the most important factors which underpinned South Korea's steady economic progress during the 1960s and the 1970s. In about two decades, the country moved from less developed economic status to the threshold of full industrialization. Press reports, for example, noted that during 1968 more than fifty large plants were opened in South Korea. Investment from the United States and Japan was followed by that from West Germany, Britain, France, and other Western countries. During 1965–77, the ROK economy expanded at an annual growth rate of 10 per cent per annum, with peak figures of 14 per cent recorded in 1973 and 1976.

During the early 1970s, the ROK's industrial progress took place against a background of global economic uncertainty. In August 1971, President Richard Nixon suspended the dollar's convertability into gold. The dollar now floated on the international currency markets. As the South Korean *won* was linked to the dollar, the subsequent fluctuations of the American currency threatened the ROK's economic stability. Another adverse factor was the 10 per cent surcharge posted on all American imports at the time of the floating of the dollar. Two years later, the quadrupling of Arab oil prices in late 1973 presented another threat to South Korea's economic prospects as the ROK is almost completely dependent on imported oil. There was rising protectionism abroad against some South Korea goods.

By now the South Korean economy was resilient enough to meet these challenges. The government adopted a programme of intensive development of certain strategic industries such as machinery, shipbuilding, petrochemicals and steel.

Development of these industries in this way served two purposes. It boosted exports, but it also provided a substitution for foreign imports, and thus helped to make South Korea self-sufficient in these basic industrial products. The net effect of this intensive and extensive development of the economy over nearly two decades meant that exports climbed from less that $40 million (as noted) in 1961 to over $15 billion in 1979; *per capita* national income during the same period increased from $82 per annum to about $1,500. The GNP jumped from $2 billion to $60 billion.

This economic progress meant that the ROK had become in effect an advanced industrial country, second only to Japan in the Far East. At the beginning of this period of expansion, in 1961, North Korea's exports and *per capita* income exceeded that of South Korea. But by 1980, the ROK had overtaken and significantly surpassed North Korea in both these indicators of national economic development.

According to a World Bank report in the late 1970s 'From a position uncomfortably close to the bottom of the international income scale and without the benefit of significant natural resources South Korea embarked on a course of industrial growth that hecame one of the outstanding success stories in international development.'

Rural Development: The Saemaul Movement

Although South Korea's economic progress during the late 1960s began to attract world-wide attention, rural development lagged behind the industrial sector. South Korean agriculture on the whole remained stagnant, the result of many factors, some traditional, some more recent.

The imbalance was a source of concern to the planners and politicians alike. For the planners agricultural investment, which had a lower priority than industrial development, was showing a poor return. But rural stagnation also represented a definite political challenge to the generally conservative regime of President Park. This government, of course, drew much of its grass-roots political support from the traditionalist rural areas of South Korea. Moreover, the North Korean regime of Kim Il Sung was claiming by the late 1950s to have solved its agricultural problems through collectivisation.

But since about 1970 South Korea's rural poverty has been progressively eliminated. This is primarily the result of an effective modernizing drive in the South Korean countryside organized under the auspices of *Saemaul Undong* (The New Community Movement). By common consent the movement has changed the whole economic potential and even the appearance of the ROK's rural areas.

The modernizing objectives of the Saemaul movement (as it is usually known) had long been an ambition of Korean reformers. In carrying out this programme the average real income of the South Korean farming family has been brought into line with average industrial earnings. The Saemaul movement moreover is a continuing programme with the overall objectives of raising both agricultural production and productivity. Why should the Saemaul movement have succeeded when similar schemes of rural regeneration in both Asia and Africa have often failed?

A very significant factor in the Saemaul movement's success lay in its inception by President Park Chung Hee. The late President Park, who was brought up in a Korean village between the two world wars, knew at first hand the problems of rural poverty in Korea. But he also believed in the resilience and capacity for hard work of the villagers. The spirit of co-operation is also one of the traditional attributes of those who farm the Korean land.

The Saemaul movement thus owes its beginnings to a speech by Park in April 1970 during which the ROK President stated that 'if we can create and cultivate the spirit of self-reliance and independence and hard work, I believe that all rural villages can be turned into beautiful and prosperous places to live. . . . We may call such a drive the *Saemaul Undong*.' In short, local initiative was to be harnessed on a national scale throughout the South Korean countryside.

President Park and his advisers then instructed South Korean provincial governors and other regional officials to outline a series of self-help measures for the countryside. It was laid down that a centralised bureaucracy was to be avoided at all costs. The ROK's Ministry of Home Affairs was to co-ordinate and fund the movement. But the President's personal interest in the programme meant that progress was possible on the governmental level which would not otherwise have occurred. On the local level, with government backing, a system of appointing village and community leaders emerged. These men, with government backing, were to oversee Saemaul projects on a day-to-day basis.

During 1970-71 a number of pilot projects were begun in selected rural areas. At this time, most of the villages in the South Korean countryside were seen as underdeveloped. Initially, the government provided simple assistance such as cement for new roads and bridges. The traditional (but leaky) thatch was replaced by tile in many villages. Slowly, in the early 1970s the immemorial appearance of the Korean village began to change. A modern agricultural landscape with well-built homes, concrete access roads, and prosperous-looking farmers began to become the norm.

As the number of underdeveloped villages began to decline in this way, so the government began to sponsor more ambitious projects aimed at increasing national wealth. These measures included the building of small rural factories and cooperatives, together with modest electrification projects. Many farms were rebuilt and running water installed. The level of rural *per capita* wealth began to rise slowly both in itself and in relation to the urban sector of the South Korean economy. By now the Saemaul movement had spread into the remotest parts of the country.

At the beginning of the 1970s, average rural earnings were little more than half the earnings of those who lived in South Korea's towns and cities. But by 1976 the gap had closed, a tribute to the movement which had as its slogan 'Self-help, Hard Work and Cooperation'. On this base, the Saemaul movement has continued to improve the rural standard of living in South Korea.

Resolving a Historic Problem

Perhaps only by a brief reference to the Korean past can the full significance of the Saemaul movement be appreciated. As we saw earlier in our story, the early Yi kings had failed in their attempt at land reform. For many centuries, Korean agriculture remained stagnant. The vested interests of the great yangban landlords and the conservative Confucian ethic precluded progressive changes in Korean farming.

After 1910, the Japanese rulers of Korea instituted a land survey, and modernized the upper, more profitable sectors of Korean agriculture. But below this level, Japanese landlords continued to exploit Korean tenant farmers. When the Japanese left Korea in 1945, two outstanding problems thus remained to be solved on the land. The first was the con-tinuing widespread existence of tenant farming which precluded incentives to improve buildings and cultivation. The second was the drastic need for modernizing investment. Meanwhile, the traditional poverty of the Korean countryside remained despite all the political changes in Seoul.

Between 1947 and 1950, large areas of South Korean farming land (once held by the Japanese) were turned over to tenants by the American Military Government and by the post-1948 Syngman Rhee government. By 1950, as significant numbers of tenants became freeholders, the old tenancy problem was on its way to being solved.

However, further progress in modernizing Korean agriculture came to a halt in 1950 with the outbreak of the Korean War. During that conflict millions of farm animals were killed, thousands of farms destroyed, and irrigation works wrecked. There were two million displaced families in South Korea in 1953, many of them farmers. Postwar reconstruction was necessarily concentrated on rebuilding the war-damaged towns and cities, and in replacing damaged communications. Following the military revolution of 1961, in circumstances we have reviewed, the government found it imperative to concentrate on industrial growth and developing an export programme. But it was soon seen that the historic problems of the Korean countryside and its associated poverty could no longer be ignored on both economic and political grounds.

During the 1950s, the South Korean agricultural population comprised about 70 per cent of the total. By 1965, as the urban, industrial sector of the economy began to expand, the agricultural population still comprised 55 per cent of the national aggregate. Yet many farms, perhaps a third of the total, were really inefficient smallholdings of less than two acres. The harsh Korean winter which precluded productive work for two or three months of the year, and Korea's hilly terrain, all compounded the difficulties of Korean farming.

Moreover, wartime damage and dislocation, combined with traditional backwardness, meant that South Korea in the late 1960s was a net importer of rice, barley and other foodstuffs. Valuable foreign exchange was being expended on these food imports so distorting the entire structure of the balance of payments. The imbalance between town and country was underlined by the fact that economic growth in the rural sector was markedly less than the 10 per cent average annual growth for the economy as a whole in the late 1960s. Modernization of South Korean farming became essential.

In line with President Park's enthusiasm for the Saemaul

movement, the Third Five Year Economic Development Plan (1972–76) stressed balanced growth between town and country. A price support system was planned which would ensure that farmers received a guaranteed minimum on rice and grain products. The government also planned to invest about $2 billion in South Korean agriculture generally and to plan for national self-sufficiency in rice and barley. As the Saemaul movement continued to raise living standards, the gap between average urban and rural incomes was closed, as already noted, in 1976. By this time the agricultural sector growth rate was over 7 per cent. By 1980, the average rural family income had reached the equivalent of about $3,000.

While the Saemaul movement was instrumental in raising rural living standards in this way, the long-term objective of national self-sufficiency in food was given a new urgency by the oil crisis of 1973. Eventually, through improved irrigation techniques, better fertilizers, and the use of new, high-yield strains, South Korea became self-sufficient in rice by 1975. By the late 1970s, self-sufficiency in barley was attained as well.

Wider national trends since the mid-1970s have continued to improve the prosperity of the farming community. Outstanding amongst these trends is the continuing movement of population away from the country to the cities, and the consequent high urban demand for food products. By 1978, the rural sector comprised only 30 per cent of South Korea's population; by the early 1990s it is expected that only 20 per cent of the population will be working on the land.

As the thorough moderization of the South Korean countryside continues in this way, the Saemaul movement remains an indispensable part of the South Korean scene. The movement is currently concerned with two outstanding objectives in the continuing drive for ever-greater agricultural efficiency.

The first of these is the plan for the long-term rationalization of South Korea's many paddy fields into larger units. The second objective is the full mechanization of agriculture with the comprehensive introduction of power-tillers, rice harvesters, and other specially-designed machines.

It seems clear from these developments in the South Korean countryside that the Saemaul movement has been instrumental in raising living standards. In the wider context national self-sufficiency in basic foodstuffs has been achieved. Perhaps most significant of all, the historic problem of Korean rural poverty has been resolved in the ROK.

Political Problems

As South Korea's economic revolution continued in town and country during the 1970s, the government of President Park faced increasing political problems. Partly these problems were due to the very success of the government's economic policies. But these issues also had long-term implications for the stability of the ROK.

Successive governments in South Korea since 1961 have considered that democracy in South Korea should develop organically from its own national roots. This widely-shared view accounts of course for much of the popularity of the Saemaul movement. Other South Koreans, an increasing number as the country's society becomes more prosperous and pluralistic, feel that there should be faster progress towards Western-style liberal democracy. Honest differences between these viewpoints underlay the events of the 1970s, and continue to affect the political debate in South Korea.

President Park and the military who had underwritten South Korea's government since 1961 believed in general, as we have seen, that democracy must be qualified in the interests of political stability, economic progress and above all national security. The latter is especially important bearing in mind the self-proclaimed ambitions of North Korea's Kim Il Sung (see below). There is the indisputable fact that since 1953 South Korea has enjoyed a truce rather than a formal peace settlement.

Following his election as President in 1963, Park Chung Hee thus ruled as a strong executive. His Democratic Republican Party (DRP) controlled the National Assembly. Park was then elected for a second four-year term in 1967, once again by popular vote. This second electoral victory was followed in 1969 by a constitutional amendment which abolished the two-term limitation on the Presidency. The amendment was strongly criticised by the opposition New Democratic Party (NDP).

Park now won office for a third term in 1971, but it was only by a relatively narrow majority that he defeated Kim Dae Jung, the opposition candidate. Strong press criticism of the President was now routine, and another form of protest came in student riots.

But fundamentally President Park remained a popular leader and the ROK economy continued to thrive.

During 1971, events both domestic and foreign combined to toughen Park's rule. Internally, there were many anti-government protests on the university campuses of South Korea. Perhaps even more important was the clearly impending American withdrawal from South Vietnam and also President Nixon's coming visit to Peking which was announced in July 1971. In President Park's view these events might well presage a change in the balance of power in East Asia.

South Korean national policy now developed in two ways. Responding to the new mood of American *rapprochement* with China, President Park sanctioned contacts between Red Cross delegates from both North and South Korea at Panmunjom. Talks between these delegates began during September 1971 with the object of uniting divided families and solving other humanitarian problems. Following an agreed agenda, substantive Red Cross talks began at Panmunjom in August 1972. Already in August 1970, on the 25th anniversary of Korea's liberation, Park had suggested that North and South Korea solve their differences by peaceful competition.

The Red Cross talks were now to lead to further political contact between the two Koreas. In the wake of President Nixon's successful visit to Peking in February 1972, North and South Korean officials met in secret. On 4 July 1972, a Joint Communique announced the creation of a high-level North-South Coordinating Committee (NSCC) which would meet to bring about peaceful Korean unification without foreign interference. After this celebrated communique, ministerial-level talks to discuss procedural matters began at Panmunjom in November 1972. A 'hot line' had earlier been set up between Seoul and Pyongyang. These developments were unprecedented since the end of the Korean War.

But while attempting to negotiate with North Korea, President Park also acted to strengthen his position and to preserve, as he saw it, the stability and security of the ROK. During October 1972, the President suspended parts of the Constitution, declared martial law, and dissolved the National Assembly. He announced a new *Yushin* (Revitalizing) Constitution which enhanced the President's powers and provided for a six-year term of office with no limit on re-election.

Controversial Yushin Constitution

Under the new *Yushin* constitution, the President was elected by a popularly-chosen electoral college, the National Conference for Unification. As Head of State he was given unrestricted power to promulgate emergency decrees. The President was also given the right to indirectly nominate one-third of the members of the National Assembly. But the *Yushin* constitution also stated that the Republic of Korea was a democratic state, and that sovereignty rested in the people.

The new Constitution was approved by a national referendum, and in December 1972 Park Chung Hee was elected to a six-year term of office. So began South Korea's 'Fourth Republic'. Yet although Park had popular support for his new constitution, there was significant opposition. Martial Law was scrapped, but the President ruled largely by decree. Limitations on freedom of speech and assembly were resented by opposition groups in the churches, the universities and in some sections of the press. The new constitution was also opposed by the opposition NDP, now led by Kim Young Sam. There was also a storm of protest when the former opposition leader, Kim Dae Jung, was kidnapped in Tokyo and forcibly returned to Korea by South Korean agents in August 1973. This incident resulted in a protest from the Japanese government.

Following the breakdown of the North-South talks at Panmunjom in August 1973 a new phase of militancy began to characterise North Korean policy. As in the past such militancy had the effect of rallying support to the South Korean government. In August 1974 Park made new comprehensive reunification proposals to Pyongyang. He advocated a mutual nonaggression pact, free all-Korean elections, and freedom of movement between the two Koreas. But illustrating the tensions of the time, Park's wife was shot dead, as the President made this speech, by an assassin aiming at Park himself. It later emerged that the assassin was trained in North Korea.

In general, the continuing prosperity of the ROK economy ensured Park's continuing popularity after the breakdown of talks with the North in 1973. But a new phase of domestic unrest developed during 1975. Following the fall of Saigon on 30 April of that year, Park promulgated Emergency Decree No. 9 on 13 May 1975. The decree banned all criticism of the government and of the *Yushin* constitution. A number of dissidents were subsequently detained, and students came under close scrutiny by the authorities.

The discovery of a series of North Korean infiltration tunnels hewn under the DMZ partly validated Park's concern with national security. The opposition continued to call for a less authoritarian government and on 1 March 1976 a demonstration at Myong-dong Cathedral in Seoul received considerable attention. But the dissidents were contained for several years after this demonstration.

Following the end of President Park's six-year term of office under the *Yushin* constitution came his re-election in 1978. However, in the elections to the National Assembly in December that year the opposition NDP polled more votes than the government party. The ruling DRP was able to maintain its hold over the Assembly because one-third of its members were Presidential nominees under the *Yushin* system.

The following year, the steady expansion of the ROK economy was affected by inflation and the first signs of the world recession. The government moved to switch investment from heavy to light industry, and tried to boost consumer demand. Responding to world market forces, South Korean industrialists and entrepreneurs were encouraged to invest in electronics and other high-technology products. The general foundations of the economy remained good, and as we have seen, there was steady progress in the rural sector. In line with the Western economies, there was a gradual shift of resources from labour-intensive industry to capital-intensive new technology plants.

President Park undoubtedly faced a serious political crisis by the summer of 1979. The opposition stepped up its attacks following the elections of the previous December, and now called for Park's resignation and the dismantling of the *Yushin* constitution. The NDP leader, Kim Young Sam, denounced the Park regime as 'dictatorial' in a *New York Times* interview during September 1979. Kim was subsequently expelled from the Assembly; during October there were serious student riots in Pusan (and nearby Masan) which had to be controlled by the army.

Park now faced the worst domestic unrest since taking office in 1961. But he was a tough, resourceful and experienced leader and there was no reason why he should not ride out the storm. The Presidential advisers were divided with some urging firmness, and others conciliation towards the opposition. Amongst the latter group was apparently the Director of the KCIA, Kim Jae Kyu.

On the evening of 26 October 1979, President Park Chung Hee was shot dead by Kim Jae Kyu at a dinner in Seoul. An intensive enquiry later concluded that Kim assassinated the President as a prelude to launching a *coup d'etat*. In the event power passed according to the constitutional process to the Prime Minister, the former diplomat Choi Kyu Hah, who now became Acting President.

President Park, although sometimes a controversial figure, had presided over the transformation of the Republic of Korea into a strong modern, industrial state. This transformation had emphasised South Korea's vital strategic position in East Asia, and also the country's growing role in the world economy. But Park was also very much aware of the values of Korea's traditional Confucian culture with its emphasis on authority.

Following Park's death, South Korea went through a period of uncertainty, but stability was soon restored. The debate over the best form of government, begun in President Park's time, remains. But restraint and security remain the order of the day in view of what most South Koreans see as the threat from North Korea. It is to developments in North Korea during the period of South Korea's economic revolution that we must now turn.

Chapter Fourteen: The Beloved and Respected Leader

Throughout the period of South Korea's continuing economic revolution, the pressures from North Korea for national reunification on Pyongyang's terms have remained unceasing. Yet although open warfare between the two Koreas has been avoided since 1953, the intense political, military and economic rivalry remains.

This continuing inter-Korean tension is inseparable from the personality and ambitions of Kim Il Sung, North Korea's unchallenged ruler since the 1950s. It is Kim's ambition over many years to reunify Korea on his own terms which gives the tension within Korea its own unique quality. The tension is underlined by Kim Il Sung's apparently successful efforts over the past fifteen years to make his son, Kim Chong Il, his heir-apparent as ruler of the DPRK.

Whether or not Kim Chong Il succeeds his father, who celebrated his seventy sixth birthday in April 1988, remains to be seen. When rumours swept the world in November 1986 that Kim Il Sung had been assassinated it was assumed in many quarters that internal tensions and resentments over the succession plan had been responsible for Kim Il Sung's death. These reports were of course premature. Thus there remains the strong possibility of an effective succession, as a result of which the ideas and attitudes of Kim Il Sung will continue to influence profoundly events in Korea.

North Korea's 'Revolutionary Base'

To understand the development of Kim Il Sung's policies we must remember that following the 1953 armistice he was primarily concerned with North Korea's postwar reconstruction and above all with consolidating his own power. By 1960 Kim Il Sung had gained undisputed mastery over the North Korean Workers' Party; his control over the government and armed forces followed inevitably. His power was further cemented in 1966 when the post of Party Chairman was abolished and Kim Il Sung became Party Secretary-General, ruling through a new six-man Presidium of the KWP Politburo.

The growing resources of the North Korean economy and the military revolution of 1961 in South Korea seem to have hardened Kim's attitudes towards reunification. The DPRK embarked on an ambitious Seven Year Economic Plan in 1961, and on its conclusion the plan was extended for another three years to 1970. The general objective was to build a militarized society in North Korea so turning the country into a 'revolutionary base' for the forthcoming reunification of Korea under Kim Il Sung's aegis. This concept has remained constant in North Korean official thinking ever since.

Although North Korea's population was less than half that of the ROK, a ratio which remains unchanged to the present day, the North Korean armed forces were built up to become significantly larger than those of the ROK. The personality cult of Kim Il Sung was also intensified during the 1960s as part of this process of political and military mobilization.

Since the mid-1960s, therefore, the fear that the North Koreans may have both the intention and the capability of again invading the South has led the ROK and its American ally to look to their own defences. Most South Koreans believe that if Kim Il Sung were presented with the opportunity, he would not hesitate to order his troops to march south.

Reunification by Insurgency?

During the late, 1960s, as Kim Il Sung continued to stress his military line of 'fortifying the whole country', Pyongyang escalated its subversive activities and infiltration against the South. From about fifty incidents along the DMZ in 1966, the number jumped to over 500 in 1967. North Korean agents entered South Korea by crossing the DMZ but also from spy boats moving down the long South Korean coastline.

In January 1968, North Korea made one of its most provocative moves in the post-Korean War period. A team of about 30 specially trained North Korean commandos crossed the DMZ north of Seoul with orders to kill President Park of South Korea. Their destination was the Blue House, the South Korean Presidential Mansion. The commandos were within a mile of their objective before they were intercepted and most of them killed by the ROK security forces. A captured commando stated that the DPRK had organised a special unit of over 2,000 men to wage guerrilla warfare in South Korea as part of North Korea's reunification campaign.

Immediately following this attempted commando raid, the North Koreans seized the USS *Pueblo* off Wonsan on 23 January 1968. The 83-man crew of this naval intelligence vessel were then kept in North Korea for nearly a year. Later in 1968 the North Korean campaign came to a peak when over 100 North Korean guerrillas were landed on the east coast of the ROK near Ulchin. The invaders then fanned out into the Taebaek mountains.

These guerrillas were quickly eliminated by the ROK security agencies. But in April 1969 came a further incident when an US Navy EC-121 electronic intelligence aircraft was shot down over the Sea of Japan by North Korean interceptors. As North Korean infiltration southwards through the DMZ continued, the DPRK media emphasised the activity of the pro-Kim Il Sung 'United Revolutionary Party' within South Korea. This group was of course not a political party in the usual sense, but a group of agents who were mostly arrested by the South Korean police.

By 1970 it was clear that North Korea's policy of 'reunification by insurgency' was completely counter productive. Kim Il Sung's agents and commandos had been rounded up by the South Koreans, while President Park had formed a new national home guard or militia of two million men so further strengthening the ROK's internal security. Abroad, North Korean policy was condemned for its militancy and as a threat to peace in the Far East. The United States sent more military aid to South Korea. These were hardly the objectives of Kim Il Sung's policy. But to consolidate further his position, Kim Il Sung became President of the DPRK in late 1972.

Moreover, there were significant changes in the political environment of the Far East during 1970–71. An American rapprochement with China was imminent, as we have seen, as well as an United States withdrawal from Indochina. The Soviet Union, for its part, was calling for 'peaceful coexistence' with the

West and pressing for a whole range of strategic agreements with the United States in particular under the general banner of *'detente'*. During August 1970, in line with the new mood in world politics, President Park called for peaceful competition between the two Koreas and urged North Korea to end its despatch of armed insurgents into South Korea.

For a short time, North Korean reunification policy seemed to follow these larger trends. The insurgency campaign was called off, and inter-Korean Red Cross talks began at Panmunjom in September 1971. Following the Joint North-South Communique of 4 July 1972, senior delegates from Seoul and Pyongyang met at Panmunjom during 1972–73 to discuss peaceful Korean reunification. But all senior delegate meetings at Panmunjom, both on the Red Cross and on the political level, were unilaterally ended by North Korea on 28 August 1973. The North Korean radio resumed its call for a South Korean revolution as a means of national reunification.

Since that time, North Korean policy towards the ROK has alternated, often bewilderingly, between threats, provocative action, and suggestions of renewed inter-Korean talks which once again resumed on a regular basis at Panmunjom and elsewhere in 1984 (see below).

But certain lines of North Korean policy remain unchanged. Thus North Korea has continued to maintain an 'independent' foreign policy between the Soviet Union and China while obtaining military aid and economic credits from both the great Communist powers. North Korea has also developed extensive diplomatic relations with third world countries in an attempt to gain international support for its reunification policies.

Above all, the removal of American forces from South Korea remains the paramount objective of North Korean policy. if American troops were withdrawn from South Korea, together with their supporting air units, the military advantage within the peninsula could tip to the North.

At the same time, North Korea promotes inter-Korean talks on a number of subjects, presumably with the objective of weakening the consistent ROK stand against North Korean reunification policies. From time to time, North Korea has stated that its reunification policy is a peaceful one. But it would be fairer to describe it as a policy which advocates both peaceful and violent means to achieve the goal of Korean reunification under Communist auspices.

The Thoughts of Kim Il Sung

North Korean policies on reunification thus often seem contradictory. But certain enduring themes emerge quite consistently over the past thirty years which must be attributed largely to Kim Il Sung himself. Current day-to-day manifestations of North Korean policy often reflect one or another of these themes, sometimes in combination.

Firstly, in order to stress that he is a creature neither of his Soviet nor of his Chinese allies Kim Il Sung claims that he has 'creatively adapted' classical Marxism-Leninism to Korean conditions through his concept of *Chuche* (Self-Reliance). Kim attributes North Korea's economic progress since the Korean War to *Chuche* as a guiding ideology.

Chuche, as an indigenous Korean approach, is contrasted with the Western, cosmopolitan sympathies of South Korea, and is thus an important factor in North Korea's reunification strategy. The promotion of *Chuche* dates back to 1955. During the 6th Korean Workers' Party Congress of 1980 it was declared officially that *Chuche* took precedence over Marxism-Leninism as the only guiding concept of the KWP.

Second, Kim Il Sung is the subject of a personality cult which claims him as a brilliant strategist and political leader who fought successfully against the Japanese colonialists and the American imperialists. He is continually referred to in North Korea as 'the genius of revolution . . . the iron-willed commander . . . the beloved and respected leader'. He is claimed as a world-class Communist leader and ideologist on the level of Marx, Lenin, Stalin and Mao. As part of this cult, Kim's birthplace at Mangyongdae, not far from Pyongyang, has been established as a national shrine. Thousands of statues of Kim Il Sung bedeck the North Korean countryside, while overlooking Pyongyang stands a statue of Kim over 500 foot tall.

The enormous claims made for Kim Il Sung usually ignore the Soviet role in liberating North Korea in 1945 and also Kim's crucial debt to the Chinese during the Korean War. But this outsize personality cult, which surpasses the devotions paid to Stalin and Mao during their lifetime, plays a central role in making North Korea probably the most highly mobil-ized and militarized country in the Communist world. Thus according to a statement issued by the Central Committee of the Korean Workers' Party in early 1976, 'The whole party, the whole country, and the entire people are firmly united like a monolithic organism breathing,

THE BELOVED AND RESPECTED LEADER 165

thinking, and acting only in accordance with the revolutionary ideas of the great leader. . . . .'

Significantly, since the mid-1970s, Kim Il Sung has developed dynastic ambitions, promoting his son Kim Chong Il to succeed him. Although details of the younger Kim's life are sparse, he was probably born in 1942, either in Manchuria or Soviet Siberia. He is believed to have studied for two years during the late 1950s at a military air force school in East Germany, and then graduated from Kim Il Sung University, Pyongyang, in 1964.

At first Kim Chong Il was referred to anonymously in the North Korean media as the 'party centre'. But in October 1980 he was given a series of key party positions all held simultaneously; the fourth position in the Presidium of the Politburo, the second position in the Party Secretariat after his father, and the third position in the Military Affairs Commission after his father and the defence minister. During 1981 Kim Chong Il was promoted to the second position in the Presidium. His emergence from anonymity combined with these high posts made him the official heir-apparent of Kim Il Sung.

Since that time Kim Chong Il has become the subject of an all-embracing personality cult which is surpassed only by the cult of his father. The succession is justified officially by the claim that Kim Chong Il has alone gone through the historic preparatory stage to emulate the Great Leader and thus the son 'is the real incarnation of Kim Il Sung'.

Third, over a period of decades North Korea has for diplomatic consumption, promoted a reunification policy based on the establishment of a confederal republic based on a loose merger of the two Korean states, in which North and South would have equal representation. In commemoration of one of the great dynasties of Korean history, this system is sometimes called the 'Democratic Confederal Republic of Koryo'. Sometimes Pyongyang advocates 'a whole nation conference' of many political parties and social organizations to discuss reunification. This policy contrasts with the South Korean official view that reunification is best promoted initially through inter-governmental contacts which would culminate in free elections. In Seoul's view, 'a whole nation conference' as advocated by Pyongyang is a propaganda device.

A *fourth* and perhaps central theme in Kim Il Sung's programme is the often-repeated call for the 'revolutionary reunification' of Korea. Essentially Kim envisages, and works for, a

Marxist-Leninist revolution in South Korea. In this upheaval, the KWP would lead an 'united front' composed of a wide spectrum of students, intellectuals and other 'democratic elements'. In doctrinal terms, this South Korean revolution would be a 'national liberation revolution' in that it would lead to the expulsion of the United States presence from Korea; but it would also be a 'people's democratic revolution' against the Korean supporters of US imperialism in particular and Western influence in general.

Following the triumph of the revolution in South Korea, national reunification would emerge as naturally as the reunification of Vietnam was accomplished after the fall of Saigon in April 1975. Thus according to a speech by Kim Il Sung in February 1968, 'Only when we use force of arms can we gain power. We cannot gain power simply by holding elections. The most decisive and positive form of struggle is the struggle with arms for the liberation of our people.' The same thought is seen in an address by the North Korean Armed Forces Chief of Staff, General Oh Guk-ryol, on 24 April 1986. He stated that his forces would achieve 'by every means possible, the national reunification of the Korean peninsula through its struggle against South Korea'.

A *fifth* constant in Kim Il Sung's reunification strategy is the belief that a revolutionary situation can be created in South Korea by the assassination of the ROK President. Thus in 1968, North Korea sent a team of commandos to kill President Park; six years later Park's wife was shot in yet another assassination attempt. The most spectacular North Korean assassination attempt came on 10 October 1983 during an official visit of South Korea's President Chun Doo Hwan to Rangoon, Burma.

In a massive bomb blast engineered by two North Korean agents, four South Korean Cabinet ministers and thirteen senior civil servants were killed. President Chun missed death by minutes. It seems reasonable to believe that these successive assassination attempts against the ROK Head of State must inevitably have had Kim Il sanction. This violent element in Pyongyang's policy was underlined when North Korean terrorists destroyed the South Korean airliner, KAL Flight 858 over the Indian Ocean on 29 November 1987, an incident which led to widespread condemnation of North Korea.

The Continuing Impasse

The remarkable range and consistency of Kim Il Sung's efforts to reunify Korea have borne little fruit over the years. The South Korean people remain resistant to all appeals from the North and in particular remember the apparently innocuous peaceful reunification proposals from Pyongyang that immediately preceded the launching of the Korean War. The assassination of 17 South Korean ministers and officials in Rangoon in October 1983 is still fresh in the public mind.

Thus ever since the breakdown of the high-level North-South Coordinating committee talks in August 1973 the deadlock between the two Koreas remains. This is despite new inter-Korean contacts since 1984 (see below). But in the context of Kim Il Sung's general approach to Korean reunification the aftermath of the 1972–73 talks is instructive.

In November 1974, South Korean soldiers discovered by chance the exit point of an infiltration tunnel leading from North Korea deep underneath the DMZ to South Korean territory. The tunnel was discovered near Korangpo, north of the Imjin in the sensitive western sector of the front. A second tunnel was discovered four months later near Chorwon, at the western corner of the strategic 'Iron Triangle' area on the central front. Later, in 1978, a third North Korean tunnel was found near Panmunjom, its exit point barely thirty miles from Seoul. During 1980 yet another North Korean tunnel under the DMZ was located north of Seoul.

All four tunnels, in the view of experts, were major engineering projects and could have been used to infiltrate commandos as well as regular North Korean troops with some of their equipment into South Korea. The very length of the tunnels, several miles long, and the evident difficulty of construction, indicates that the tunnelling programme was probably begun during the early 1970s, and continued during the North-South 'peaceful reunification' talks of 1972–73. Since 1975, the sound of muffled explosions has been heard along the DMZ indicating that the tunnelling programme probably continues. Kim Il Sung has told Japanese visitors to Pyongyang that the existing tunnels were built to evacuate 'patriots' from South Korea in case of war.

The discovery of this North Korean tunnelling programme at the end of 1974 was followed a few months later in April 1975 by the collapse of South Vietnam. In a public speech in Peking, Kim Il Sung stated that if a revolution took place in South Korea,

North Korea would 'strongly support the Korean people'. If the enemy were to start a war, Kim went on, North Korea would answer the challenge with war. Korea would then be reunited.

In an effort to defuse the tension created by this speech, the American Defence Secretary, James Schlesinger, visited Seoul in May 1975. He reaffirmed the American commitment to South Korea, and stated that in the event of an attack from the North, the use of tactical atomic weapons could not be ruled out. Schlesinger later said that in a new Korean conflict, the United States would not become involved in 'endless ancillary military operations' but rather 'go for the heart' of its opponent's power. In this way the commitment of the United States to South Korea was emphasised in a way that Kim Il Sung could not ignore.

Subsequently, the advent of the Jimmy Carter administration in January 1977 was followed by a pledge to withdraw American ground forces from South Korea. The American-South Korean Mutual Defence Treaty of 1953 was to remain in force, but many South Koreans and high American officials as well were profoundly uneasy at this policy given the ambiguities in North Korean reunification policy. Pressure also from Japan was responsible for the reversal of the troop withdrawal policy in 1979.

With the arrival of Ronald Reagan in the White House in January 1981, there came a new affirmation of the American commitment to South Korea. President Chun Doo Hwan visited Washington, and testified that the friendship between the two countries was as strong as during the Korean War. Later, in November 1983, President Reagan visited South Korea, including the DMZ, and again reaffirmed America's commitment, stating for good measure that South Korea's security was vital to peace and stability in North East Asia and to America's defence.

For obvious, political, military, and strategic reasons, there can be little doubt that over a period of many years Kim Il Sung has seen in the United States the most formidable barrier to his many plans for Korean reunification. The United States fills a special place in North Korean demonology, for without an American withdrawal from South Korea all Kim Il Sung's reunification proposals remain a dream.

During 1974, North Korea attempted to overcome this problem by proposing direct talks with the United States to conclude a non-aggression agreement and the withdrawal of American forces from South Korea. But South Korea would only attend these talks as an observer. Subsequently Presidents Ford, Carter and Reagan all affirmed that the United States would not negotiate with North Korea in the absence of South Korea.

Eventually, after an entire decade, in January 1984 North Korea proposed in its 'Tripartite Conference Proposal' that the two Koreas and the United States should all negotiate as equal partners to solve the Korean problem. In Pyongyang's view, a formal peace treaty between North Korea and the United States would be followed by an American withdrawal from South Korea, and a non-aggression treaty between the two Koreas. These developments would lead to a reunification dialogue between Pyongyang and Seoul.

Although the North Korean intentions behind such proposals remain in doubt given the history of the past forty years, some limited progress has been made in recent years in renewed inter-Korean contacts. Such contacts are in line with Seoul's belief that only gradual negotiations between the two Koreas can lead to a meaningful easing of tension in Korea.

Thus during 1985 three plenary or full-scale Red Cross meetings were held between North and South Korea, as well as four rounds of economic talks, and two contacts on the possibility of holding parliamentary talks between the two Koreas. These talks were held in Seoul, Pyongyang, and Panmunjom, but no substantive progress was possible on the economic and parliamentary issues. The one result achieved was a Red Cross agreement for the exchange of a limited number of visitors and performing artists to Seoul and Pyongyang.

In addition during October 1985 talks between North and South Korea were held at Lausanne, Switzerland, to discuss the possible co-hosting of the 1988 Seoul Olympics. After four meetings (the last in July 1987), no agreement was reached. Later North Korean statements referred to the Olympics as the product of an imperialist plan to divide the Korean peninsula. However, North Korea appeared isolated on this issue when, in January 1988, the Soviet Union and China announced their intention to compete in the Seoul Olympics. In early 1986, North Korea once again broke off the inter-Korean dialogue giving as its reason the annual 'Team Spirit' defensive exercises held by the South Koreans and the United States.

Underlying all North Korea's reunification proposals over past decades is the belief that in the general political and economic arena North Korea's system would win the implied competition between the two Koreas.

These hopes of Kim Il Sung's have not materialized. South Korea has emerged as a major regional power in East Asia, while during the 1970s North Korea's command economy reached an impasse due to the very rigidity of the system combined with over-high defence spending. During the 1970s, North Korea had to default on many of its international loans, so precluding any further foreign borrowing on a significant scale.

The disparity between the two economies was sharply shown in the trade figures for 1980 when overall South Korean trade, both imports and exports, reached $40 billion. The corresponding figure for North Korea was $2 billion. According to the National Unification Board in Seoul, in 1984 the Gross National Product of South Korea was $81 billion, that of North Korea $14 billion. The *per capita* GNP of the South in the same year was $1,999, that of the North $762. Other estimates broadly concur with these figures. Thus the contrast between the vigorously expanding southern economy and the stagnation of the north has become an apparently permanent feature.

In political and economic terms, therefore, the race for modernization between North Korea's command economy and South Korea's market economy has been won decisively by the ROK. North Korea's reunification proposals, for some of the reasons outlined here, have no appeal in South Korea. But the implied threat of violence and force in Kim Il Sung's reunification policies, pursued over many years, makes it impossible for South Korea to ignore events in Pyongyang.

Thus over forty years after the division of Korea in 1945 the problem which above all preoccupies the leaders of South Korea is not political, constitutional, or economic, central as these issues are to the future of the ROK. The overriding problem for South Korea is the problem of security, and it is with this fundamental issue that we close our story.

Chapter Fifteen:
The Problem of Security

Following the death of President Park Chung Hee on 26 October 1979, South Korea went through a very difficult period of political and economic uncertainty. Park's immediate successor, as we have seen, was the former Premier Choi Kyu Hah, who now became Acting President. The government quickly decided that under the 1972 Constitution the electoral college, the National Conference on Unification, should meet to elect a new President with full powers. Choi was then formally elected President on 6 December 1979. He was legally entitled to serve out the rest of Park's term of office and so could stay as President until 1984.

The election of President Choi gave a firm legitimacy to subsequent events, but his term of office very soon became an interregnum. Inevitably, President Choi, a former diplomat, lacked a power base. His predecessor, President Park, had dominated the political and economic power centres of the Republic as well as the bureaucracy, and above all Park had the confidence of the military elite from which he had emerged. President Choi had none of these vital attributes.

President Choi was also faced with an increasingly vocal demand from the political parties for a swift move away from the authoritarian *Yushin* constitution of 1972 towards full, Western-style democracy. In the van of the parties were 'the three Kims': Kim Chong Pil, who was elected leader of the ruling Democratic Republican Party in place of Park; Kim Young Sam, the resourceful leader of the opposition New Democratic Party; and Kim Dae Jung, the opposition leader who had narrowly defeated Park in the 1971 presidential election, and who was now a rival of Kim Young Sam's.

In the weeks following Park's death there was thus an increasing consensus in the National Assembly on the necessity of reform. In particular the opposition parties called for a new constitution based on a popularly-elected President, the reduction of the presidential term from 6 to 4 years; and a restriction on the emergency powers of the Executive.

President Choi was in favour of some reform, and immediately following his election he rescinded Emergency Decree No. 9, Park's unpopular catch-all decree, and said that detainees under this measure would be released. But Choi was also a cautious politician, and in his inaugural speech on 21 December 1979 he promised a new constitution in about a year followed by elections. This new constitution, the President stressed, must preserve both national security and social justice.

But events were now to demonstrate that there was no national agreement within South Korea on a rapid advance to Western-style democracy. The political parties were divided on the speed of this process, while the military elite who had underwritten the Park regime believed that national security would be fundamentally compromised if reform went too quickly. At the same time, the unfolding of the world recession, and the development of economic trends that antedated Park's death meant that the South Korean economy was in trouble. Production was beginning to fall, and inflation rising. Another major problem was the rising price of imported oil at the end of 1979.

The Advent of Chun Doo Hwan

On 12 December 1979, about six weeks after the death of President Park, troops under the command of Major General Chun Doo Hwan, the Head of the Defence Security Command, arrested General Chung Seung Hwa, the Army Chief of Staff. Combat troops loyal to Chun Doo Hwan then occupied the area of key government offices including the Presidential Blue House in central Seoul.

General Chun's command was a high-level counter-intelligence agency and he had been in charge of the investigation into Park's death. The Army Chief of Staff was arrested, with the approval of President Choi, because of his alleged involvement in the death of President Park. General Chung was later sentenced to ten years in jail, but afterwards pardoned.

THE PROBLEM OF SECURITY

General Chung's arrest on 12 December 1979 had two important effects. The first was that Major General Chun Doo Hwan became the dominant personality within the South Korean armed forces. The second was that the military as a whole had moved to fill the power vacuum that had developed in the aftermath of President Park's death. General Chun was born in 1931, and came from a farming family near Taegu. He represented a powerful group of professional military officers, the core of whom like himself had graduated with the eleventh class of 1955 from the Korean Military Academy. This was the first class to take a full four-year course.

Following Chun's coup within the military establishment, over thirty senior officers were removed or retired, and the intelligence and security services reorganised. In particular, the KCIA, centrally implicated in Park's death, was downgraded and placed under the command of a senior Army officer loyal to General Chun.

As General Chun consolidated his power, political unrest in South Korea gathered momentum. During May 1980, large-scale student riots in Seoul and other cities were followed by a rising in Kwangju, the capital of South Cholla province in south-west Korea.

Responding to these events, on 17 May 1980 President Choi promulgated a decree establishing a state of 'extraordinary martial law'. With the President as Chairman, a 'Special Committee for National Security Measures' took over the direction of the government. A majority of this Special Committee was composed of senior military men; its 'Standing Committee', an executive group, was chaired by General Chun. President Choi, meanwhile, stated that social unrest would only encourage North Korea to attack the ROK.

This latter factor was undoubtedly in the minds of General Chun and his associates who now took strong measures to end the spreading unrest. Mass student rioting was for the most part stopped by the expedient of closing most universities. The Kwangju rising was suppressed by army units, but with a severity that continues to make this unhappy event a controversial episode in recent South Korean history. Kim Chong Pil and Kim Young Sam were investigated and forced to resign as the heads of the two main political parties. Other leading officials from both parties were accused of corruption. Kim Dae Jung was arrested and charged with offences against the national security law, including sedition. he was sentenced to death (but later reprieved). In effect, the two main political parties of the Park era were dissolved.

With General Chun's approval, a widespread 'purification campaign' was launched against corrupt officials, bureaucrats and politicians. This campaign was seen by the military as a cleansing of the body politic and was analagous to the earlier campaign sponsored by General Park and his associates during 1961–62. The press and the media generally were also affected by this purification campaign which altogether resulted in thousands of dismissals.

During August 1980, Chun now emerged as President of South Korea. He was first promoted a full, four-star general, and following the resignation of President Choi on 16 August, Chun was given the endorsement as next President by the ROK Chiefs of Staff, a necessary ritual. Chun then formally retired from the Army and was elected President on 27 August by the electoral college, the National Conference for Unification. The Acting Premier, Park Choong Hoon, was Acting President during the transition.

In his inaugural speech a few days later the new President, wbo was now also Commander-in-Chief, pledged himself to the creation of a democratic welfare state, the drafting of a new constitution, and elections in early 1981. Like Park, Chun promised to work for peaceful Korean reunification, and like Park again the new President stressed that political democracy in South Korea would have to develop in conformity with Korea's own traditions.

The new draft constitution reflected criticisms of the years with no provision for re-election, there was a limit on the proposed emergency powers of the Presidency, but provision was also made for indirect Presidential election by a popularly chosen electoral college. This constitution was approved by a national referendum on 22 October 1980. Political parties were now allowed again. in the national elections for the new electoral college in February 1981, Chun's newly Democratic Justice Party had a large majority.

In early March 1981, Chun Doo Hwan was formally elected President for seven years under the new constitution of the ROK's 'Fifth Republic'. Chun was also the fifth President of South Korea since its founding in 1948.

South Korea During the 1980s

President Chun Doo Hwan assumed his high office when South Korea was adversely affected by the world recession. But by administrative reforms, by reducing the government's role in economic matters, and by stressing market competition in order to make more efficient use of existing resources, the South Korean economy has continued to expand in both the industrial and rural sectors. By 1985 the *per capita* gross national product was over $2,000.

Barring unforseen events, there seems no reason why the economic progress of the 1960s and the 1970s should not be sustained. The Sixth Five Year Economic Development Plan (1987–91) envisages a growth rate of over 7 per cent. Underwritten by hard work and indigenous South Korean skills and entrepreneurial talent, the ROK economy has become an integral and valued part of the world economy as a whole.

In the arena of South Korea's political development, President Chun faced perhaps an even more difficult task than lifting the economy out of the downturn of the early 1980s. He repeatedly stated that the peaceful transition of power after his seven-year term as President ended in February 1988 was the central test of his administration. Only by such peaceful transition will it be possible to claim that democracy has taken root in South Korea.

President Chun also attempted to steer a firm path between the traditionalist, authoritarian ethos of the military elite and the ever-increasing demand for full Western-style democracy with a directly-elected President. This course has not been easy. In April 1986 Chun indicated that early constitutional change might be possible. But on 13 April 1987 Chun stated that no changes in the current constitutional system would be contemplated until after the 1988 Summer Olympics were held at Seoul. The reason given for this decision was to avoid the appearance of national disunity in the run-up to the Olympics. Until then, the present method of indirect presidential election through an electoral college was to remain.

The opposing viewpoints on political reform in South Korea are not purely a result of the events of the past thirty years. There is a much older context for these differences. In line with the teachings of Confucius Korean traditionalists see personal freedom in the Western sense as one, but only one, of the prerequisites of virtue which also assumes social harmony and individual restraint. The opposition to President Chun believed with equal conviction that South Korea's social and economic progress in the past generation must be matched by decisive measures of reform.

Yet it should be stressed that more than any political or constitutional issue it is the problem of security that pre-occupies the government of the Republic of Korea. That is why the widespread student riots which followed President Chun's postponement of the constitutional dialogue in April 1987 aroused such apprehension in the governing elite. However, such was the scale of these demonstrations that President Chun reversed his earlier position and agreed to constitutional reform. As a result a new South Korean president was chosen in December 1987 by direct elections. But whatever the political regime in the ROK, the risk remains that internal dissent plays into the hands of an implacable enemy in a precariously divided country, and that the final result of such dissent could be chaos and war.

The Korean Military Balance

It is in this context of security that we end our story as we began it. For in our introduction we noted that Korea's traditional position as a land bridge between the Asian continent and the Pacific Ocean has long made the country a focus of rivalry between more powerful neighbours. Today four of the largest nations in the world, China, the Soviet Union, Japan and the United States are involved in one way or another with events in Korea. Since the present division of Korea along the Military Demarcation Line represents the current balance of power in the Far East generally any forcible attempt to alter this balance would probably have global repercussions. Korea has been the scene of three wars since the late nineteenth century and today the country has become one of the most heavily armed areas in the world.

It is this reality that underlies South Korean concern 'with North Korean policy. The cost of a new Korean War would be beyond calculation bearing in mind that the conflict of 1950–53 resulted in about four million casualties.

This complex and dangerous security problem has two broad aspects. There is firstly the military balance within Korea itself and secondly the wider balance of power in the Far East generally. Both are intimately related.

According to *The Military Balance* for 1985–86 published by the

London-based International Institute for Strategic Studies, the opposing sides in the Korean peninsula are roughly equivalent. Neither side possesses the capability of launching a major offensive against the other without foreign assistance. Yet despite North Korea's population of slightly less than half that of the ROK, its total armed forces number about 838,000 as opposed to South Korea's 598,000. North Korea has 24 infantry divisions, as opposed to South Korea's 19 divisions, a larger air force, and signigicantly greater numbers of tanks and artillery. *The Military Balance* notes that North Korea has over 3,000 tanks, as opposed to about 1,200 deployed by the ROK.

There is also the factor that North Korea possesses large unconventional forces wbich could be deployed, at least in theory, behind the DMZ through tunnels or landed on the South Korean coastline. Given North Korea's appreciable industrial base, Kim Il Sung has the capability of fighting a brief, blitzkrieg war against South Korea without external resupply.

The chief security problem facing the ROK is the unique vulnerability of Seoul. For the political and industrial heart of South Korea, a city of over eight million, lies only thirty miles south of the DMZ. The population and industrial centres of North Korea, on the contrary, are about 150 miles north of the DMZ. A North Korean surprise attack across the DMZ in the western sector might therefore result in at least a partial occupation of Seoul with all the dislocation consequent upon such an event.

Yet South Korea possesses some distinct defensive advantages. Between the DMZ and Seoul lies the barrier of the Imjin River. A North Korean armoured attack would probably have to be channelled along the two historic invasion corridors which lead to Seoul. The first of these avenues leads from Kaesong to Munsan, and the second from Chorwon southwards to Uijongbu. Both these corridors, as we have seen, were used by the North Koreans in 1950. Needless to say, both these approaches are heavily and effectively fortified by South Korean and American troops, which was not the case in 1950. The hilly terrain between these invasion routes also favours the defence, providing the weather allowed full deployment of the ROK and American air forces.

Additionally, South Korea has a larger, more flexible, and more sophisticated economy than the North. The ROK population base is twice that of North Korea, which has probably reached its maximum, optimal military posture in relation to the

South. North Korea has already lost the modernization contest with the South, and after the end of the 1980s its relative military advantages, despite its intense, totalitarian mobilization measures, will inevitably decline. Moreover, there can be no assurance that China and Russia will support Kim Il Sung as they did in 1950. But some analysts consider that as time works against North Korea in this way, so grows the possibility of a desperate, pre-emptive offensive against the ROK.

Central to any assessment of the military balance in Korea is the role of the United States in offsetting North Korea's military advantages. America helps its South Korean ally in three ways. There is the Mutual Defence Treaty of 1953 which promises the full moral and political help of the United States in the event of an external armed attack. Secondly, there is a wide-ranging American Military Assistance Programme aimed at the full modernization of the ROK armed forces. Under this category, the latest aircraft, missiles, tanks, and other equipment are supplied under successive five-year programmes.

Most important of all is the American deployment of ground forces in South Korea. About 40,000 men are involved in this deployment, the heart of the American commitment. Some 15,000 men of the US 2nd Infantry Division are placed south of the Imjin along the access route from North Korea through Kaesong and Munsan to Seoul. One battalion is based north of the Imjin, on the south of the DMZ, so providing a guard detail for the United Nations personnel stationed at Panmunjom.

The American forces in South Korea also include about 8,000 personnel from the US Air Force which maintains the equivalent of a full wing of tactical fighter aircraft, some based at Kunsan, on the south-west coast of Korea, and others at Osan, south of Seoul. Other American forces provide intelligence, logistic, communications, and other specialized assistance to the ROK armed forces. US Navy personnel in South Korea liase with the ROK Navy and arrange coordination with the US Seventh Fleet.

Contingency planning over many years covers the possibility of rapid American ground, sea, and air reinforcement from Japan, bases in the Pacific Command, and even from the continental United States. The deliberate placing of the 2nd Division covering Seoul means that in the event of a North Korean invasion these American troops would inevitably act as a strategic tripwire.

The deployment of American ground troops in South Korea

for deterrence and defence is underwritten by an unified command structure through which most of the South Korean armed forces come under US command and control. These arrangements go back to the early days of the Korean War. In the event of war, the decisions of the President of the United States would devolve through the Commanding General, US Forces, Korea. This four-star general is also Commander of the US Eighth Army, and Commander-in-Chief of the United Nations Command which, composed of South Korean troops and token contingents from the Korean War allies, oversees the truce in the DMZ.

Through this chain of command orders would descend in an emergency from the American Commander in Korea to the American Lieutenant General who heads the ROK/US Combined Forces Command (CFC). This command comprises most of the South Korean army, as well as the US 2nd Division.

Finally, the American forces in Korea include a tactical nuclear weapons capability which probably comprises about 700 or more nuclear warheads. Precise details are naturally a secret. The warheads are shared between American Army and Air Force bases in South Korea, deployed some distance south of the DMZ. Delivery systems include Honest John surface-to-surface missiles, F-4 Phantoms of the US Air Force, and 155mm artillery of the US Army. The 7th Fleet, which often sails in Korean waters, also has nuclear capability.

It is through all these means that the military balance, and peace, are preserved in Korea.

The Shifting Balance of Power

The military balance in Korea which we have outlined is but part of the wider balance of power in the Far East which comprises the finely balanced security interests of the four great regional powers. Historically this wider balance of power dates from the defeat of Imperial Japan in 1945. The United States then established a virtual protectorate over Japan and the Western Pacific.

By its defence of South Korea during 1950–53 the United States demonstrated its belief that the security of Japan and the ROK were closely linked. It was also shown that a stable political order in North East Asia was inseparable from American security interests and above all that a Communist-controlled Korea would decisively threaten the regional balance of power. The Japanese peace treaty of 1951, the simultaneous Japanese-American security pact, and the 1953 defence treaty between America and South Korea were the diplomatic underpinnings of a new regional security system that has lasted to the present.

It remains true that a Korean peninsula controlled by Pyongyang would be as grave a threat to the regional balance as in 1950. The American control of the maritime perimeter extending from the Aleutians through Japan to the Philippines would be compromised. It is control of this zone that enables the United States to maintain the regional balance of power. The growing commercial importance of the Asia-Pacific basin only underlines these strategic factors. So Korea retains its age-old strategic importance in the region.

Since about 1975, the continuing buildup of Soviet forces by land, sea and air in the region threatens this wider balance of power. The United States is therefore doubly sensitive to developments in Korea. Especially as in an age of a shifting power balance there can no longer be any obligatory assumption of American military superiority in the Western Pacific. But how do Japan, China, and the Soviet Union see their security interests in this intricate pattern at the centre of which lies Korea?

There can be little doubt that Japan sees its strategic interests as largely those of the United States. Although Japan is naturally hesitant for obvious historical reasons about making pronouncements on Korea's strategic importance, relations between Tokyo and Seoul grow closer. In 1969, the joint communique between President Nixon and the then Japanese premier, Eisaku Sato, stated that the security of the Republic of Korea was vital to Japan.

Successive Japanese administrations have reaffirmed this policy, especially as Japan is now committed tentatively to defending the 'straits and sea-lanes' around its islands against the USSR, a policy not possible without South Korean help.

In the political arena, President Chun Doo Hwan's Tokyo visit in September 1984 was notable for apologetic words from Emperor Hirohito and Prime Minister Yasuhiro Nakasone over Japan's past role in Korea. South Korea's current defence policy was also supported by the Japanese in a joint communique published at this time. As regional defence planning becomes increasingly elaborate between Japan and the United States, so the existing military balance in Korea becomes vital for Tokyo.

Japanese commercial interest in South Korea increases from year to year. Japanese historians point out that in the past, and with the exception of the Pacific War, all significant threats to Japan came from the north through Korea. To be sure, the current Soviet buildup in the Kurile Islands, immediately north of Hokkaido, is an important matter to Tokyo. But Korea remains the historic route through which continental powers could mortally threaten Japan.

Thus for Japan the emergence of an unified Korea under Communist auspices would present a major strategic, political and economic challenge. Hence the identity of interest between the United States and Japan in supporting the integrity of the Republic of Korea.

Although Moscow and Peking support formally the concept of peaceful Korean reunification under Pyongyang, there can be little doubt that both China and Russia prefer, for the time being, the *status quo* in Korea. Both countries have, indeed, developed tentative contacts with the ROK. The Chinese and Russian leaders probably believe that any change in the existing situation in Korea might play into the other's hands. For both Moscow and Peking, a Korea unified under the other's auspices would present a major security problem. So the Sino-Soviet rivalry helps to maintain the balance of forces in the Korean peninsula.

There are however, differences of emphasis in the attitudes of Moscow and Peking to North Korea. For racial, cultural, and historical reasons the relationship between China and North Korea is very close. But on the other hand, China's growing links with the United States and Japan, and its determined efforts to become a part of the international community gives Peking a vested interest in the maintenance of the *status quo* in Korea.

As opposed to these increasingly shared interests between America, Japan and China, the Soviet Union works slowly but certainly to undermine the American-sponsored balance of power in the Far East.

The Soviets make no secret of their objectives. The modern, late-model armaments which North Korea uses to threaten South Korea are mostly of Soviet manufacture. Since 1975, Soviet vessels have used Najin (Rashin) in north-east Korea as a transit port; since 1985 Soviet military aircraft have overflown North Korean air space en route from Vladivostok to Soviet bases in Indochina. It was reported during 1986 that Soviet naval vessels may now visit Nampo (formerly Chinnampo) on North

Korea's west coast, another sign of the growing military links between the two countries. There is a clear community of strategic interest between Moscow and Pyongyang.

A time may come, therefore, when the Soviet Union will take the risk of backing a North Korean adventure against the ROK. It seems unlikely that the Soviet leaders have forgotten the strategic benefits that their Czarist predecessors saw in southern Korean ports.

For the time being, however, that contingency lies in the future. At present the interests of the great powers in the Far East lie in the continued division of Korea. Yet this entire, somewhat flimsy structure could be menaced with quite unforseeable results if North Korea attempted to implement forcibly its self-proclaimed reunification policies. With the passing of Kim Il Sung the situation may change. Conceivably relations between North and South Korea will improve. Alternatively, with the effective succession of Kim Il Sung's son, the present uneasy truce will continue indefinitely.

In sum, it seems inconceivable that after so many centuries as an united country Korea will stay partitioned between North and South. But our story must end with the conclusion that for the forseeable future the Land of the Morning Calm will remain divided.

Epilogue:
Seoul Past and Present

When President Ronald Reagan visited South Korea in November 1983, he said that the Republic of Korea had become 'an industrial power, a major trading nation, and an economic model for developing nations throughout the world'. The President went on to say that the growing respect of the international community was shown by South Korea's plans to host the Asian Games in 1986 and the Summer Olympics two years later in 1988. So South Korea takes its place in the world.

The official policies of the government of the Republic of Korea have no doubt played a very important part in this development. But many observers believe that there is another factor, not always generally recognised, that also plays a central role in South Korea's transformation in the past quarter of a century. This is the remarkable resilience and resoucefulness of the Korean character. We need only mention the negative legacy of colonialism, national partition, and the Korean War to see that something very remarkable has occurred in South Korea in recent decades that is not attributable to purely economic factors.

This resilience of the Korean character has long been apparent to discerning foreign observers. In the last decade of the nineteenth century that intrepid Englishwoman, Isabella Bird Bishop, visited Korea and went not only to Seoul but into the central mountains as far as Chorwon. It was a time when there were the beginnings of a national awakening against contemporary isolation and stagnation.

She later wrote in *Korea and Her Neighbours* (1898) that my 'first impression was that Korea was the most uninteresting country that I had ever travelled in, but recent events have given me an intense interest in it; while Korean character and industry have enlightened me as to the better possibilities which may await the nation in the future'.

These were prophetic words. Another Western observer of the Korean scene, Horace G. Underwood, an American who grew up in Korea and who now teaches in a Korean University, believes that the Korean character has undergone little change. He has recently written that 'the vigour, the independence, the respect for authority combined with a healthy scepticism of that authority . . . the innate courtesy towards friends, the deep desire to be left just to be Korean in Korea's way has not changed at all, although some of the specific manifestations may have changed from time to time. Receptive as the nation is to new ideas, new ways and practices, they have always become Korean ideas, ways and practices, with sometimes subtle and sometimes deep variations stamped on them by Korea.' (*Korean Newsletter*, London, November 1983.)

These distinct Korean virtues are surely strikingly exemplified in the dramatic rise of Seoul over the past thirty years. From the ashes of the Korean War, when the capital of Korea changed hands no less than four times, there has arisen phoenix-like a new metropolis. This is the political, commercial, educational and artistic centre of the Republic of Korea, a still-growing city of nearly nine million people, a city that now approaches even Tokyo in its size and above all its vitality.

Some elementary facts about the rise of Seoul give an idea of its transformation. In 1949, immediately before the Korean War, the population of Seoul was 1.5 million. Wartime occupation and damage reduced this figure to only 200,000 in 1951. Although rebuilding and restoration of services began before the end of the Korean War, by 1960 there were no buildings of more than ten storeys in Seoul.

But by the early 1970s, as Seoul entered a phase of headlong development, scores of buildings of more than twenty storeys had been built, streets widened, subways excavated, and new Expressways constructed to link Seoul with all parts of South Korea. By 1980, the population was 8.4 million. The pace of development and innovation has continued to this day.

Yet despite this emergence of a modern city, much of old Seoul has survived, to be zealously conserved. The old and the new coexist in harmony, and it is still possible to see the outlines of the old royal capital of the Yi dynasty. We must remember, moreover, that although Seoul was founded a century before Christopher Columbus discovered America, it is still a young city by Korean standards of antiquity.

Originally, the old city of Seoul was surrounded by a stone wall. But today only fragments remain on Pugak-San and Nam-San, the two commanding mountains to the north and south of Seoul respectively. These fragments have however been restored. But of the original nine gates into Seoul, five still stand. The two largest, Namdae-mun (Great South Gate) and Tongnae-mun (Great East Gate) are striking reminders of the past.

The centre of royal government for the first two hundred years of the Yi dynasty was the Kyongbok Palace (The Palace of the Shining Happiness). It was burnt down in 1592, and lay in ruins until the 1860s. It was then restored on the original foundations and once again became a royal residence. In the Palace grounds stands a thirteen-storey pagoda, which was built originally in about 1340 during the Koryo dynasty, and moved to Seoul from Kaesong.

Since 1986, the Kyongbok Palace has been the home of the National Folklore Museum of Korea. Many items in the life of the people in past centuries are on display, including examples of the movable metal type that was invented in late Koryo times.

To the immediate south of the Kyongbok Palace is the large, modern Capitol Building, where the Republic of Korea was proclaimed in 1948, and which was then the home of the National Assembly for over thirty years. A striking new building has recently been opened for the Assembly in the Seoul suburb of Yongdungpo, on the south bank of the Han River.

The Capitol Building is now the home of the National Museum of Korea. Here are the great art treasures of the Korean past from the age of the Three Kingdoms through the Silla and Koryo periods to the Yi dynasty. In particular there are many beautiful celadons from the Silla and Koryo periods, and memorable examples of painting and calligraphy from the Yi period. A collection of artefacts projects Korea's cultural history in relation to its closest East Asian neighbours, China and Japan. The collection of national treasures housed here, over 7,000 items altogether, is exceeded in size only by the collections in the British Museum and the Louvre in Paris.

Immediately south of the Kyongbok Palace and the Capitol lie the government buildings, business offices and hotels of downtown Seoul with their world-wide connections. The Presidential Mansion, the Blue House, is also near the Kyongbok Palace.

Further south again Chong-no (Bell Street) is a wide East-West avenue, the original main street of old Seoul. Here during the centuries of the Yi dynasty was hung a great bell which signalled the curfew and the closing and opening of the city gates. The bell has long since vanished, but Chong-no was also famous for its street traders over the centuries and these remain in the smaller roads that run off this main thoroughfare.

To the south of Chong-no, and opposite the modern City Hall, lie the grounds of the Toksu Palace (The Palace of the Virtuous Longevity). As we have seen, the palace was originally known as the Kyongun Palace. The buildings and gardens are traditional Yi period in style. The Palace was originally built as a royal villa, but after the Japanese invasions of the 1590s King Sonjo, the 14th Yi king, moved here as the other royal residences had been destroyed.

Three centuries later, after the murder of Queen Min in 1896, the 26th and penultimate Yi king, Kojong, fled to the Russian legation in Seoul. The following year he moved to the Kyongun, as it was still known, which was near the foreign quarters of Seoul. Kojong continued to live here until his death in 1919. But after his abdication in 1907, the palace was renamed the Toksu Palace, and it is still known by this name.

The third great royal palace which survives in modern Seoul lies east of the Kyongbok. This is the Changdok Palace (The Palace of Illustrious Virtue), which was originally built in 1405, very soon after the founding of Seoul by King Taejo. The palace was destroyed during the Japanese invasions of the 1590s, and then later rebuilt in 1611. From then on it served as the official residence of most of the Yi kings, including Sunjong, the last Korean king who abdicated in 1910 in the face of Japanese pressure. But Sunjong continued to live at the Changdok Palace until his death in 1926.

The extensive grounds of the Changdok Palace contain the Piwon, or secret garden, the royal family's private park with woods, ponds, bridges, and ornate pleasure pavilions. A small complex nearby still houses the descendents of the Yi royal family.

To the south of the Changdok Palace lies Chongmyo (The Royal Ancestral Shrine). Here a walled complex with two long buildings contains, in line with traditional Confucian requirements, the ancestral tablets listing the achievements of all 27 Yi kings from Taejo to Sunjong.

During the Yi dynasty Confucian rituals (*Chongmyo Cherye*) were held here five times a year, in the first month of each season and in the twelfth lunar month. Ceremonial music was played, incense lit, and stylised greetings made to each departed king. These ancient ceremonies have now been partially revived, and are re-enacted each year on the first Sunday in May by descendants of the Yi kings. Here, perhaps more than anywhere else in modern Seoul, the sense and feeling of Korea's royal past is found.

Two great religious centres are found in central Seoul, One Buddhist, one Christian. Chogye-sa is a large Buddhist temple and the centre of Buddhism in Korea. The temple lies to the south of the Kyongbok Palace, and is busy throughout the year. Each evening, believers come to buy paper lanterns and candles for Buddhist rituals. Other worshippers light incense in the temple in front of the golden replica of Buddha. Chogye-sa is one of the great Buddhist shrines of the Far East.

Half a mile to the south of Chogye-sa lies the Myong-dong area of central Seoul, one of the historic districts of the capital known for its banks, finance houses, and precious metals markets. Here stands the great Myong-dong Cathedral, the centre of Roman Catholicism in Korea, and a place of special interest to foreign visitors. But as the Cathedral stands in the heart of Seoul, it is surrounded not only by modern high-rise offices but by small shops, taverns, and restaurants which are alive with people at almost all hours of the day.

Like all great cities, Seoul has a foreign quarter. When the first Westerners came to Korea in the nineteenth century they were forbidden to live in the old city. Later, in the 1880s and 1890s, these diplomats, missionaries and businessmen were permitted to purchase land and settle in the Chong-dong district immediately west of the Toksu Palace.

The foreign connections of the area, one of the most pleasant in Seoul, remain. Here is the home of the American ambassador and also the British embassy, a red brick building in nineteenth century colonial style. Nearby is the Anglican cathedral, a tasteful Romanesque building with a tower. Not far away is the Chong-dong Methodist Church, and the Ewha Girl's High School, the foundation of which dates to the late nineteenth century.

In much more recent times, since the Korean War, many Westerners have come to live in the Yongsan district near Nam-San (South Mountain), one of the pivotal hills in the founding of

Seoul. High-rise apartment blocks and Western-style bungalows have been built on the slopes of South Mountain, so giving splendid views of the Han River and the mountains to the south of Seoul. To the south-west lies the Seoul suburb of Chamsil, with the recently-constructed Seoul sports Complex and the Olympic stadium.

Officially, Seoul is designated a special city by the ROK government, along with Pusan, Inchon, and Taegu, so putting its administration on a provincial level.

But Seoul remains unique, both in Korea and in the Far East generally. The sense and feeling of the past is everywhere. Yet at the same time the old walled capital of the Korean kings has become one of the great cities of the modern world.

Select Bibliography

ACHESON, Dean. *Present at the Creation*, Norton, New York, 1969.
ALLEN, Richard C. *Korea's Syngman Rhee: An Unauthorized Portrait*, Tuttle, Tokyo, 1960.
APPLEMAN, Roy E. *US Army in the Korean War: South to the Naktong, North to the Yalu*, US Government Printing Office, 1961.
BUSS, Claude A. *The United States and the Republic of Korea: Background for Policy*, Hoover Institution Press, Stanford, 1982.
CHO, Soon Sung. *Korea in World Politics 1945–1950*, University of California Press, Berkeley, 1967.
CONROY, F. Hilary. *The Japanese Seizure of Korea 1868–1910*, University of Pennsylvania Press, Philadelphia, 1960.
CUMINGS, Bruce. *The Origins of the Korean War: Liberation and the Emergence of Separate Regimes, 1945–1947*, Princeton University Press, 1981.
HAN, Woo-Keun. *The History of Korea*, University of Hawaii Press, Honolulu, 1971.
Handbook of Korea, Korean Overseas Information Service, Seoul, 1982.
HASTINGS, Max. *The Korean War*, Michael Joseph, London, 1987.
HENDERSON, Gregory. *Korea: The Politics of the Vortex*, Harvard University Press, 1968.
HENTHORN, William E. *A History of Korea*, Free Press, New York, 1971.
HERMES, W. G. *US Army in the Korean War: Truce Tent and Fighting Front*, USGPO, 1966.
KIM, Se-Jin & CHO, Chang H. (Eds.). *Government and Politics of Korea*, Research Institute on Korean Affairs, Silver Spring, Maryland, 1972.
KIM, Se-Jin (Ed.). *Korean Reunification: Source Materials with Introduction*, Research Centre for Peace and Unification, Seoul, 1976.

SELECT BIBLIOGRAPHY

LEE, Chong-Sik, *The Politics of Korean Nationalism*, University of California Press, Berkeley, 1963.
LOWE, Peter. *The Origins of the Korean War*, Longman, London, 1986.
MARSHALL, S. L. A. *The River and the Gauntlet*, Morrow, New York, 1953.
MCCUNE, George. *Korea Today*, Harvard University Press, 1950.
MEADE, E. Grant. *American Military Government in Korea*, King's Crown Press, New York, 1951.
NELSON, M. Frederick. *Korea and the Old Orders in Eastern Asia*, Louisiana State University Press, Baton Rouge, 1946.
PAIGE, Glenn, *The Korean People's Democratic Republic*, Hoover Institution Press, Stanford, 1966.
REES, David. *Korea: The Limited War*, Macmillan, London, 1964.
– (Ed.). *The Korean War: History and Tactics*, Orbis, London, 1984.
REEVE, W. D. *The Republic of Korea*, Oxford University Press, 1963.
REISCHAUER, Edwin & FAIRBANK, J. K. *East Asia: The Great Tradition*, Houghton Mifflin, Boston, 1960.
REISCHAUER, E., FAIRBANK, J. K. & CRAIG, A. *East Asia: The Modern Transformation*, Allen & Unwin, London, 1965.
SCALAPINO, Robert A. & LEE, Chong-Sik. *Communism in Korea*, University of California Press, Berkeley, 1972.
SCHNABEL, James F. *US Army in the Korean War: Policy and Direction: The First Year*, USGPO, 1978 ed.
STORRY, RICHARD. *A History of Modern Japan*, Penguin, London, 1979 ed.
SUH, Dae Suk. *The Korean Communist Movement 1918–1948*, Princeton University Press, 1967.
TRUMAN, Harry S. *Years of Trial and Hope*, Doubleday, New York, 1956.
US Department of State. *Foreign Relations of the US: The Conferences at Cairo and Teheran, 1943*, 1960.
– *The Record on Korean Unification 1943–1960: Narrative Summary with Documents*, 1961.
– *The Korean Problem at the Geneva Conference, 25 April–15 June 1954*, 1954.
WHITE, John. *The Diplomacy of the Russo–Japanese War*, Princeton University Press, 1964.
WHITING, ALLEN S. *China Crosses the Yalu*, Macmillan, New York, 1960.

Index

Acheson, Dean, 93–94, 95, 99, 119, 122, 130
Aigun, Treaty of, 36
Almond, Edward (Major Gen.), 106, 109, 111, 114
Annexation Treaty, 62
Atlee, Clement, 101–102, 115

Bevin, Ernest (UK Foreign Sec.), 86, 109
Bishop, Isabella Bird, 183
Bonesteel, Charles H. (Col.), 79
Bradley, Omar (Gen.), 119, 122
Buddhism, 6, 10, 11, 15, 16, 17, 37
Byrnes, James F. (US Sec. of State), 78, 86

Carter, Jimmy, 168
Capitol Hill, 127
Catholic Church, 34–35, 37–38, 39, 42
Celadon (porcelain), 15, 25
Changdock Palace, 186
Chang Do Yung (Lt. Gen.), 144
Chang John (Chang Myon), 142–143, 145
Changjin, 71
Changjin Reservoir, 111–113
Chang Son (artist), 33
Chen yi (Marshal), 113
Cheju Island, 92

Chiang Kai Shek, 69, 73, 74, 92
China, 5–9, 10, 12–13, 14, 15, 16, 18, 27, 29, 30, 31, 34, 35–37, 42–50, 51, 57, 69, 70, 73–75, 111–133, 163, 164, 169, 181
Chinese Eastern Railway, 46
Chipyong-ni, 117
Ch'oe Che-u, 37, 46–47
Chogye-sa, 187
Choi Kyn Hah (President), 159, 171–174
Ch'olchong (King, d. 1864), 38
Cho Man-sik (Nationalist Leader), 86, 88
Chando-gyo (Society of Heavenly Way), 66
Chongjo (King, 1776–1800), 32
Chonju, 48
Chongchin, 70, 78, 110
Chongmyo (Royal Ancestral Shrine), 52, 186
Chonmin (menial class), 22
Chorwon, 118, 122, 124, 127, 167, 177, 183
Choryong Is., 54, 55, 57
Chosan, 111
Chosin, see Changjin
Chosan, 5, 18
Chosan, Ancient, 5
Chou En-Lai (Chinese Foreign Minister), 109, 130

Chou Wen Min (Catholic Priest), 34
Chuche (Self Reliance) Policy, 140, 164
Chu Hsi (Chinese Sage), 15, 17
Chun chon, 81, 96, 116
Chun Doo Hwan (President), 4, 166, 168, 172–176, 180
Chungin (Middle Class), 23
Chungjong (King, 1506–44), 26
Chungking, 69, 73, 83–84
Chung Seung Hwa (Gen.), 172–173
Churchill, Winston, 74–76
Clark, Mark (Gen.), 130, 133
Class structure, 22
Collins, Lawton J. (Gen.), 107, 115, 117
Confucianism, 6, 8, 12–13, 15, 16, 17, 20–23, 31, 32, 33, 37, 38, 42, 44, 45, 159

Dairen, 57, 59, 75
Dean, William (Major Gen.), 102
Doyle, James (Rear Adm.), 106, 107
Dulles, John Foster (US Sec. of State), 131, 136

Eden, Anthony (UK Foreign Sec.), 73, 136
Eisenhower, Dwight, D., 130, 131, 132, 135

Fairbank, John K. (Historian), 31, 61
Flying Fish Channel, 106, 107
Ford, Gerald, 169
Formosa (Taiwan), 49, 73, 74, 122
France, 35–36, 37, 39, 42, 51, 54, 149
Futrell, Robert F. (Historian), 128–129

General Sherman, USS, 39
Germany, 42, 51, 130, 149

Ghengis Khan, 15
Goro, Minra (Japanese Minister), 53
Great Britain, 35–36, 42, 45, 46, 51, 54, 60, 70, 73–76, 86, 101–102, 105, 107, 109, 115, 120, 136–137, 149

Hangul (Korean Alphabet), 23–24, 54, 56
Hanmun (Chinese language), 23
Harbin, 57, 61
Harrison, William K. (Major Gen.), 127, 131, 132
Henderson, Gregory (Historian), 4
Hideyoshi, Toyotomi, 27–28
Hirohito, Emperor, 180
Hiroshima, 72, 78
Hodge, John R. (Lt. Gen.), 80, 88, 91
Hokkaido, 59, 80, 181
Hongchan, 116
Hook, The, 127
Hopkins, Harry, 75, 76
Hsieh Fang (Chinese Gen.), 123
Hull, John (Lt. Gen.), 77
Hungnam, 71, 111, 112, 114, 128
Hunmin Chongum, *see* Hangul
Hwachon Reservoir, 120
Hyesanjin, 111

Independence Club (Tongnip Hyophoe), 54–56
Independence Party, 43, 44
Independent, The (Tongnip Shinmun), 54–56
Imjin River, Battle of, 120
Inchon, 41, 42, 44, 48, 53, 58, 77, 81, 96, 105–108, 109, 127, 188
Inje, 120
Injo (King, 1623–49), 29, 30
Injong (King, 1122–46), 15
Iron Triangle, 118, 122, 167
Ito Hirobumi, 60–16
Iwon, 111

INDEX 193

Japan, 2, 3, 10, 16, 18, 20, 26–28, 30, 34, 35, 36, 37, 39–40, 41–50, 51–54, 56–62, 63–72, 75–82, 130, 141, 146, 148, 149, 180–181
Johnson, Lyndon, 79
Joy, Turner (Vice Adm.), 123, 126
Jurched (Mongols), 14, 29

Kaesong, 13, 16, 18, 81
Kaewha (modernising reform), 42
Kanggye, 111
Kanghwa Island, 16, 29–30, 39, 40
Kanghwa, Treaty of, 41–42
Kansas–Wyoming Line, 122
Kansong, 122, 134
Kapsan group, 139
Kasan, 105
Katsura, Count (Japanese Premier), 59–60
Kaya tribe, 6
Kennedy, John F., 79
Khitan tribe, 14
Khrushchev, Nikita, 94
Kim Chong Il, 160, 165
Kim Chong Pil, 171, 173
Kim Dae Jong, 155, 157, 171, 173
Kim Hang-do (painter), 33
Kim Il Sung, 69, 86, 89, 91, 93–95, 96, 108, 111, 118, 119, 133, 138–140, 143, 150, 155, 160–170, 177–178, 182
Kim Jae Kyn, 159
Kim Kue, 68, 69, 83–85
Kim Ok-kyun, 44
Kim Sung Chu, *see* Kim Il Sung
Kim Tae-song, 10–12
Kim Young Sam, 157, 158, 171, 173
Koguryo, 6–9
Kojong (King, Emperor, 1864–1907), 38, 40, 43–44, 47–48, 52–54, 55, 60–61
Komun Island, *see* Port Hamilton
Kongju, 49
Korangpo, 167

Koryo, 13–17
Kowshing, Ferry Boat, 48
Kumchon, 103
Kumhwa, 118, 122, 127
Kumsong, 124
Kunuri Pass, 114
Kunsan, 103, 178
Kurile Islands, 78, 181
Kwanju, 173, 174
Kyondok (King, 742–764), 10, 11
Kyongju, 9, 10
Kyongsun (King), 13

Lausanne Talks, 169
League of Nations, 69
Lenin, 68, 163
Liaotung Peninsula, 49, 51, 57, 59
Li Hung-chang (Chinese statesman), 43
Lin Piao (Marshal), 112
Lobanoff, Alexei (Russian Foreign Min.), 56
Lushan, 54

MacArthur, Douglas (Gen.), 80–81, 84, 91, 93, 99–102, 105–122, 138
Malik, Jacob (Soviet UN Delegate), 102, 123
Manchukuo, 70, 144
Mangyongdae, 164
Mao Tse-tung, 69, 88, 112, 139, 164
Marshall, George C. (Gen. US Sec. of State), 70, 90, 109, 119, 122
Marshall, S. L. A. (Historian), 113
Martin, Joe (US Congressman), 119
Masan, 57, 104–105, 146
Masatake, Terauchi (Gen.), 61
McCune, George (US scholar), 4
Meiji (Emperor), 39
Mikoyan, Anastas (Soviet Statesman), 139
Min (Queen), 43, 44, 48–49, 52–53, 186

Mokpo, 103
Molotov, V. M. (Soviet Foreign Min.), 86, 136
Mongols, 13, 15–16, 29, 30
Moscow Protocol, 86–87
Muccio, John J. (US Ambassador), 95
Mu-Hak (Buddhist Monk), 18
Mukden, 30, 58, 70, 113, 118
Munsan, 123, 124, 133, 135, 177, 178

Najin, 181
Nakasone, Yasuhiro (Japanese Premier), 180
Nam Il (Gen.), 123, 131, 132
Nampo, 182
Nam-San, 18, 185, 187
National Museum of Korea, 15, 185
Nelson, M. Frederick (Historian), 12
Netherlands, The, 30, 36
New Korea Society (Shinganhoe), 68
Nixon, Richard, 149, 156, 180
Noron (Elder Group), 32

Oda Nobunaga, 26–27
Oh Guk-ryol (Gen.), 166
Okinawa, 78, 81
Old Baldy, 127
Onjong, 111
Opium War, 35
Osan, 102, 107, 117, 178

Paekche, 6–9
Pak Hon-yong, 138–139
Panmunjon, site of truce talks, 124
Parhae (Korean state), 9, 13, 14
Park Choong Hoon, 174
Park Chung Hee, 144–146, 151, 153, 155–159, 162, 163, 166, 171
Pearl Harbor, 69, 73
Peking, Treaty of, 36–37

Peng Teh-huai (Gen.), 118, 123, 133, 139
Perry, Matthew (Comd.), 36
Pibyonsa (State Council), 31
Port Arthur, 49, 51, 52, 57, 58, 59, 75
Port Hamilton, 47
Portsmouth, Treaty of, 59
Potsdam Conference, 72, 75, 76–78, 80
Pueblo USS, 162
Pujon, 71
Pulguk-sa Temple, 10
Pusan, 26, 27, 30, 39, 41, 42, 46, 54, 55, 57, 59, 77, 99, 100, 102–107, 108, 109, 114, 158, 188
Pyonggang, 118, 122
Pyongyang, 9, 27, 29, 49, 59, 70, 81, 86, 94, 108, 110, 111, 114, 139, 164

Rangoon, 167
Reagan, Ronald, 169, 183
Ricci, Matteo (Missionary), 34
Ridgway, Matthew B. (Lt. Gen.), 115-117, 119, 120–121, 122, 123, 124, 125, 130
Roh Tae Woo, 4
Roosevelt, Franklin D., 73–75
Rusk, Dean (Col.), 79
Russia (USSR), 35–36, 42, 46, 50, 52, 53–54, 55, 56–59, 74, 77–82, 85–89, 91, 98, 101–102, 131, 138, 139, 169, 181–182

Saemaul Undong (New Community Movement), 150–154
Sakhalin, 58, 78
Sangmin (common people), 22
Sariwon, 110
Sato, Eisaku (Japanese Premier), 180
Schlesinger, James (US Def. Sec.), 168

INDEX

Se-Jin Kim (Historian), 143
Sejo (King, 1455–68), 25
Sejong (King, 1418–50), 20, 23, 25
Seoul, Early, 18, 19, 27, 29, 30, 33, Korean War, 98, 107, 116, 117
Silla, 2, 6–14, 185
Sinanju, 111, 113
Sinuija, 59, 110, 116
Sin Yun-bok (painter), 33
Sirhak (practical learning) Movement, 33
So Chae-pil (Philip Jaisohn), 54–56
Sohak (Western Learning), 34
Sohyon (Crown Prince), 30
Sokkuram Temple, 10
Sone Atasuke, 61
Songjin, 128
Songjong (King, 1469–94), 25
Soron (younger group), 32
South Manchurian Railway, 57, 59
Sowon (Confucion Academies), 31, 38
Stalin, Joseph, 74–78, 80, 94, 131
Struble, A. D. (Vice Adm.), 106, 107
Sudong, 112
Suiho, 71
Sunchon, 92, 114
Sunjong, Emperor, 61, 62, 187
Supung dom, 71
Suwon, 99, 100, 105, 107, 128
Sherman, Forrest (Adm.), 107
Shimonseki, Treaty of, 49–50, 51
Syngman Rhee, 55, 67–68, 69, 73–74, 83, 84, 88–89, 91, 92, 95, 97, 101, 132, 136, 140–142, 153

Taegu, 38, 92, 102, 104, 116, 144, 173, 188
Taejo (King, Wang Kon), 14
Taejo (King, Yi Song-gye), 17–20, 187
Taejon, 103

Taejong (King, 1400–18), 21
Taewongun (Yi Ha-ung, Regent), 37–39, 40
Taft, William H. (US Sec. of State), 59
Taiping Rebellion, 37
Taoism, 18, 37
Tienstin, Treaty (Sino–Russian), 36, (Sino–Japanese), 44, 48
Toksu Palace, 55, 87, 186
Tonghak (Eastern Learning), 37–38, 46–48, 66
Tongnae, 39–40
Trans-Siberian Railway, 51, 58
Treaties of the Five Powers, 36
Triangle Hill, 127
Tripitaka, 15
Triple Intervention, 51, 52
Truman, Harry, 74, 75–77, 80, 93, 99–101, 109, 110, 115, 116–117, 119–122, 130
Trygve Lie (UN Sec. Gen.), 98
Tun-gunwanggon, 5
Tunnels, North Korean, 167, 177
Turtle Ships, 27

Uijongbu Corridor, 30, 96, 116, 177
Uijn, 30, 54
Ulchin, 162
Ullong Island, 55, 57
Underwood, Horace G. (US Academic), 184
United Nations, 90–92, 97–98, 100–102, 108, 110, 123, 130, 133, 137, 143
United Nations Command, 101–135
United States of America, 35, 36, 39, 42, 45, 54, 59–60, 66, 67–68, 69, 73–82, 84, 86–90, 92, 93, 95, 96–133, 136–137, 140–141, 148, 149, 162–163, 166, 168–169, 176–181, 183
Unggi, 78
Unsan, 111–112

Vandenberg, Hoyt S. (Gen.), 117
Van Fleet, James (Gen.), 119, 120, 124
Vladivostok, 37, 46, 78, 128, 181–182

Waegwan, 104
Walker, Walton H. (Lt. Gen.), 103–106, 110–111, 113, 114, 115
White Horse Hill, 127
Wilson, Woodrow, 66
Wolmi Island, 106, 107
Wonju, 116, 117
Wonsan, 41, 42, 46, 86, 109, 111, 128, 162

Woo Keun Han (Historian), 8, 21, 32

Yangban (aristocratic class), 14, 17–18, 21, 22, 25–26, 31–33, 34, 37, 52, 61, 64
Yi Sun-sin (Adm.), 27
Yi dynasty, founded, 16
Yi Sung-man, *see* Syngman Rhee
Yongampo, 57
Yongjo (King, 1724–76), 32
Yosu, 92
Yuan Shih-k'ai (Gen.), 43–45, 49
Yun Po-sun, 142, 144, 145
Yushin (Revitalising) Constitution, 156–158, 171